PRAISE FOR AMY E. REICHERT
THE SIMPLICITY OF CIDER

"Reichert captures the food, relationships, and unique settings of the Midwest at their best. I was absolutely charmed by *The Simplicity of Cider*."

— J. Ryan Stradal, *New York Times* bestselling author of *Kitchens of the Great Midwest*

"*The Simplicity of Cider* will quench your thirst for a smart, poignant tale of people who find their true selves, and in the process each other, in the most unexpected places. A sparkling tale of creating family where you need it, and learning to let go of the things that hold you back from your best life."

—Stacey Ballis, author of *Wedding Girl* and *Recipe for Disaster*

"Reichert has once again delivered a surefire hit with *The Simplicity of Cider*. It's charming, heartwarming, and magical."

—Nina Bocci, *USA Today* bestselling author of *Roman Crazy*

"*The Simplicity of Cider* is the perfect blend of sweet, smart, and immensely satisfying. If foodie fiction is a thing, Amy E. Reichert is the grand master."

—Colleen Oakley, author of *Close Enough to Touch*

"Deep family secrets and undeniable attraction collide in this wonderfully atmospheric and heartwarming tale of a father trying to save his son, a woman trying to save her family's land, and the way that the two of them might just save each other if they can stop the past from destroying their future. As deliciously satisfying as a crisp glass of the cider Amy E. Reichert so masterfully describes."

— Kristin Harmel, internationally bestselling author of *The Sweetness of Forgetting*, *The Life Intended*, and *When We Meet Again*

"With a dreamy setting and lovable characters, *The Simplicity of Cider* is so good you can practically taste it. Read it in the shade of an apple tree, near a perfectly dry bottle of cider, or wherever—just read it!"

—Kelly Harms, author of *The Good Luck Girls of Shipwreck Lane*

2/18

"Reichert's writing is like the song in your heart, at once lilting and joyous yet aching and real. *The Simplicity of Cider* is a comforting and layered read with a cast of well-developed characters who feel both unique and authentic, and a setting that will have you yearning for a trip to Door County and a mug of cider."

—Sonali Dev, author of *A Change of Heart*

"*The Simplicity of Cider* is a novel as delicious as cider and as enchanting as magic—both of which are found in measured doses throughout the book. Amy Reichert has a way of writing about complicated relationships and seemingly impossible situations with a strong thread of hope that is both uplifting and substantive. This is a lovely book, meant to be savored."

—Karen White, *New York Times* bestselling author of *The Guests on South Battery*

LUCK, LOVE & LEMON PIE

"Laugh-out-loud, hold-on-to-your-panties women's fiction. The characters are game for anything when it comes to getting back what they think they have lost. Reichert is a talented author."

—*RT Book Reviews* (four-star review)

"Amy E. Reichert serves up another delicious serving of fresh wit and lots of fun in this charming tale of a woman determined to fix her marriage gone stale. This heartfelt novel is as funny as it is tender—in other words, the perfect summer read."

—Colleen Oakley, author of *Close Enough to Touch* and *Before I Go*

"As irresistible and delicious as an actual slice of lemon pie, *Luck, Love & Lemon Pie* has all of the sweet ingredients that make a book impossible to put down. Amy E. Reichert has a flair for writing heartwarming fiction that will give you sweet cravings!"

—Liz Fenton and Lisa Steinke, authors of *The Year We Turned Forty* and *The Status of All Things*

"*Luck, Love & Lemon Pie* is touching, clever, and a hell of a lot of fun. Amy E. Reichert somehow manages to not only tell a stirring story

about modern marriage, but also transport you poolside in Vegas. Simply put, *Luck, Love & Lemon Pie* is a great bet."
—Taylor Jenkins Reid, author of *Maybe in Another Life* and *After I Do*

"With relatable characters and a lot of heart, Reichert delivers a story that is both entertaining and wise, and leaves you believing that, when it comes to true happiness, you can create your own luck."
—Karma Brown, bestselling author of *Come Away with Me*

"Charming."
—*People*

"Reichert's second novel, after the popular *The Coincidence of Coconut Cake* (2015), will appeal to readers who enjoy a lighter look at self-discovery, family, and friendship."
—*Booklist*

"An enjoyable and thought-provoking exploration of a modern-day marriage in midlife crisis."
—*Kirkus Reviews*

THE COINCIDENCE OF COCONUT CAKE

"A delectable novel."
—*Bookreporter*

"Deliciously entertaining! Amy E. Reichert's voice is warm and funny in this delightful ode to second chances and the healing power of a meal cooked with love."
—Meg Donohue, *USA Today* bestselling author of *All the Summer Girls* and *How to Eat a Cupcake*

"Amy E. Reichert writes like your best friend and reading her words is like having that friend whisper them into your ear. *The Coincidence of Coconut Cake* is a delicious story of food, love, and a wink at what people will do to have their cake and eat it, too."
—Ann Garvin, author of *The Dog Year* and *On Maggie's Watch*

"Highly recommended that you eat before reading this book . . . a light, fun read that feels a bit like eating dessert for dinner."

—*RT Book Reviews*

"Amy E. Reichert whips up the perfect recipe for a deliciously fun read. Combine humor and romance with a dash of drama, then let it simmer. The sprinkle of Wisconsin pride is icing on an already irresistible cake. Warning: do not read this book hungry!"

—Elizabeth Eulberg, author of *The Lonely Hearts Club* and
Better Off Friends

"What a wonderful treat! Delicious descriptions of food and love and Milwaukee (I know! Who knew?). A sweet, endearing read."

—Megan Mulry, *USA Today* bestselling author of *A Royal Pain*

"*The Coincidence of Coconut Cake* is a smart and delicious debut—a read as satisfying as the last bite of dessert after a lovingly prepared meal."

—Susan Gloss, author of *Vintage*

"Well-developed secondary characters and detailed descriptions of the Milwaukee food scene will leave readers hungry for more. Fans of Stacey Ballis and Erica Bauermeister will find lots to love."

—*Booklist*

"Amy Reichert brings sweetness and substance to her delicious debut. Sign me up for second helpings!"

—Lisa Patton, bestselling author of *Whistlin' Dixie in a Nor'easter*

"Amy E. Reichert takes the cake with this charming tale of food, friendship, and fate."

—Beth Harbison, *New York Times* bestselling author of
If I Could Turn Back Time

"Reichert's quirky and endearing debut skillfully and slyly examines identity and community while its characters find love in surprising places. Clever, creative, and sweetly delicious."

—*Kirkus Reviews*

ALSO BY AMY E. REICHERT

Luck, Love & Lemon Pie
The Coincidence of Coconut Cake

the Simplicity of Cider

AMY E. REICHERT

GALLERY BOOKS

NEW YORK   LONDON   TORONTO   SYDNEY   NEW DELHI

G

Gallery Books
An Imprint of Simon & Schuster, Inc.
1230 Avenue of the Americas
New York, NY 10020

First Gallery Books trade paperback edition May 2017

GALLERY BOOKS and colophon are registered trademarks of Simon & Schuster, Inc.

For information about special discounts for bulk purchases, please contact Simon & Schuster Special Sales at 1-866-506-1949 or business@simonandschuster.com.

The Simon & Schuster Speakers Bureau can bring authors to your live event. For more information or to book an event, contact the Simon & Schuster Speakers Bureau at 1-866-248-3049 or visit our website at www.simonspeakers.com.

Manufactured in the United States of America

10 9 8 7 6 5 4 3 2 1

Library of Congress Cataloging-in-Publication Data
Names: Reichert, Amy E., 1974- author.
Title: The simplicity of cider / Amy E. Reichert.
Description: First Gallery Books trade paperback edition. | New York : Gallery Books, 2017.
Identifiers: LCCN 2016050277| ISBN 9781501154928 (paperback) | ISBN 9781501154935 (ebook)
Subjects: | BISAC: FICTION / Contemporary Women. | FICTION / Romance / Contemporary. | FICTION / Family Life. | GSAFD: Love stories.
Classification: LCC PS3618.E52385 S56 2017 | DDC 813/.6—dc23
LC record available at https://lccn.loc.gov/2016050277

ISBN 978-1-5011-5492-8
ISBN 978-1-5011-5493-5 (ebook)

the
Simplicity of
Cider

To my Sam, for being my real-life inspiration.
To John, thank you.

The art of making a good cider is of great simplicity.
—L. DE BOUTTEVILLE AND A. HAUCHECORNE,
LE CIDRE, 1875

CHAPTER ONE

Sanna Lund's thoughts of apple blossoms and new cider blends stuttered to an end with the grunt of her dad's snore. Einars rumbled from the squashy armchair in front of the huge fieldstone fireplace framed by large picture windows, afternoon sun blanketing him. The stones had come from their orchard, unearthed when the first generation of Lunds began planting the orchard four generations ago. The stones varied in color and shape, from light gray limestone to rusty red granite, each highlighted by the golden light. Above the inset wooden mantel hung a huge collage of watercolor paintings, comprised of six-inch squares, each showcasing a different variety of apple grown in the orchard set against a distinguishing hue.

Sanna closed the refrigerator and set on the kitchen counter the baggie of sticks she'd been retrieving and walked across the huge great room to where her dad slept. His long legs stretched out in front of him, like roots expanding their reach. Everything about him was stretched, like taffy pulled slightly too far. His head tilted back enough for his gaping mouth to emit another snort. An open shoe box full of weathered photos and yellowing paper sat on his lap, while he clutched a single photo to his chest.

An afternoon nap was a common enough scene in other homes, but Sanna couldn't remember ever watching her father sleep. Einars was a man of action, always in the middle of three different chores at once, making it all seem effortless. Age spots dotted his face from too many years in the sun before sunscreen was as recommended as the proverbial apple, wrinkles traced exactly where his smile would be if he were awake, and fluttering eyelids hid his sparkling blue eyes. Dark smudges pooled under his pale eyelashes, evidence of the late-night pacing that had become a habit during the last year. Sanna shoved away her guilt that she might be partially to blame for that, deep into the mental cave normally reserved for what people thought of her, dawdling tourists, and small talk.

When he'd come in from the trees, he had told her he would start their dinner. That was forty-five minutes ago. Sanna had been so immersed in grafting old branches to new trees, she hadn't noticed how long he'd been gone. If she hadn't come in to retrieve the scions—the twigs from older trees she was hoping to graft—from the house fridge, she wouldn't have found him dozing.

Thinking she should wake him, Sanna smiled down at the man who was her world. He'd taken care of her through colds, puberty, growing pains that would have knocked an elephant to its knees. He taught her how to climb a tree, determine the exact right day to pick an apple, drive a stick-shift truck through the bumpy aisles of an orchard, and dip crispy french fries into her chocolate shakes from Wilson's. She pulled the picture he was gripping out of his long fingers and glanced at the faded image, then dropped it as soon as she saw what it was, not wanting to hold it even a second longer. The four smiling faces beaming at her fluttered into the battered box. Her father, her brother, Anders, herself, and the Egg Donor. Sanna wouldn't even shorten it to the friendlier acronym, TED.

She'd often seen the box tucked under her dad's bed, but she'd never been curious about the contents. Her dad had always respected her privacy and given her space, so she had always offered him the same courtesy. At that moment, though, destructive urges boiled inside her—shoving all else to the side. Merely throwing away the box of photos wasn't permanent enough. It deserved a more dramatic demise. She wanted to drive it to Gills Rock and toss it into the Death's Door waters, where it could live with all the other shipwrecks. That's where that box belonged.

Rational thought prevailed—she didn't snatch the box and run away to destroy it—but it did little to calm her roiling emotions. She gently lifted the box, but her careful movements caused her dad to twitch awake, his hands pulling the box back to his lap.

"I've got it," he said, the words still mushy with sleep.

Sanna straightened and watched as her dad fumbled to cover the box and pull it close to his plaid-coated chest.

"Why are you wasting time with that, Dad? There's nothing worth remembering in there."

He blinked away the sleep still muffling his senses and covered the box protectively with his arms. Einars smiled that annoying grin of elders who know better.

"Happiness is always worth remembering, even when it was temporary."

Back in her happy place, the barn, Sanna snapped one of the sticks she'd grabbed from the fridge and searched for any sign of green inside. Nothing—only dry, dead wood. She tossed the branch onto her cluttered stainless steel workbench already strewn with beakers, plastic tubing, her journal—tools of her woefully unsuccessful cider-making business. And now, she failed again to graft her beloved heirloom apple trees onto newer stock.

After waking her dad, she'd returned to the safety of her barn, but the pain welling inside her wouldn't go back down. The barn, complete with the fresh sawdust scent of new construction, was built into a small hill across a gravel-covered parking area from their house. The bottom level was used as the farm stand during the fall and a garage during the winter, while her workspace and cidery comprised the second level. She could get to the bottom story two ways: by taking the spiral stairs in the corner or by exiting the garage door on the opposite wall and walking around the building and down the hill. She'd bounded up the spiral steps two at a time just now, her long legs and resentment carrying her even more briskly than usual. She hadn't been prepared to see the Donor's smiling face, though she knew enough to know preparation wouldn't have helped. Her day had been perfectly scheduled and productive, everything as expected. Awake at six, breakfast by six thirty, in the trees by seven with a thermos of black tea and a packed lunch, then to the cidery after lunch for an afternoon of quiet, peaceful work. That's where she'd been before she found her dad, in the content corner of her mind full of trees and flavors—when she was ripped out of it like a fish flopping on a hook.

At thirty-two, she knew she should be over the betrayal. And she wanted to forget about the Donor, but, even after all these years, she could never forgive her.

"Didn't keep?" her dad said, and pointed to where she had flung the branch. He stood in the doorway of her second-story workspace, his lanky frame outlined by the warm June sunlight behind him. Einars wore his usual work jeans and a lightweight long-sleeve work shirt over a tee. The vitality that had been notably absent during his nap vibrated off him now.

"No," she said. "Not the ones I had in the house, or the ones I stored out here. All dead wood." She had hoped to graft these twigs onto the root stock she'd been saving, to see if she could foster new trees from the heirloom stock in the back of the orchard. "I was able to graft the Honeycrisps and Galas with sticks I harvested the same day. I don't know what else to try."

She threw the twig and a Ziploc full of dead sticks into the large garbage can, then leaned against the counter to face her dad. Her large workbench spanned an entire wall in the mostly empty main room of the orchard's barn. Later in the season, she'd share the space with giant crates of apples for the visiting tourists shopping their farm stand on the lower level. This early in the season, though, the wooden crates were empty, leaving space for her towers of waiting carboys—the five-gallon glass jugs she used to make her hard cider. Adjacent to her workbench was a refrigerated room and walk-in freezer, where she stored the juice she had pressed during the previous season in neatly labeled freezer bags and five-gallon buckets. Still waiting along one of the walls was the much larger press and new tanks her father had purchased this year, silent judges of her failure. She'd been trying for two years to sell her small-batch hard cider, but only a few locals seemed interested. Instead, the cooler overflowed with her finished products, carefully sorted according to batch.

Einars plucked the broken twig out of the garbage with long, thin fingers speckled from sun and age. He'd be seventy soon, but he didn't act like it. He could spray a row of trees, trim branches, and make a delicious apple dessert all before one in the afternoon. They worked hard, but Idun's Orchard thrived under their care—perhaps not as well as when the Lund population topped their meager two, but well enough they could support themselves. It was a decent life.

"You kept it hydrated? But not too wet?" he asked.

Sanna stared back.

"I take that as a yes." Einars let the twig drop. "Maybe we need some fresh blood around here. You can't expect the trees to give their best for just the two of us."

"Pa, we don't need more people complicating our system. If it's not broken and all that. Besides, the trees don't know any better."

Einars looked out the window behind the workbench at the orchard below them.

"You'd be surprised. They say plants respond to singing and the moods of their owners, why not trees?"

Sanna returned her grafting tools to their proper places and pulled out beakers and measuring cups.

"I'm not singing to the trees."

Einars stretched his fingers a few times, like a pianist before a solo.

"I need to get the spraying done in the Earlies. Can you run to Shopko to pick up some toilet paper and ibuprofen—just get the store brand."

Sanna played with her necklace, a flat wooden circle strung on a silver chain, the wood worn smooth from years of twisting it with her fingers. Her mind sought the solitary peace of work to pacify the shock and failure of the day.

"I can't today, Pa." She opened her journal to where she had left off. Maybe creating something new would ease the disappointment in her chest. "I need to blend a new cider. I'll see you at dinner."

She disappeared into the walk-in cooler to get the juices she would need. When she emerged, her dad still stood next to her bench, now with the bag of sticks in his hands, pulling each one out and inspecting it.

"What if we clipped fresh twigs and did the grafting now?" he asked, then dropped the sticks back in the bin.

"I tried that last year, and they didn't take. That's why I used clippings that had a full season of growth in them. I thought they might be more robust."

Sanna set the frozen juice blocks on the counter, already considering her dad's proposition.

"How did you graft them?"

"Whip graft."

"Let's try the cleft graft on the understock you have, and a few side grafts onto some older trees. Maybe the scions want a more mature tree to grow with. What do you think?"

His idea could work—Sanna wanted to try it. She needed to know she could make more of those trees, that they wouldn't die out under her watch after living for over a hundred years.

"What about the Earlies?"

"I can spray them tomorrow—this seems more important."

That was good enough for her. She grabbed her grafting tools and led the way out of the barn, determined to be successful. She would discover the secret to grafting these finicky trees.

CHAPTER TWO

Dad, come look. I think I can see California."

Isaac Banks looked up from the magazine cover he'd grabbed downstairs from a line of free travel brochures. He'd gotten himself and his son to the Midwest and wasn't sure where to go next. Sebastian—Bass—had hopped up on the sloped ledge to get his face closer to the glass in the observation deck of the St. Louis Arch. Twenty other people crowded around the panes to see the sprawling city below them.

Isaac tucked the magazine under his arm and joined Bass at the window.

The horizon blurred in the distance.

"I'm not sure that's quite California, Guppy."

"How do you know?"

"Logic. We're too far away."

Bass hopped off the ledge, already bored with the view. Keeping a ten-year-old boy entertained required stamina and creativity, especially when going on the third week of a cross-country road trip. Stamina, creativity, and a fair bit of patience.

"That's just sad," Bass said.

"Geography is sad?"

"If we're this far up, we should at least be able to see the Rockies. It'd be cool if we could see Pike's Peak. Those trams were boss. And the sheep with the big horns bonking their heads together."

He held his hands to the side of his head as if holding giant cinnamon rolls over his ears while a new batch of tourists joined them in the already crowded space, jostling them into the wall.

"Ready to go back down, Wahoo? There's a frozen yogurt place in our hotel. We could get some, then order pizza, and swim in the pool."

Bass took one last look out the glass and nodded. They joined the line for the descending elevators, Isaac keeping his eye on the back of Bass's head and one hand on his shoulder. He crouched to fit inside the elevator pod, which they shared with a young couple, still in the early days of their romance to judge by the amount of kissing. Each pod contained only five seats and a small window through which Bass watched their descent—occasionally commenting on all the steps they'd have to walk down if the elevator got stuck. Isaac kept himself occupied with the magazine, paging through articles about the best burger in the Midwest and how to get upgraded to first class without using miles.

Isaac had taken enough time to finish up his last project and for Bass to finish the school year, then they'd started out for their summer adventure—or at least that was what Bass thought. In the eighteen days since they'd left home, they'd shouted into the Grand Canyon, ridden horses in Estes Park, and watched the Oakland A's trounce the Royals in Kansas City. Though he'd lived in California all his life, it had been easy to leave San Jose, where too many people—like his mother, who texted daily—knew about their troubles. Bass had grumbled about missing his summer baseball league until Isaac had promised they could catch a few games while on the trip, hence the A's game. He had no qualms using some judicious bribery to start their journey in a good mood.

Isaac watched Bass's breath fog up the window, his legs bouncing—even an elevator ride couldn't contain his need for perpetual motion. The little-boy cheeks had sharpened into those of a young man sometime in the last year. Big feet didn't match the skinny legs they were attached to, his still-high voice disarmed his dad with an occasionally good argument for why he should get to stay up later, and a little sprig of hair on the crown of his head still refused to lay flat—and Bass didn't care, yet. Isaac's innocent little boy grew up more each day, and he was bound and determined that they would have this last summer of simple boyhood.

"Where're we going next?" Bass said, sitting so close to him that he was almost on his lap. Isaac put an arm around him and flipped the magazine's page. The headline read "Ten Best Places to Get Away from It All." He scanned the article. Most were coastal, like Key West or Malibu. No, thank you. But number two. Number two had potential.

"How about here?"

He pointed to the words *Door County, Wisconsin* next to photos of a towering white lighthouse, a winding road through an autumnal tunnel of arching trees, and isolated rocky shores with a single kayaker exploring the nooks and crannies. The article described a rural, remote peninsula where people spent their days in leisure amid orchards and ice cream shops—the perfect place for an idyllic, postcard American childhood summer.

As they emerged from the visitor's center, the afternoon sunshine reflecting off the mirrored surface of the structure above them, Isaac's phone whistled that a new text message had arrived. Bass scampered ahead, all cowlick and sincerity, onto a wide field beneath the monument where a few people lay on their backs to take photos. They could go home, Isaac thought. It wasn't too late for Bass to join his friends on the team or sign up for a few camps—but the reality of everything that came with that decision caused his heartbeat to quicken and skip in panic.

They would try their luck in Door County, Wisconsin.

His phone whistled again.

He didn't need to check. He knew who it was. He'd ignored all the daily messages and phone calls from Bass's grandma, his mom. He had not given her any warning that Bass and he were going on a trip, where, or for how long they would be gone. He still didn't know. They'd be gone as long as it took for Isaac to figure out how to tell Bass his mom was dead.

Sometime in the last thirty minutes, Isaac and Bass had driven over an invisible line—or maybe it was the Sturgeon Bay Bridge. Traffic had slowed, radio stations wavered, and the tension that had pinched his right shoulder since leaving California eased. Farm fields traded places with orchards, which traded places with magical patches of forest. Bikers hugged the edge of the road as cars patiently weaved around them. No one hurried—except one dick in a giant Suburban hauling a trailered speedboat.

Already Isaac knew this was the right place for them. He hadn't seen a fast-food restaurant since crossing the bridge, and the most garish tourist attraction seemed to be the mini-golf courses. Since deciding to head in this direction in St. Louis, he'd done some research. Door County was Wisconsin's thumb, a peninsula that jutted out into Lake Michigan. Much of the land was dedicated to farming and local tourism, mainly orchards and forests. To the northwest was Green Bay, not the city but the body of water. To the southeast was Lake Michigan. Because of its pastoral setting, it had also become a vacation getaway for those wanting a slower pace and a reason to spend the days outdoors. Perfect.

Orchard stores advertising cherries and apples, fresh baked goods, and gifts appeared along the road. Some promised the best cider donuts or cherry pie, others had outdoor activities where children could burn off some energy, and yet others offered to let you pick your own cherries when the season started. As they approached a store offering a wide selection of samples, Isaac pulled into the parking lot. It seemed like a good time to stretch their legs and grab a snack at the same time.

"Let's see what we've gotten ourselves into, Barracuda," Isaac said.

He stepped onto the gravel parking lot, the rocks shifting under his flip-flops. Minivans, SUVs, and cars, many bearing out-of-state plates, filled the lot. Inside the store, freezers contained frozen cherries, apple juice from last season, and pies. Fresh baked goods lined shelves, and quippy signs hung from the walls that said things like IF I HAD KNOWN GRAND-KIDS WERE SO MUCH FUN, I WOULD HAVE HAD THEM FIRST and I ENJOY A GLASS OF WINE EACH NIGHT FOR THE HEALTH BENEFITS. THE REST ARE FOR MY WITTY COMEBACKS AND FLAWLESS DANCE MOVES. Bass slid his hand into Isaac's as they walked around the store, staying close to him as they sampled pretzels with cherry-studded dips and homemade jams. A café sold freshly roasted Door County–brand coffee and cherry sodas made with Door County cherry juice.

In the bakery area, Isaac picked up a container of apple

turnovers still warm from the oven—they would be a tasty breakfast in their motel room tomorrow.

"Good choice," a small older woman said. She had come up beside him quietly. Her smile and bright skin contrasted with the silver hair pulled into a knot at the back of her head. She had kind blue eyes that crinkled as she smiled up at him. "They're the best in the county, other than my own of course."

She stood a few feet from him, close enough to talk comfortably, but not so close that he felt encroached on by a stranger— though he couldn't imagine anyone feeling cramped by this tiny woman who radiated a gentle spirit. "Well, how do I get yours?" Isaac said.

"Charmer." From her arm dangled a shopping basket containing a pound of coffee and a bag of frozen cherries as she took him in from head to toe. She looked around him at Bass, who was doing his best to remain unnoticed. "Are you here for vacation?"

"I think so?" Isaac meant it as a statement, but it sounded more like a question.

"You don't sound too sure. How long are you staying?"

"I'm not too sure about that, either. We came here on a whim and aren't too sure what to do next." Maybe she could share some pointers on where to stay more long term and how they could pass their time. "Can I treat you to a coffee in exchange for more local tips?" He pointed to the four-table café at the back of the store.

The older woman studied him. He envisioned her judging prize cattle at a state fair, her skilled eye seeing below the surface to the quality underneath. She nodded and let him pay for two coffees and one cherry soda for Bass.

As they settled onto their chairs, Isaac stuck out his hand. "I'm Isaac. Isaac Banks. This is Bass."

She shook it with her soft, warm hands.

"I'm Mrs. Dibble." She poured a generous amount of cream and sugar into her coffee, unabashedly. "So, where are you staying?"

"We have reservations at Cherrywood Motel."

She nodded and tapped a short, wrinkled finger to her lips.

"That's a lovely place if you're here for a weekend or so. But if you're looking to stay longer, you might want to try something other than staying at a motel—even those get pricey here during the summer."

"What else is there?"

"Some people rent their houses, but that's not cheap either. If you're looking to make a little money, though, a lot of the orchards hire extra help during the summer. Some provide housing."

Isaac liked the idea of spending the rest of the summer here. Already it seemed a million miles away from home, away from having to deal with his ex-wife's death. On the flip side, staying still might give the truth time to catch up to him. He shook the thought away. He thought about where they could go next—maybe south through the Appalachians—and the muscle in his right shoulder twitched in protest. He rubbed it with his left hand. While he had enough money saved to finance a month or two on the road, earning some income meant they could stay as long as they needed. Plus, having some work would also keep his mind from dwelling on the past.

"That would be great. Where would I find a list of places hiring? Is there a website?"

Mrs. Dibble chuckled.

"We're not so fancy. I happen to know of a perfect orchard that might suit you. It's not too big—run by a small family. They don't normally hire help until the harvest, but I know the owner is looking for someone now." She clicked her tongue. "You might just be perfect. And I know they love kids."

She nodded toward Bass. Warmth spread up Isaac's arms—a sure sign this idea had merit.

"Do you have a number?"

She wrote it down and handed it to him.

"You'll get his answering machine, but he'll call you back after dinner. He's always very good about returning phone calls." Her lips curved into a soft smile.

"Thank you."

"Don't mention it. I'm sure you'll be seeing more of me." Sending a quick smile toward Bass, Mrs. Dibble rose from the table and said her good-byes.

Isaac turned to Bass, who was gulping the last of his cherry soda.

"What do you think, Tuna? Should we check it out?"

Bass's quick nod reaffirmed his own thoughts. The muscle twitch, the fortuitous meeting of Mrs. Dibble, and the overall easing of tension all colluded as if by design. Isaac dialed the number feeling more certain than he had in years.

CHAPTER THREE

Sanna measured the apple juice into a large glass beaker and added it to the carboy, swirling a cheery red—like Santa's suit. She wrote down the amount in her notebook and did the same with the next juice, this one a bold sapphire blue, which mixed with the red into a vivid purple. When it came to cider, colors and flavors blended together for her. She knew she had the right blend when it matched the color she had envisioned. It wasn't scientific—and it didn't happen with anything else Sanna tasted—but here, with her beloved trees, it worked. She carefully tracked the blends in her journal. The sun streamed through the window, lighting up the colors in the carboy like Christmas lights. She was close—one more juice should do it. She closed her eyes, calling to mind all the juices in the barn's cooler and their corresponding colors.

Every juice she tasted from their apples had a slightly different hue, differing among individual varieties, but even varying slightly from tree to tree. When she was twenty-four, she had stood at the tall kitchen counter tasting freshly pressed juices she had made for the first time with the press she had unearthed from the old barn. Her plan had originally been to sell them in the farm stand, but she wanted to pick the best. As she sipped each one, an unmistakable color came to mind—different for each juice—and she finally understood the watercolor apple portraits above the fireplace. They were proof she wasn't the only family member who could see the colors. After she explained it to her dad, he smiled.

"I thought you might have the gift."

"You knew about this?"

"It's family legend. My dad said Grandpa could taste colors in the apples, but no one in my lifetime has been able to, so I thought it might be myth. When you returned home after college—the way you were drawn to Idun's—I thought you might have it." He had put his hands on the side of her face. "This means something good, Sanna."

"Why didn't you say anything? Why didn't I know before?"

"Would you have believed me?"

"I've had apple juice from the Rundstroms a thousand times. Why can't I see it with theirs?"

"I think it has something to do with apples from our land. We're connected to it, and it to us."

Sanna had always appreciated the sanctuary of the orchard, and this revelation bonded Sanna like another root digging into the soil, finding nourishment. She'd never leave.

After a few years of making and selling apple juice, Sanna strolled through the Looms wondering how these older trees still produced apples, even though they couldn't sell them. They didn't make for good eating or baking—Einars called them spitters. Over the years, the family had stopped paying attention to the sprawling trees since no one would buy their fruit—customers only wanted attractive, sweet produce. Other than the art above the mantel, they had lost track of what varieties they had, but with a bit of research and a lot of comparing and contrasting to the watercolors and online photos, Sanna discovered they had a treasure trove of cider-making apples—Kingston Black, Ashton Bitter, Medaille d'Or, Foxwhelp, her favorite Rambo tree, and so many more. The first Lunds had brought these trees to make cider, but had to stop during Prohibition, packing away the equipment in the back of their barn for Sanna to find so many years later.

She spent years experimenting with small batches, understanding the colors, using their existing press and carboys to ferment. Then, last year, Einars surprised her with plans to rebuild the barn, complete with huge fermentation tanks and modern mills and presses. Sanna could use her talent and passion to help move their orchard into a new phase . . . or so they both hoped.

Sanna poured a small amount of her purple blend into a beaker, where she could experiment on the tinier amount before risking the entire batch. She'd almost found the exact shade of purple she'd been trying to create when it disappeared in a flood of apple juice and crystalline shards. The cause—a hard, green apple thrown through the closed window and into her cider.

Sanna blinked as the daylight pushed the last tatters of lavender from her vision, replacing it with harsh afternoon yellow and floating dust motes set loose by the interruption. She watched the combination of juices swoosh to the floor until just a few violet drips were left. She sighed and plucked the fruit from the broken and wet equipment, careful not to cut herself. With each crunch of glass underfoot, she got angrier and angrier. Some moron had ruined her beautiful purple cider by chucking an apple—an apple that should have been safely left to grow on the branch—through her window. Sanna gripped the sphere and looked down through the broken pane.

Outside, Einars spoke to a handsome dark-haired man. The breeze pulled at his unruly brown curls. At his side stood a miniature version; the man's hand gripped the boy's shoulder with one hand as he gestured toward the window with the other, his apologetic smile matching the one of amusement on her father's face.

Heat rose up her neck. Breaking her window was no laughing matter. In a few efficient moves, she swept the broken glass off the counter to the floor, careful not to step in it, and mopped up the ruined blend of juice before it made the counter sticky. She squeezed the apple in her fist, its flesh still too immature to give more than a few drops of juice where the skin had broken on impact. In a righteous fury, she left the barn that still smelled of sawdust from the recent remodel.

As she approached the threesome, the man and boy stopped talking. Einars smiled wider when she halted in front of them. He was the only man she ever had to look up to, and right now his pale eyes twinkled. He was planning something. Her own crisp blue eyes squinted in suspicion. His thin and transparent hair lifted off his head in the soft, early-summer breeze. The boy stepped shyly behind his father as she held up the orb of destruction to accuse.

"This apple broke my window," she said, her lips tightened to clip the words short.

Einars ignored her, instead holding open his arms. "Sanna, come meet Isaac Banks. He'll be helping at the orchard this season."

Helping? Sanna was confused. They never took on extra hands until the harvest, which was months from now—and even then it was generally one or two neighbors they'd known for years. Perhaps she had misunderstood her father.

Isaac held out his hand in greeting as his eyes took in all

six feet three inches of her. Sanna girded herself for the comments, switched the apple to her other hand, and shook the offered palm out of habit, realizing only when they touched that she hadn't bothered to wipe off the few drops of apple juice. His big hand encircled hers and was warm and dry, like it had been buried in the sand. His deep brown eyes, fringed in lush lashes, sparkled under strong brows. His olive skin already had a bronze glow, countering the silver flecks in his thick, dark beard. His temples crinkled as his lips curved into a warm, homey smile. Sanna's mouth went dry. This man sparkled, brightening everything around him, too. If her window hadn't just been broken, she might have tested her very rusty flirtation skills. Instead, she pulled herself a little taller.

"Hi, Sanna, pleasure to meet you." He said her name like the sounds were new and he was rolling them over his tongue, learning and liking the way they felt. The warmth of his hand nearly burned on hers, which was still cool from an afternoon in the chilly barn, and sticky from the juice drying on her skin. Even though neither of them had moved, she seemed closer to him, or maybe she wanted to be closer to him. Her focused ire threatened to scatter, and she maintained contact with him for a second longer. She pulled her hand back, their skin briefly sticking together from the apple juice.

Sanna nodded briskly, pulled her eyes away from where they lingered on his smile, turned to her dad, and held the apple in front of her.

"What are we going to do about this?"

Isaac's lips thinned as Einars plucked the apple from Sanna's grip and tossed it into the orchard.

"Calm down, Sanna-who." Sanna cringed. Her dad—who liked to joke they were "Scanda-whovians"—had been calling her Sanna-who ever since she was a barefoot, sun-bleached child running through the orchard. She didn't mind it when they were alone, but in front of strangers? Too personal. "The boy was just being a boy. It's nothing that can't be fixed."

"That carelessness broke some of my equipment and ruined a batch I was blending."

With Isaac's eyes watching her every move, she struggled to maintain her anger, even though she was in the right. She knew she was coming off harsh, but she didn't dare speak more words than were necessary.

Einars took a moment to look at Sanna, then at the boy. "Then he'll have to help you until the equipment and window are paid for. He'll be your assistant," Einars said.

That brought her back to her senses. He may as well have slapped her, the impact was the same—bracing and immobilizing. She couldn't even manage a gasp, though her eyebrows stretched up toward her hairline. Spending time with this whelp of . . . she couldn't even tell how old he was. Eight? Twelve? All kids looked the same to her. Dirty and noisy and annoying.

"That won't be necessary," she finally said. She expected her father to respond, but instead Isaac spoke up.

"No, I insist. Einars is right. Bass needs to take responsibility for his actions."

Sanna squinted at him, not sure she'd heard correctly. He had his hands on his son's shoulders, sturdy and guiding, making it clear where his priorities were.

"Bass? Like a fish?"

The boy snorted, then covered his mouth to hide a giggle. That wasn't the response she had hoped for.

"His name is Sebastian, but that's a bit of a mouthful. He responds to most fish names, don't you, Trout?" Isaac ruffled Bass's moppish curls, and he mumbled "Dad" as he stepped out of reach.

Isaac's face glowed as he looked at his son, now kicking at the rocks in the orchard's parking lot, then he shifted back to her—obviously expecting her to object again. She couldn't work with someone who had the attention span of a gnat—but she'd make her objections clear to her father at dinner. Having spent time with her spoiled nieces, Gabby and Sarah—Anders had completely ruined those girls, they didn't even know how to climb a tree—she didn't want to spend any more time with Fish-Boy than she had to. She'd just lie low and her father would forget about it. Besides, he never made her do things she didn't want to.

"Fine. I'm heading back to work." She turned to go back to the barn without another word—avoiding making eye contact with Isaac.

"Sanna," her father said, "don't clean up the mess. That can be Bass's first job." She gave a little wave to acknowledge she had heard him and kept walking to the barn. What would she do to keep a kid busy all day—assuming she could keep it together in front of his dad? Before she opened the side door closest to the stairs, she paused to look over Idun's Orchard. The straight lines of trees, cocooned in fresh green leaves that hid the small apples in various states of growth. She couldn't quite see the trailer behind all the trees, the place where Isaac and Bass—what an absurd nickname—would be living while they stayed on. There was no way to avoid working with Isaac—and she wasn't entirely sure she wanted to, which bothered her—but with some strategic planning, she could avoid the kid.

Behind her, on the other side of the gravel driveway, was the Lund family home, an enormous two-story farmhouse in the shape of an L, covered in white painted wood siding. They could shelter a small village in the large home, and practically had in the past when generations of Lunds had lived there to-gether. Now it was only the two of them.

Sanna could still hear Isaac and Einars talking from around the corner, Isaac's loud, unbridled laughter competing with her father's boisterous voice. She could even hear the skittering of rocks as Bass continued to kick them. While intrigued by the appearance of this undeniably handsome man, she was unsettled by all these changes in one day. Hired help before harvest? What would this do to their finely tuned routines? Was there even enough work to make the help worthwhile? All the uncertainty blocked her usual confidence and command. She sighed, letting her shoulders slump as she climbed the stairs to the loft.

The season was only five months long, she told herself bracingly, then everything would go back to normal.

Sanna walked up the four steps from the back door into the kitchen, the screen door slamming behind her as she reached the top. The kitchen was half of the airy great room that made up the heart of the house. A long counter hugged the wall, hous-ing the sink, stove, and cabinets, with a window overlooking the giant oak tree, patio, and the orchard's barn and parking lot. A massive island served as both countertop and eating spot—six inches taller than a traditional counter to accommodate the generations of tall Lunds. Separating the kitchen from the great room was an ancient farm table that could easily seat ten, worn from years of family dinners, frequent scrubbings, and dropped objects. Like with so many pieces in the house, she could recall the history in each scratch and dent. Each held a story that had been told to her by her father as she grew up, like the half-inch divot where her grandfather dropped an entire cast-iron pot on the table when his wife went into labor, or the crayon scribbles on the underside of every piece of furniture—she herself had scrawled the entire alphabet on the coffee table.

Sanna pulled off her boots and tucked them into a wooden cubby, one of many lining the wall at the top of the steps. Above the cubbies hung the range of all-weather gear she and her dad needed—raincoats and pants, wide-brimmed hats, thick leather gloves, and warm winter jackets. Weather didn't stop work on a farm. She slipped into her indoor clogs made of boiled wool and lined with soft lamb's wool and strode across the bright room to the bathroom she shared with Einars.

Since it was just the two of them, they only used a small part of the sprawling house. They had converted the office and den near the great room into bedrooms, leaving the rest of the house closed off to conserve energy. The closed-off wing contained bedrooms full of sheet-covered furniture—it was where Sanna had spent her early years, when her grandparents were still alive and the Donor and Anders had rounded out their family, but she preferred the central part of the house now. She loved that instead of building a traditional second floor, they had left the loft open, amplifying the airiness of the space. A spiral staircase of pale-gray painted wood led to the large open room. On one side of the loft, she could look down on the activity in the great room and kitchen, or she could sit on one of the squashy couches or chairs that faced the large windows overlooking the northern side of the orchard. From up there, she could see her favorite tree— one of the oldest in the orchard—a meandering Rambo with sweeping arched branches that sat in the center of the Looms, rising above all the other trees. When she was a child, it was her favorite to climb. She could scramble higher because its center limb was never trimmed back but allowed to grow straight. From its branches, she could see over the tops of all the other trees, the way she towered over the other kids at school.

Perhaps she'd read in the loft tonight, but for now she needed to clean up for the dinner her dad would have on the table at six fifteen sharp. With efficient movements, she showered and swapped her sturdy work clothes for comfortable cotton men's pajama pants and a soft, worn T-shirt. As she went through the familiar motions, she pondered how to bring up the issue of the new residents with Einars. With her hair still wet and sending a few errant drops down the back of her neck, she joined her dad in the kitchen with five minutes to spare.

"Hey, Pa, what's for dinner?"

Einars pulled a square, white dish from the top oven and set it on a blue and white ceramic trivet. Sanna grabbed two plates and a serving spoon, preparing to start scooping.

"Let it cool. You can pick out the veg." He pointed his oven-mitted hand to the freezer. She opened the door and grabbed the bag on top—green beans. She tossed them into the microwave and turned back to her father as he pulled a second dish out of the bottom oven; this one scented the room with cinnamon and apples. Einars had long insisted on an apple dessert every day, their reward for tending the orchard so carefully, or so he told her. She thought he just wanted a sweet every night.

"Cheesy chicken noodle and cobbler?" Sanna pointed her chin to the potato chip–topped casserole and toasty brown pan.

He nodded. When their veggies dinged, they scooped out servings and poured drinks in a synchronized routine, ending with them sitting at the table in silence, Sanna's mind wandering to the fresh bottles waiting to be filled with a new batch. Between bites, Einars cleared his throat and pulled her back to dinner.

"Anders called today," Einars said.

Sanna kept chewing—she didn't trust herself to not make snide comments about her absentee brother.

"He invited us to Thanksgiving at their house this year."

Sanna swallowed before she choked on her food, gulping it down with her milk. She couldn't contain a small cough, which her dad interpreted as intentional.

"He's trying to stay in touch. It wouldn't kill you to reach out to him, too."

"Pa, I'm not going to argue about him. You know how I feel."

Sanna took a big bite so she could avoid saying more about her brother.

"I told Bass he'd start with you, tomorrow."

But this was not the topic change she was hoping for. Sanna stopped chewing and took another drink of her milk.

"I'm not dealing with him. He can help you or his dad. I don't want him near the cider stuff."

"You will deal with him." Einars pointed his fork at her. "He broke your equipment and he needs to work it off."

"I don't like kids."

"You don't know any. Besides your nieces, who are, frankly, pretty spoiled. Not all kids are like that—you were an okay kid, once. He's working with you, and that's final."

Einars went back to scooping forkfuls of chicken and noodles into his mouth, ignoring Sanna's blinking. She couldn't remember the last time he'd issued a direct order. Maybe never.

"Fine. I'll teach him curse words. Even the really bad ones."

"At ten, he'll probably be teaching you a few." Einars snorted a laugh. "And you'll need to cancel any plans you might have for tomorrow, Isaac and Bass are going to have dinner with us here."

Sanna shrugged. Thad wouldn't care if she canceled. Their mutual apathy was one of her favorite things about their weekly outings.

"Besides, since when do we hire help in June?"

Einars looked quickly at his plate, trying to spear a green bean on his fork. "I'm not so young anymore. I can't do what I used to."

Ridiculous. Just last week she'd seen him install her new fermentation tanks. This was absurdity. There was no reason for him to mess with their routine. It had worked great for a decade, and there were no grounds to change it now.

She cleared their plates when they were done and set them next to the sink. Their deal was he would make dinner and she would clean the dishes—though he cleaned while he cooked, so her job was easy. With a quick peck on his cheek, she shooed him from the kitchen with a plate of cobbler in his hands, set her own plate next to her journal, then filled the sink with steaming water and fluffy bubbles—doing the dishes by hand gave her time to think.

The journal itself was one of many bound notebooks she had. This one had a faux lizard cover and a ribbon placeholder. Each one was a little different, wide lines, no lines, leather bound. Whenever she found one she liked, she bought it. They were the place where she scribbled every thought, every experiment, every success, and every failure of her cider making. The early ones overflowed with more failures than successes, but lately the drawings had evolved. She pulled out her colored pencils and started layering colors, stopping long enough to turn off the water and set the dishes in the water to soak.

She wasn't particularly artistic, but without thought she knew the combination that would get her the color she wanted. Last night she'd arrived at a rich royal made up of layered cobalt blue and indigo, and she knew exactly what it would taste like. Dry, but not bitter, with a bold apple finish. Not shy of what it was, but proud and majestic.

Tonight the greens she sketched spoke to her of gentle whis-

pers and a soft sweetness, with just a lilt of apple, but very refreshing. She'd need to finish her orchard chores with Bass early
if she'd get a chance to play with this. She'd met him for two
minutes and was already annoyed by the little beast. Frustrated,
she slammed the journal cover closed, causing a scrap of paper
to escape and flutter to the floor. She had a routine, a life, and
babysitting a little boy did not fit into it. Giving up on her journal,
she scooped a bite of her dessert and turned to the dishes in the
sink, taking regular breaks for another bite of cobbler—leaving a
trail of water from the sink to the counter. As the sun took its last
few breaths before night, the answer to the Bass problem hit her.

Kids didn't like her! Her nieces had made it abundantly
clear that her short hair and mannish clothes made her a loser,
as did her lack of knowledge of any current movies or shows.
Not to mention, on more than one occasion she'd made them
cry with her blunt opinion on their spoiled behavior. She'd just
be her normal self, and the kid would most likely beg his dad to
get away from her.

Standing at the counter, solid with her decision, she scraped
the last of the cinnamon sauce from the plate and set it in the
deflating bubbles. Just being herself was the perfect solution.
She picked up her dad's empty plate from the end table next to
where he shuffled through orchard paperwork, reading glasses
perched on the end of his nose. She finished washing their
dishes, retrieved her novel, and curled into a chair, confident
tomorrow would put an end to needless disruptions.

CHAPTER FOUR

The key turned in the lock easily; a sheen of WD-40 glinting in the afternoon sun revealed the reason why. Isaac expected a waft of stale air to assault his nose when he swung open the door to the trailer, but was greeted with fresh air with a hint of bleach. A quick glance to the windows explained why—they were all open, letting the evening air circulate. With Bass's hand clutching tight to his, he led them both into their home for the next few months.

The trailers of his youth were musty, dingy hovels, but the temporary worker housing at Idun's was crisp and efficient, with a palette of pale wood trim, whites, and grays. They stood in a small entry—directly in front of them was a closet with a stacked washer and dryer. To the right of that was the door to the bathroom—the source of the bleach scent—complete with an actual tub. The toilet didn't even have rust stains. Farther right was a walk-through kitchen; the cupboards already housed a few dishes. He dropped the keys onto the white counter and opened the fridge, smiling to see a fresh jug of milk, a few cold waters, and some apples. He tossed one to

Bass and took one for himself, biting it with a crunch, sucking the juices so they didn't dribble into his beard—the hazards of facial hair. A peek into the pantry revealed a few boxes of cereal and cans of soup. He couldn't imagine the brisk Sanna stocking the cupboards, so it must have been Einars—or Sanna on Einars's orders. Though he had trouble envisioning Sanna taking orders from anyone.

A small table rounded out the kitchen, tucked tightly against a bank of windows that looked out onto the back property line, with more trees in neat lines on the other side. On the end of the trailer was a snug living room with a worn but clean sofa. A peek under the cushions proved it to be a hide-a-bed. Next to the window, a folded blanket lay on the back of a slim recliner. It was spare but cozy.

"Where's the TV?" Bass asked.

Isaac looked for a cabinet or spot where one could be hidden, but didn't see one.

"I think we are sans TV for the summer." Bass's face fell in disappointment. "TVs are where you watch other people's adventures. We're going to be having our own." Bass perked up a bit, but Isaac knew it would be a long summer, especially since the trailer wouldn't have Wi-Fi either, per his request during his phone call with Einars.

Before going out to get their luggage, he stuck his head in the bedroom, which took up the back third of the house and contained a queen bed and a built-in dresser.

"Looks like you'll be bunking with me, Sardine," he said, giving Bass's hand a little squeeze. "Let's get our stuff."

In one trip, they carried the couple of duffel bags and Bass's backpack from the black Prius. Bass unzipped his bag and pulled out a green fuzzy object, setting it on the right pillow of the bed, his preferred sleeping side.

"Snarf make the trip okay?" Isaac asked.

"He's a stuffed animal, he's fine." Bass rolled his eyes, but moved the dragon a bit farther from the bed's edge before dumping the rest of the backpack's contents out. Sprawled across the clean white comforter was his son's life—everything he had deemed important enough to bring on their trip: a stack of baseball cards, books four and five in the Amulet series, his baseball glove and a baseball, a *Mad Libs* book they had bought somewhere in Kansas in which all nouns entered were either *fart* or *butt*, his iPad, and a handful of superhero action figures.

But Snarf was the prize possession, a gift from his mother, Paige, shortly after she and Isaac had divorced. It was a squishy green dragon with hidden pockets to keep secret treasures. Snarf's pockets were filled with sticky notes written by both Isaac and Paige for Bass's kindergarten lunch box during the last year of their marriage. Bass wasn't aware that Isaac knew he'd kept them. Isaac had discovered them before Snarf got his first bath after falling in a mud puddle. Before tossing it into the washing machine, he'd dutifully checked all the pockets, each note a sad reminder of the year they tried to make it work even as Paige had slipped away. Some notes were in his precise print—simple reminders on how to spell their last name and that Q came after P in the alphabet, followed by a dozen Xs and Os to show his love. Paige's notes were in a wobbly cursive, illegible to a six-year-old, but treasured all the same.

As Bass sorted his treasures and found them homes along the windowsills, Isaac dumped out the duffels onto the bed to organize their clothes in the dresser, careful not to let the envelope of papers, one of which was Paige's death certificate, fall out. With a subtle glance to make sure Bass hadn't seen, he closed the now-empty duffel and slid it under the bed. Bass was still too young.

After devouring the frozen pizza Isaac found in the freezer, Isaac and Bass tidied up the kitchen. With so little space, they would need to keep things clean, which wouldn't be too difficult with the little they had brought with them.

"Time for bed," Isaac said.

Bass slid the last dried plate into the cupboard and yawned. "Not tired."

"Dude, you just yawned big enough an ostrich could have run in and out of your mouth and you wouldn't have noticed." He paused, walking back toward the bedroom, knowing he was pulling Bass in his wake. "It's been a long day, and tomorrow we actually have work to do."

He opened the dresser drawer and pulled out Bass's pajamas.

"I don't want to work with her." Bass crossed his arms.

"You have to. You broke the window and some of her equipment. Since you don't have money, you need to work it off. Besides, you might even learn something."

They both got into pajamas and went into the bathroom to brush their teeth. It had become their routine to do it together.

"She doesn't like me."

Isaac was a little worried about this, too. Sanna didn't seem like the most warm and fuzzy person, but it would be good for Bass to learn how to interact with different types of people. He would make sure to spend some time with her, too, make sure the prickly woman was giving Bass a fair chance—or at least that was the level of interest he was willing to admit to himself tonight.

"She doesn't know you." He squirted toothpaste onto each of their toothbrushes.

"She's really tall. As tall as you," Bass said around the tooth-brush in his mouth, spraying white foam onto the mirror.

Isaac smiled and wiped it off. He loved hearing Bass's take on events. For some magical reason—or more likely the not-so-magical reason of trying to extend his bedtime—Bass always became more talkative at this time of night, and Isaac found it impossible to resist the conversation. It wouldn't be long until the surly teen years, might as well soak up the conversation now. He spit out his toothpaste.

"I noticed."

"Do you think she needs a ladder to pick apples?" Tooth-paste foam dribbled out of his mouth as he spoke. Isaac resisted the urge to wipe his chin.

"You can ask her tomorrow. I bet she'd tell you."

"What do you think about her?"

He wiped his mouth and held out the towel for Bass to do the same, buying some time before answering. His first thought was what he wouldn't call her to his son: sexy, luminous, or even pretty. Those weren't exactly the words he wanted, but she was undeniably attractive, the way an incoming storm could take your breath away with its ferocity and purpose. He couldn't give that answer to Bass.

"I think she's smart and knows how she likes to do things around here, so you'll need to listen carefully and follow her instructions. Now into bed."

After waiting as Bass slid under the covers and tucked Snarf into the crook of his arm, he covered them both with the com-forter and turned to go out to the living room. He needed to check some messages on his phone—needed to send his mom something to placate her—and maybe start one of the well-worn paperbacks he had seen tucked into a cupboard.

"You aren't coming to bed?" Bass asked, his voice tiny in the dim light. Isaac could hear the uncertainty in his voice. It was a new bed in a new place, and for the first time in three weeks, he had the space to stay up past Bass's bedtime in a different room rather than turn out the motel room's lights so he could fall asleep. Leaves rustled in the night breeze, and the occasional bug thwapped against the screen trying to get to the lights—the only sounds that broke through the blanket of quiet in this corner of the orchard.

He understood.

Bass had never gone this long without seeing his mom. Even with her roller-coaster emotions and frustrating highs and lows, she was the only mom he had, and he knew Bass missed her. That combined with the new and unfamiliar bed rattled his little boy's courage. Of course Bass would want to keep his dad as close as possible.

"I am." He took a quick glance at his phone to confirm there wasn't anything that couldn't wait until morning. "Just turning off the lights and locking up."

When Isaac lay down next to Bass, he was barely settled before Bass's little body and lanky limbs were draped all over Isaac—one arm still clutching Snarf, the other wrapped around Isaac's arm so he couldn't sneak away without Bass noticing. Isaac used his free arm to rub Bass's shoulder. So much had changed over the last few weeks, and so much could never go back to the way it was. He still couldn't process it all. As Bass snuggled in closer, his breath already easing into the first layers of sleep, Isaac let the closeness burrow into him, too. He kissed the top of Bass's head—somehow it always smelled like the air right after it rained, earthy and damp but never unpleasant—grateful that at least this had not changed.

Dew soaked Isaac's and Bass's feet in moments, and they weren't even past the first line of trees from the trailer's doorstep. The sun hadn't risen high enough to dry it yet, though the day promised to be warm and breezy. Isaac would need to get them some sturdier footwear or their feet would be perpetually wet. Bass had already discovered how slick the dew made the long grass, running and sliding across it. Seeing the natural escalation too slowly, Isaac could only groan. There wasn't time to stop it. Bass had already started his next dash, this time diving face-first like he would on a Slip'N Slide, gliding a few feet before stopping. When he popped up, his shirt and pants were drenched and a sloppy grin beamed off his face.

"Hey, Wahoo, how about we try and make a decent good impression?" He helped Bass brush off the dead leaves that clung to his now soggy shirt. With the way the sun was coming up, he'd dry off in no time. It wasn't worth heading back for a change of clothes—especially when he'd just find another way to get messy.

"What do you think I'm going to be doing?" Bass asked.

"Not sure. Whatever Miss Lund asks you to do."

"But what do you think? Maybe I'll get to drive a tractor."

Isaac laughed.

"We aren't on that kind of farm—and you're too young to be driving anything other than a broom around the floor."

They walked for a few moments in silence as the white farmhouse became visible between the trees.

"That house is huge. Are they rich?" Bass asked.

"Don't ask Miss Lund that." Isaac bit his cheek to keep from smiling at Bass's innocent yet impertinent question. "If I were to guess, I bet they used to have a lot more people living there than just them. If you look at the bottom, that's the foundation and it's made from fieldstone, not concrete blocks, so you can tell it's been around for a while. People don't really use fieldstone in construction anymore."

He had noticed it yesterday, too. The house was hard to miss, rising out of the trees like a mountain—or a nice-sized hill. He had been surprised to learn that only Sanna and Einars lived there, running the entire orchard themselves. Envisioning them working long days, then bumping around an empty house painted the entire orchard with a melancholy patina.

It seemed a lonely life.

He touched the dangling branches, the spring bright leaves hiding baby green apples, a first glimpse at the harvest to come. Everything around him was new and fresh with so much growing left to do. Yet with all the new growth, the trees had aged bark, wrinkled and scarred where branches had been trimmed off. He could almost feel the roots winding deeper into the earth, stretching themselves ever farther while their crowns reached to the sun.

Sometimes Bass grew the same way. He'd put him to bed with pants that fit perfectly, then wake in the morning to see two inches more of ankle. Some nights they'd put bags of ice on his shins to freeze out the growing pains.

Isaac took a deep breath, filling his lungs with the clean air, not the stagnant, stinky feet fug of their car. With each breath, the tension of the last few weeks eased out, like the shaking out of a rug. Each breath released more of the dirt. He'd never get all of it out, but he felt cleaner than he had since he decided to take Bass on this journey. He shoved the sadness that lingered down deep. No amount of shaking could remove it, so he'd need to keep it hidden.

His priorities now were to make sure Bass enjoyed this adventure as much as possible. The fresh air, the blue skies, the warm water at the beach in the nearby state park. He wanted his son to learn how to climb a tree and catch fireflies, maybe how to grill a hamburger on the Weber he had seen behind the trailer. This time needed to be so wonderful that Bass would forgive Isaac for not telling him the truth about Paige right away.

Bass started tilting his head in a rhythm, and Isaac knew what was coming.

"Farts and butts and farts and butts and farts and butts," Bass chanted in time to the head tilts.

Isaac couldn't help but smile before he nipped this latest verbal tick.

"Perhaps you should keep the backside commentary to a minimum until the Lunds get used to us. As shocking as you may find it, not everyone thinks farts are as funny as you do. Got it?"

"Got it."

With a skip, Bass took off at a run to weave between the apple trees, juking back and forth. Isaac wasn't sure if he was envisioning an epic lightsaber battle or an end-of-game touchdown run, but he knew it had nothing to do with their actual surroundings. But it was the surroundings that Isaac was counting on to give the two of them some much-needed sanctuary.

Watching Bass's unbridled play, Isaac knew he had done the right thing. He didn't need to know the truth yet. One more summer of innocence.

As they approached the tree line, Issac saw Einars and Sanna waiting for them at the same time Bass did. He stopped running and returned to his dad's side, walking half a step behind him, still not ready to leave the safety of his dad's shadow. Isaac wasn't used to this reticent side of Bass—but what else could he expect when he took him from everything that was familiar?

Einars and Sanna stood on gravel, twin stalks of denim and plaid. Einars's wispy gray hair shook in the morning breeze while Sanna's didn't move. It was pale with a hint of red, like the first blush on a ripening apple. You had to see it in the sunlight to make sure it was really there.

They hadn't spotted them yet, so Isaac took a moment to watch her as she plucked weeds from the gravel drive. When she stood, she was almost as tall as her father and she owned every inch. Her spine was straight and challenging, her movements concise and efficient as she bent at her waist and tore the plants up in quick yanks. She moved as much as she needed to, exactly as she needed to. There was a certain unselfconscious grace in it. Her mouth was a straight line on her pale, smooth skin. For someone who must spend a lot of time out of doors, this seemed a mystery until she put on a floppy, wide-brimmed hat with open weaving and a long strap to keep it from falling off.

He wanted to stand there all day drinking her in, enchanted. Before taking his first step onto the gravel parking lot, Isaac paused, his feet still buried in the damp grass of the orchard. He could feel a pull from behind his navel drawing him straight toward her. He hadn't noticed it in yesterday's introductions, he'd been too focused on Bass and getting him settled into a new place. But today there was no question.

Good Lord, he had a full-blown, five-alarm crush on the boss's daughter.

He stepped back, bumping into Bass.

"Dad!" he yelped.

Both Einars and Sanna turned to them. Isaac's chest thumped as her eyes hit his, then turned to Bass without even a pause, no recognition that she felt a pull in his direction. He straightened his shoulders and gave in to the magical tow line drawing him forward. Not like he had a choice—he couldn't exactly go back to the trailer. As soon as he gave in, a smile spread across his face and his steps lightened.

"Morning," Einars said as Bass and Isaac joined them. "Sleep well?"

"Very. It's been a long time since I fell asleep to the sound of leaves rustling outside my window." He watched Sanna out of the side of his eye. She stood still, watching her dad speak but clearly mentally somewhere else.

"Good, good." He nodded, his blue eyes flicking from Isaac to Sanna. "You'll start the day with me and the young man can help Sanna clean up the mess from yesterday. Isn't that right, Sanna?"

Sanna jolted at the sound of her name and looked from her father to Bass to Isaac. Isaac gave a little smile to her, but she looked back at Bass, who was standing so close to Isaac he was stepping on his foot. Isaac gave his shoulder a little squeeze to reassure him, and himself. Why couldn't Sanna be a bit more friendly toward Bass? He was a good kid and obviously uncomfortable with the prospect of being alone with her. Was she completely oblivious to it?

"Yes," she said. "Follow me." She turned and walked toward the barn. Bass looked up at Isaac, and he winked.

"Just listen to her instructions and be friendly. I'll see you in a bit." Bass nodded, swallowed, then ran to catch up before she disappeared into the barn. Isaac felt a pang as the two walked into the shadows. She was like a thistle, regal from a distance, but get too close and it would prick you. She had better not hurt Bass—crush or not.

"Good luck," Einars said. Isaac turned to look at him.

"Pardon?" he asked.

"Good luck. I mean it. I looked at my wife the same way you're looking at my daughter now, and my Sanna won't make it easy."

He was looking at her in a certain way? Had she noticed?

"You think . . . Ha! No. Bass is a little nervous so I was making sure he was okay." And that was partly true.

Einars sucked on his teeth as he took in Isaac's lie, deciding if he'd let him get away with it.

"Sure." He grinned. "Let me show you around the place."

Isaac gave the barn one last glance before following after the older man toward the head of the parking lot. Einars stopped and turned to face the orchard.

"Here's a quick lay of the land. Nearest the road on the south side." He pointed to his right. "These are the Earlies—the apples designed to ripen first. As you get farther back, the apples ripen later and later in the season. The same is true for the north side on the rear of the house." He moved his hand to indicate between the house and the barn. "In the far northeast corner are our oldest trees—the Looms. Those are Sanna's trees, so defer to her on those. We have about nine thousand trees total, from just grafted a few days ago to very old. This land has been in our family since 1870, and we've been growing apples ever since."

Einars's eyes scanned across the landscape in front of them and landed on Isaac, taking his measure in response to this information. Isaac sensed the pride and something even more important in Einars's words. This place wasn't just trees and dirt, it was a legacy and a home—in the truest sense of the word.

"I'm honored you're letting Bass and me help out here."

Einars nodded and clapped him on the shoulder with more strength than he'd expected from those wiry limbs.

"Now, let me show you my new ride," Einars said, his blue eyes sparkling.

CHAPTER FIVE

Sanna could see the boy formulating the thought. She saw that look every time she met someone new. This kid wouldn't be any different. "How's the weather up there?" was ever popular, as was "Do you play basketball?" The little boy's eyes traced the long journey from her tan work boots, over her worn blue jeans and faded plaid shirt, to the hat she had pushed off her head once they walked into the barn. Bass's eyes scrunched up as he finally met her level gaze. His mouth opened, as if tilting his head so far back made it impossible to keep his lips together at the same time. He took a quick breath, and she knew the inevitable comment about her height was about to come.

"Do you smell farts up there?"

At least that was a new one. Sanna's mouth opened to respond, but she had no words.

"Because hot air rises, but you're really up there, so I didn't know if they made it that far," Bass continued.

She blinked and recovered.

"No, I get what you're trying to say. And yeah, I do." She eyed him. "Is that gonna be a problem with you?"

Bass gave his butt a little wiggle.

"Not yet, but give me some time."

Sanna pressed her lips tightly to keep from smiling. Perhaps this kid wouldn't be as awful as her nieces.

She looked out the broken window to the orchard and could see her dad and Isaac walking across the parking lot to the first row of trees. Isaac kept his eyes trained on Einars as he explained about tree care, nodding and asking questions. Even though his pathetic sneakers were soaked, he looked at home in the orchard, unbothered by the buzzing insects and lack of technology. When he laughed at something Einars said, his head kicked back a little like the recoil of a gun—his joy shooting out into the world and through the open pane in front of her. Why was he so happy? His white teeth flashed in the sunlight, stark against his trim, dark beard. He squinted into the sun, not knowing enough to have brought a hat with him. He'd learn.

Everything about him was vivid: pink lips, brown twinkling eyes, even his cheeks were a bit rosy. The trees around him popped with emerald, bolder and stronger than ever. His dark waves absorbed the light, beaming it back through his skin. His long fingers wrapped around a tree branch and even from this distance she could tell he had the right combination of gentle and firm, careful not to damage any of the leaves or growing apples.

And her dad ate it up—laughing at his jokes, answering his questions, sharing his knowledge. The two of them walked to the green and yellow ATV Einars used to cruise around the orchard, and he gave the keys to Isaac. Sanna narrowed her eyes. He rarely let her drive it.

"Humph."

"Did you just burp?" Bass asked.

Sanna turned away from the light-filled window into the dim barn and the small person in front of her.

"No."

The kid's floppy curls were an unruly version of his father's, each one winding in a different direction. His shirt and pants were damp from who-knows-what, and he was about to blow into a length of plastic tubing she had sanitized for bottling. She grabbed it from his hands before his slobbery maw could make contact.

"Don't touch anything."

She set it on the counter next to her beakers and funnels—the ones the apple hadn't broken yesterday. Bass stuffed his hands in his pockets and looked around, nonplussed by her reprimand. He must hear that a lot. He walked toward a wall of glass carboys, putting his eye up to one of the holes as if looking in a telescope, breathing his hot, muggy breath on the glass.

"I said not to touch things."

"I'm not touching it." He straightened up. "There's a dead spider in there."

Sanna peeked into it and saw the curved legs of a brown spider. Yuck. She picked it up, careful to have a good grip so she didn't drop it, and shook the offending carcass loose. Bass had already wandered off to inspect a stack of wooden crates containing empty bottles, ready and waiting for the batch of cider she planned to bottle. He reached out to touch the topmost crate, stretching on his tiptoes. Didn't he ever just stand still?

"Stop . . ." Did he actually want to be named after a fish? ". . . Kid."

He froze.

"Come over here."

He walked and stood directly in front of her like a soldier.

"First, which name do you prefer? Bass or Sebastian?"

"Bass. No one ever calls me Sebastian."

Sanna nodded. If he was okay with it, then she would be, too.

"Second. Stop touching things. Those are filled with glass."

"I'm supposed to be helping."

Sanna looked around. This was what she dreaded. She didn't know how to talk to this kid. She didn't know how to keep him occupied, and what could he do to help her? She really didn't want him touching her stuff. Everything was precisely how and where she wanted it—already in these few minutes, he'd threatened her entire setup. Not even her dad meddled with her barn. Then she spotted the broom.

"There. Sweep the room carefully, and make sure to get all the glass bits from the corners." She pointed to where she had pushed all the broken window and beaker glass yesterday when she was preoccupied with the spilled juice.

In moments, Bass was quietly shushing around the dust and shards, so Sanna took a deep breath to focus on what she wanted to accomplish, grasping her journal. While he swept, she could pick up where she left off yesterday or maybe dive into that lovely greenish cider she'd dreamed of last night. Opening the pages and pulling out her notes, she ran her finger down the paper, refreshing her memory. Only once she picked up her pen to jot a few ideas down did she notice the sound of sweeping had stopped.

Bass stood staring at her, the broom tucked into the crook of his arm as if it were holding him up.

"What are you doing?" he asked before she could mutter the same words to him.

"I'm working."

"But I thought you were making beer. That just looks like you're writing."

If Sanna had been a bird, all of her feathers would have ruffled immediately. Topmost of her—admittedly many—pet peeves: people who treated the world like their personal ashtray, reckless Illinois drivers, neighbors who thought it was okay to ask when she planned to marry. But above all of those annoyances, the king of all pet peeves were people who didn't know the difference between beer and cider. Ignoring the fact that Bass was ten and shouldn't know about alcoholic anything anyway, Sanna prepared her speech.

"First, I make cider, not beer. Beer is made from grains and hops. Cider is made from apples. Saying they are the same thing is like saying a loaf of bread and applesauce are the same. You wouldn't do that, would you?" Bass shook his head, his eyes wide from the fervor in her tone. "Other than the fact that they both come in the same kind of bottles and are both fermented liquids, there aren't many similarities. Never confuse the two again."

She took a breath. "And to answer your question, I take notes of what I'm doing. That way if something goes wrong or really right, I know what I did and can try to replicate it."

"Like a scientist?"

"Yes, like a scientist. There is some chemistry involved, but it's more than that. There is a fair amount of instinct, too." Code for "seeing colors in apple juice," but he didn't need to know that part. "Let's get back to work."

Bass pushed the broom around with gusto for a few more minutes, then stopped again.

"Have you always lived here?"

"Yes."

"Do you like it?"

"Yes."

"Do you like apples?"

"Of course."

"What's your favorite?"

"Depends."

"On what?"

"On what I'm using them for. Now quiet."

The sweeping didn't resume, and Sanna, eyes back on her notebook, girded herself for another onslaught.

"You don't like me very much, do you?"

Surprised by the question, Sanna jerked her pen across the page. She turned to give him her full attention, taking in his floppy hair and dust-smudged legs. She could almost smell his little-boy smell from this distance, and her nose crinkled.

"It's not personal. I don't really like any children."

She wasn't sure what she expected him to do. Cry. Call her names. Stomp off and tell his dad. He did none of the above. He nodded his head and went back to sweeping.

"Maybe I'll be the first."

Sanna stared at him. Unlike her nieces, who had bluntly refused to do anything resembling work the few times they visited the orchard, Bass seemed okay, he'd done a good job on the sweeping and was using the dustpan as though he'd done it before. Maybe he could handle something a bit more interesting. She tucked away her journal, retrieved one of the carboys full of clear cider from the cooler, and set it on her workbench. Removing the S-shaped glass airlock that allowed gas out while keeping new air from entering, she set it aside to wash later.

"Bass, when you're finished sweeping, bring me four of those crates. Careful not to break any and don't touch the inside or near the lip of the bottles. Those are sanitized and ready for cider."

While he did that, she prepped the cider for the next step— bottling and carbonation—measuring out sugar with a food scale.

"Does all that sugar make the cider sweet?"

"Nope, it's food for the yeast. Once we put it in the bottles, the fresh yeast I'm going to add will eat the sugar, making carbon dioxide bubbles for a fizzy cider."

Bass's eyebrows scrunched together.

"Bubbles are yeast farts?"

Sanna bit her lip as she measured out the right amount of sugar, then dissolved it in water over a small burner.

"I'd never thought of it quite that way, but basically, yes, you're right."

"Cool."

While the sugar mix warmed, she prepared the fresh yeast and put both the yeast and sugar water into a sanitized bucket. Finally, she transferred the cider out of the glass carboy and into a bucket, letting the sugar and yeast mix as the cider flowed.

"Why are you moving it if you're just going to put it in bottles right away?"

Sanna took a deep breath, not used to so many interruptions. She reached for a blank notebook page and a pen.

"First, so that I don't bottle any of the lees." She pointed to the sediment at the bottom of the glass. "This is leftover yeast and sediment that I don't want to bottle. Second, this is the work zone. Anytime you have a question—don't interrupt when we're in the work zone. I have to be very careful with my measurements or the bottles could explode—that's happened before. Instead, write down the questions, and I'll answer them all at the end of the day." She handed him a small notebook and pen, both of which he shoved in his back pocket.

"Now comes the fun part. Get all the bottles out and lined up on the workbench." She pointed to where she wanted them. While he did that, she set the bucket on a special shelf that would raise the bottom of the bucket above the tops of the bottles. Then she lined up the bottle capper and the sanitized caps. "Here's what's going to happen. I'm going to fill the bottles, and you're going to cap them. We'll do a few practice ones on empty bottles."

She grabbed a bottle and fitted a cap onto the top. She set it on the capper and pulled down the lever, which crimped the cap onto the bottle.

"See how that worked?" Bass nodded. "Now you try." She handed him a bottle and pointed to the caps. He did it perfectly on his first try. Not too shabby. It had taken her dad three tries to get it right. "Good. Ready to start?"

"Bring it." Bass's eyes focused on each bottle as she handed it to him, his mouth set in a grim line of concentration. Working together, it didn't take long to fill all the bottles, and Sanna— much to her surprise—was a little disappointed it didn't take longer.

CHAPTER SIX

Sanna and Bass had finished their work, and she'd sent him off with a snack and permission to run wild in the trees—as long as he could still see the house. She didn't want to be responsible for losing him on the first day.

She opened the driver's-side door of her truck and pulled hard on a lever until she heard the hood pop, then twisted the key, the engine sputtering a few times before catching. Before closing the door, she straightened the red wool blanket, which covered the torn vinyl seats held together with duct tape and positive thoughts. This beloved, frequently broken-down pickup was the truck her dad had used around the farm all her life—a dark forest green on the top and bottom thirds with a creamy white in the middle. Years of driving around the orchard meant scratches, which she regularly coated with rust preventer to keep chemistry from dissolving her beloved Elliot, named after the dragon in *Pete's Dragon* she had loved so much as a kid.

When her father bought his fancy new John Deere ATV to zoom around the orchard, he planned to sell the "old heap," given that more often than not it wouldn't start. Sanna staged a sit-in on the bed the day he wanted to bring it to the junkyard. Perhaps her tactic was a bit juvenile, but she had gotten what she wanted—the truck. Too many memories lived in it to let it go to scrap. She remembered picking apples while standing in the bed, cruising down the rows, bouncing as it hit exposed tree roots, and laying down mounds of blankets to watch the Fourth of July fireworks with her brother, seeing who could slurp from their gas station cherry slushie longest before the brain freeze hit—Sanna always won, still a point of pride.

She hoisted the heavy green hood, watching the engine chug and rumble. After all this time, he never let her down. Years of grease and dirt clung in the corners, but Sanna did her best to keep Elliot's engine presentable. She did most of the repairs herself, since he was from a time when cars were a series of gears and belts, and not the confusing jumble of electronics like in newer vehicles. She shuddered at the idea of a car without an engine, without something she could take apart and understand. Sure, they might have safety features or good gas mileage, but she preferred working with hardware.

"Okay, Elliot, what's making you cough?" she said.

"Does it ever answer back?" a deep voice said from behind her. There went her quiet time. Sanna turned to face Isaac.

"He's not an it." She walked around and turned off the engine, wary of this newcomer.

"He?" Isaac asked. "I assume he has a name as well, then?"

"Elliot."

"He looks like an Elliot."

They both stared at each other. Sanna didn't like to make small talk. It's why she avoided people as a general rule. She didn't feel the need to fill the silence with inane chatter about weather and annoying tourists, so she didn't. Maybe if she didn't speak, he'd go away. She turned back to the engine and began checking fluid levels—meaningless, but it gave her something to do while she waited him out.

"Need some help?" Isaac stepped beside her.

"Know anything about trucks?"

"Not really, but I learn fast. In IT, you have to troubleshoot a lot." He shrugged. "And I follow orders really well."

Sanna sighed. He wasn't going to go away. She could do the repairs tomorrow. She gently let the hood drop, letting gravity and the heavy metal do the work for her. A computer guy wouldn't be much help with Elliot.

"I'm done for today. I need to order parts so there isn't anything else I can do. What did you do in IT?"

"I've done everything from coding to design to management. Lately, I'm in the social media end of things—Facebook, Twitter, Instagram, websites—that sort of thing. Companies hire me to help them streamline their online brands."

He gave a little shrug at the end, as if to say "No biggie." She nodded, yet Sanna couldn't imagine working with things she couldn't see or touch, something so removed from real life. Isaac came from a different world. She gave the muted green hood a pat and opened the door to climb in.

"I've got to check the Looms." She meant it as a means of dismissing him.

"Really? Your dad mentioned them, but we didn't get out there. Mind if I come with you?" So much for her dismissal.

Sanna looked at Isaac, standing on the other side of the door like a puppy, smiling like he was eager to jump in the passenger seat. She turned the ignition, and Elliot purred to life, smoother than he had done in months. She opened her mouth to say no, but the truck gave a little chug at exactly that moment, interrupting her.

Inwardly grumbling, but unable to take her eyes off his smile, she muttered, "Hop in."

Isaac's grin sparkled at her. Did his cheeks perpetually hurt from all his smiling? He jogged around the front of Elliot and slid into the passenger's seat like he was meant to be there. When he firmly shut the door, the radio kicked on. It hadn't worked in years and now it was playing Jewel's "You Were Meant for Me," of all things. He may have never let her down, but right now Elliot seemed to have a mind of his own.

Without a word, she smashed her foot on the clutch and shifted into first, rumbling down the nearest row of trees toward her favorite place in the orchard . . . maybe in the world. Elliot bounced over the bumpy ground to the northeast corner. As they went deeper, the tree bark grew more wrinkles, the branches stretched wider and thicker, and the trees were spaced farther apart to make room for their larger footprints. A thick carpet of grass and wildflowers blanketed the orchard floor, and the air tingled Sanna's skin and sang in her ears like it always did.

"So, what exactly are the Looms?" Isaac asked, holding on to the roof handle over his window as they bounced over roots.

Sanna couldn't help but smile a little, thinking about her special trees.

"They're the heirloom trees, but we've always called them the Looms. You can tell you're in them because the leaves aren't as full as the younger, newer trees. They produce fewer, smaller, and weirder-shaped apples than the rest of our trees."

They were why Sanna would never leave the orchard.

As a child, she had always been drawn to the oldest trees, the ones from her great-great-great-grandpa. The craggy branches whispered stories of the past as she had scrambled up the limbs, her bare legs scraping against the aging bark. She'd learned quickly that the bitter apples from the old trees didn't make for good snacking, falling and rotting on the ground as the autumn turned colder. The lost harvest disappeared to hungry animals and time. Back then, she didn't understand why they would even keep these trees. Why plant apples you can't eat? But once she'd grown up and realized these bitter apples were meant for cider, she was determined to put them to use. She never wanted to give her father a reason to cut them down and plant new, fancy hybrid varieties that tourists would pay ridiculous amounts of money for.

Sanna stopped the truck and hopped out without waiting for Isaac, her face tilted to the sun, her hat slung around her neck. Insects buzzed around, a fat bumblebee hopped from flower to flower, and the grass already stretched up to her calves. They would need to mow soon, letting the clippings act as natural fertilizer. Even her unexpected company couldn't disrupt the peace that thrummed to her bones.

"So, these are the Looms." Though she wasn't about to shush him, Isaac's voice seemed louder than necessary. Whispered voices always felt more appropriate out here, as though it were an outdoor cathedral. "I thought there'd be more bees in the orchard."

"We're way past bee season. The ones that are here are sipping from the flowers." Sanna brushed the nearest branch. "The L1s brought these trees when they came from Sweden." She noticed the confused look on Isaac's face. "Oh, it's a biology thing I picked up in college, a way to track generations. L1s are first-generation Lunds. Dad's an L4. I'm an L5. Anyway, most of the original trees have been replaced. But this little nook is still all original. We don't know why they're still alive, let alone still producing. Most apple trees are productive for forty to fifty years. These are almost a hundred and fifty years old and still giving us apples every year."

Sanna ducked into the tree's canopy and rubbed the trunk.

The bark practically buzzed with life under her hand, reassuring her of its vitality. This was one of the trees she and her dad had taken a branch from to graft new stock a few days ago. Above her head, tiny apples the size of marbles loaded the branches that remained, still green, a few clinging to petals that hadn't found their way to the ground.

She looked back over her shoulder at Isaac, who wasn't studying the tree as she was, but instead had his eyes on her. The buzzing she'd felt in the tree moved under her own skin, up through her hand to her arm, and vibrated through her to the ends of her hair and the tips of her toes. She became aware of her dry, almost chapped lips, and her hair tangling in the branches above her head. But, quickly distracted from thoughts of herself, she noticed the flecks of silver in his dark hair, both in his curls and his beard, complementing the smile wrinkles at the corners of his eyes. He was the kind of man who would get more attractive with each passing year.

Sanna licked her lips, shocked at the thought that had just popped into her mind.

"I should check some trees we just grafted." She skirted around Isaac back to Elliot, where she had a few moments to pull herself together before he joined her. By the time they'd reached the newly grafted trees, on the east side of the barn, she'd gotten control of her irrational thoughts.

The afternoon shade from the barn on the tiny trees made it hard to tell what was off about them—but something was definitely wrong. The trees were as she had left them, tiny sticks in black pots, coated in wax until the scion fused to the root stock and new growth started. She closed her eyes to let them adjust and moved so she would be in the shade, too, to help her see. But her pulse skipped as she bent down to touch them, disbelieving her eyes. Her heart stopped when she easily snapped one in two. What should have been still green and supple was already dry and brittle. A quick walk down the line revealed they had lost all twenty.

"No," she whispered. Isaac picked up on the change in her.

"What?"

She held up the broken twig, but Isaac only looked more confused.

"They're dead. All of them."

Sanna sat down, leaning against the barn and letting the defeat sink in.

"I'm sorry. Is there anything we can do?"

Isaac plopped down next to her. The genuine concern clear on his face touched her more than she wanted to admit. She shook her head and tried to explain.

"These were yet another failed attempt to expand the Looms. Each time I try to graft them, it fails. With the trees so old, it's only a matter of time before they start dying and we're already well beyond it—I need to know I can make more."

"What about the seeds from the apples? Can't you plant those?"

It was a fair question from someone unfamiliar with apple husbandry, so Sanna did her best to not sound testy.

"Not if I want to get the same apples. Apple seeds are a product of two trees: the tree where the apple grows, and the tree that supplied the pollen. When an apple blossom is fertilized, there is no guarantee that the pollen came from the same species of tree, so the seeds will most likely not be what you want. The only way to guarantee the same kind of tree is to graft, to take some of the tree itself and marry it to other stock—but I, apparently, can't do that with the Looms."

Isaac awkwardly patted her arm, evaporating her need to mourn the lost saplings. Alone by the shady side of the barn, those gentle touches pushed at her carefully constructed barriers. She fought the urge to lean into his shoulder.

This wouldn't do. They'd only met yesterday.

She stood and briskly wiped dirt from her backside. "Come on. I'll show you how to trim the trees." Sanna left him to follow in her dust.

CHAPTER SEVEN

B ass carried the bucket full of soapy water, careful to not slosh too much out. Mr. Lund had spotted him juking in and out of the trees and promised that if he helped him wash the mud off the ATV, he'd get to drive it. He totally won that deal. He would have washed all the cars and the house and the barn for a chance to drive that sweet thing. It was way better than the golf cart his dad had let him drive a few weeks ago. He had checked the speedometer, and the ATV could go over fifty.

As he dipped the sponge into the warm water, he envisioned himself behind the wheel, tearing through the orchard, flying over bumps so all four tires left the ground. It would be baller. He squeezed out most of the water and started on the tires, the dirt turning to muddy rivulets as it ran down the sides.

"Start at the top and work your way down, son," Mr. Lund said. He towered over him. Bass wondered if he had two of himself and if one stood on the other's shoulders, would he be as tall as Mr. Lund? Did he see dust in spots that other people didn't?

Before his mom had moved out of their house, he remembered her frantic cleaning sessions. She'd haul a ladder from room to room, washing every inch with soapy water, even the ceilings. It would go on for a couple of days, then his mom would sleep. He knew to be quiet on the sleeping days. Dad had told him, too, but he knew. If he did make an extra-loud noise, Mom would get really angry and storm out of the bedroom with wild hair and wearing an overlarge T-shirt.

"Here, let me show you." Mr. Lund held his own sponge that he dipped into the water and started soaping the top where it was only dusty, then stopped when he got to a spot where Bass could reach. "Now you finish this side, and I'll go around to the other sides, okay?"

Bass nodded. He kind of wished there were more kids here, but he didn't mind Mr. Lund. And it was pretty cool to be staying at an orchard. It was like having an entire forest to himself where he could act out the very best battle scenes from *Star Wars*. Miss Lund even said she'd show him how to climb the trees without hurting them. With all the land to explore, the summer would be over before he had discovered all the best hiding spots.

"How did it go with Sanna?" Mr. Lund asked.

"Good. She's funny."

Mr. Lund stopped washing.

"She's funny? That's a new one. Why do you think that?"

"She doesn't lie to me."

"How can you tell?"

"Well, Miss Lund told me she doesn't really like kids and she's only working with me because she has to. Why would she say that if it wasn't the truth?"

Mr. Lund laughed.

"You are right. She didn't lie to you. And you weren't upset?"

"Nah. She answered my questions anyway. And gave me a notebook where I could write down more questions to ask her later."

Bass slopped now-dirty water all over his clothes and kept scrubbing, enjoying how the dirt came off so easily. This didn't even seem like a chore. They washed in silence for a few moments.

"Do you like being tall?" Bass finally asked. He had wanted to ask Miss Lund, too, but hadn't worked up the courage yet. Maybe tomorrow. Mr. Lund was different. He smiled all the time and laughed a lot. He seemed like the kind of guy who would buy him cotton candy and ice cream at the same time— just because.

Mr. Lund straightened to his full height. "I love being tall. I can pick most apples without a ladder, I can reach the top shelf in the cupboard, and I can tell which of my friends are hiding bald spots with a comb-over."

"What's a comb-over?"

Mr. Lund bent at his waist so Bass could see the top of his head, then pushed some hair to the side to reveal a smaller patch of bare skin.

"A comb-over is when you comb your hair over the bald spot on your head so people still think you have all your hair." He smoothed his hair back where it had been and straightened up. "But I'm so tall, no one but you knows that I do that. Think you can keep that between us?"

He winked at Bass, and Bass held out his hand with his pinkie raised.

"Pinkie swear."

Mr. Lund reached out his own little finger and they shook on it. Bass returned to his now very muddy water and looked for another spot to wash. Mr. Lund came to stand next to him.

"Looks like we're finished. You do good work. I'm glad you're helping us this summer. We'll have to add you to the payroll."

"For real? Like real money? Will I make the same as my dad?"

As Mr. Lund chuckled, his thin frame shook like a tall tree in a windstorm.

"That might be pushing it, and I'll need to talk to your dad about it. How about ten bucks a day?"

Bass thought about that. It would be fifty dollars a week, maybe more if he helped out on Saturdays and Sundays. He could buy his mom a really nice present when they got home. He hadn't seen her as much since his parents didn't live together anymore, so he wanted it to be something good. He last saw her the week before he and his dad left for this trip. She had been really sick and skinny looking. She had had dark circles under her eyes and was really shaky. Bass had worried he would hug her too tight and break her. He had kissed her gently on the cheek and tucked blankets around her. She had promised to take him to Disneyland when she felt better. When they left, his dad had warned that it might take her a long time to feel better, but, duh, Bass already knew that.

A week later, they had left.

Bass looked up at Mr. Lund.

"Twenty," he said with as much confidence as he could, like he had heard the men on the *American Pickers* show say it.

Mr. Lund looked down at him, pulled a bandana from his back pocket, and wiped some sweat from his forehead, causing his comb-over to go in different directions.

"Eleven."

Bass's mouth gaped.

"That's not how it goes, you split the difference. You're supposed to say fifteen."

"Not when I don't have to hire you in the first place. I have the leverage. Do you know what that means?"

"Yeeeeessssss. How about twelve?" He paused. "And I get to drive the ATV once a week."

Mr. Lund looked down at him, and his shaggy hair that kept blowing in his eyes. Finally, Mr. Lund extended his hand.

"Twelve and I'll let you drive the ATV, but only if I think you did exceptional work. If I see you sleeping in the Looms, then no driving."

"Done." Bass shook his hand. "What are the Looms?"

Mr. Lund's mouth curved into a smaller smile than normal, like he was looking through a fog and liked what he saw.

"Ask Sanna."

CHAPTER EIGHT

Isaac hoisted the bucket of trimmed branches into the back of the truck, setting the clippers alongside it. Then he reached for Sanna's bucket, accidentally bumping fingers, resulting in a quick intake of breath from both of them. Somehow they'd settled into a graceless dance of accidental contact and mounting unspoken tension. He could address it directly, let her know he was attracted to her, and risk ruining any hope at a congenial working relationship. Or he could try and push past these feelings. They would be working together, and he wanted to get along, maybe have a few laughs and some good conversation.

After they both climbed back into the truck and closed their doors, he gave it his best effort.

"Did Bass do a good job for you today?"

Sanna turned the key in the ignition, but the engine sputtered, not the quick purr it had earlier. Without looking at him, she responded.

"He didn't break anything."

"Glowing praise."

Sanna turned the key again, and it coughed, then silence.

"Guess we're stuck out here," Isaac said. Sanna's nostrils twitched, and she gently placed her head against the headrest. He would swear she counted to ten. Every inch of her reacted to the world around her—she didn't hide one ounce of emotion or sugarcoat her words. While refreshing, it was a little disarming. Yes, he was attracted to her, but he was also intrigued. Sanna was an interesting person, and he wanted to know more—friendship was the right path, the safe path.

"Do you want me to look under the hood for you?"

Sanna finally looked at him, her eyes wide. This time, when she turned the ignition, she gave the dashboard a sound whack and stomped on the floor. Though science and every auto engineer in America would argue it shouldn't have made any difference, the truck rumbled to life, and Sanna actually smiled.

"Not stuck after all," she said, then paused. "I imagine Bass will miss his mom this summer."

Though Isaac was grateful she was contributing to the conversation, he just wished she had picked a different topic.

"She's sick a lot, so he's used to spending time apart from her, especially since we divorced a few years ago."

Sanna's lips made a silent O. *Way to shut down the conversation, idiot*, Isaac thought helplessly.

The sun ebbed toward the horizon, spreading reds and oranges like a kindergarten finger painting, large swaths of bold color. There were worse places to spend some time, and the Lunds seemed like good people who had hosted enough temporary workers to know not to pry into their past. The quiet open air and days spent in the sun would suit him just fine. His only worry was if Bass would stay out of trouble without friends and technology to keep him occupied. And a small part of him wondered if he had made the right choice in the first place. Would Bass have been better off knowing the truth right away, spending this summer grieving but surrounded by familiar people and places? But wondering was useless. He'd already made the decision and now he needed to live with it.

Isaac waited to make sure the engine didn't conk out before trying conversation again.

"So what did you have Bass doing?"

Sanna slowed to drive over an especially large bump in the aisle. They'd moved from the larger, older trees to the younger, smaller trees and the space between the trunks barely allowed for the truck to pass unscathed. A branch poked through his window, whipping him in the face with its leaves. Sanna's lips quirked and she cleared her throat.

"He swept up the glass from the broken window, then helped me bottle a new batch of cider. He did a good job but he talks a lot."

"You should see him after a Mountain Dew and a candy bar."

"I'd rather not."

"As long as he's not contained within four walls, it's actually quite the spectacle. The best is when the effects wear off. More than once I've had to carry him into bed because he'd burned through all his energy and couldn't go one more step. It's kind of adorable."

"I'll have to trust you." Sanna focused on maneuvering the truck, clearly knowing every bump and overgrown branch, which made him suspicious of the one that had made it through the window.

"What did he talk about? Did he ask a lot of questions? Because he always does that."

"He wanted to know if I still smell farts even though I'm so tall."

Isaac laughed, and even Sanna broke into a smile. What a Bass question to ask. "I'm sorry, I told him to keep the fart talk to a minimum, but I imagine he couldn't resist."

"It's fine. It's better than my nieces and their yammering about some tween show they watch or boy band they listen to."

"At least he didn't sing the Farts and Butts chant."

"Chant?"

"Oh yes, it's as repetitive and earwormy as you'd imagine. I'll spare you."

This time she chuckled a little as she replied.

"I appreciate it. I never cared for an earworm."

They emerged from the trees, and Sanna slowed the truck behind the barn, killing the engine and giving the truck a gentle pat before getting out. Isaac felt like he was making some progress, he just wasn't sure toward what.

As the sun began to set behind the trees, Isaac and Bass returned to the trailer, showered, and changed clothes before dinner at the Lunds' house. Wanting to show they cleaned up well, they both wore khaki shorts and polos, trying to dress the best they could with the clothes they had packed. Bass even stayed clean all the way across the orchard—a minor miracle Isaac knew enough to savor while it lasted.

They knocked on the door, and in moments Sanna swung it open wearing a simple blue, button-front dress, collared and tied at the waist, in which her figure—he noticed immediately—appeared more curvy than in her normal jeans and flannel work shirt. Her short hair, still damp from her shower, had a few new curls, softening her face, and her lips shone with a gentle sheen of gloss. Isaac nudged Bass.

"You look pretty, Miss Lund," he said, giving her the flowers they had brought. Just wildflowers—weeds really—from near the trailer, but it was the best he could do.

Sanna's mouth opened to respond, but had no words at the ready. She stepped back to let them in.

"Thank you," she said. A smile finally broke her daze, and she pointed up the steps.

In the kitchen, Einars was setting out bowls full of food, plates, and silverware on a long wooden table that echoed the equally long counter separating the kitchen from the rest of the high-ceilinged room. The two-story ceiling reminded him of his grandparents' barn.

"There's the young man, all spiffed up," Einars said. "Come help me finish dessert so it can bake while we eat."

Bass went to help him while Sanna put the flowers in water. Isaac studied the huge, airy room and went to stand in front of a wall of watercolor apples—each one was set off by a colored background ranging from deep blue to fluorescent green to soft pink. He turned to ask Sanna about it, but she was still in the kitchen, pulling salt-crusted baked potatoes from the oven.

Bass kneeled on a bar stool and stirred sliced apples with cinnamon and sugar. On the counter were the fixings for a baked potato bar, with cheese, bacon, broccoli, sour cream, and minced chives.

"Are the apples above the fireplace meaningful?"

Einars bent lower to talk to Bass, as they layered the apples into a dish, forcing Sanna to answer the question.

"Those are all the apples we grow in our orchard."

There were at least thirty. He hadn't even known there were that many varieties of apple in the world.

"Did you paint them?"

"Some of them. Most were done by much older relatives."

Sanna assembled her potato, piling it with cheese, bacon, and broccoli, then set the potato on a baking sheet. Isaac followed her lead, making one for himself and Bass—adding extra cheese to Bass's—and setting them next to Sanna's potato. Once all four potatoes were ready, she slid them into the oven to melt the cheese. While they waited, Einars ushered them to the huge table where he sat at the head with Sanna to his right, Isaac to his left, and Bass next to Isaac. Einars pulled their gooey dinners from the oven and served them onto waiting plates.

"Where's your mom, Miss Lund?" Bass asked, a string of cheese dangling from his mouth. Isaac reached out to pull it from his lip. He looked to Sanna, curious about her response. But her lovely face was granite.

"We don't talk about her."

Bass looked down at his lap, and Einars coughed but didn't acknowledge her terse response.

"It's just a question, Sanna. He's a curious boy, not a criminal," Isaac said. He put his arm around Bass.

"Sorry." Sanna said it, then quickly stuffed a huge bite into her mouth, eager to move past the question. Isaac kept his eyes on her, waiting for more. He didn't like the way she brushed off Bass, especially if he was to spend so much time with her. She kept her eyes away from his. After their afternoon together, Isaac was starting to understand a bit more about her. She liked to keep people at arm's length—shying away from his touch, smiling then shutting down. She could do that with him, but not with Bass.

"Tell me more about what you did in California," Einars said.

Isaac pulled his eyes from Sanna to look at Einars. Bass, resilient, was back to devouring his dinner like nothing had happened.

"I work with companies to develop their online presence. Sometimes that means social media, sometimes that means a website, sometimes that means all of the above. I'll learn about their business and customers, then develop a plan for them.

I work with contractors to set up the websites and accounts they need and train their employees to use them."

"Very interesting." Einars chewed his food and nodded. "Social media, huh?"

He saw Sanna roll her eyes.

"Stuff like Facebook, Pa. Where Anders posts pictures of the girls."

He nodded.

"Oh yah. We don't use that."

"And that's why I get paid to do what I do. A lot of small businesses can't be bothered to learn how to do it on their own, but it can make a huge difference in driving customers to your website and the brick-and-mortar business." As he spoke, he started moving his arms. "For example, you cater to tourists. A lot of them like to take pictures and share them on Instagram or Facebook—so those are great places to have your business, especially so they can tag your orchard in their pictures and then other people can learn about you. And you could post photos of the apples as they grow. Customers love to see behind the scenes."

"What do you think, Sanna?" Einars asked.

Isaac turned to face her and caught her eyes following his hands with every excited gesture.

"It could work. Anything is better than what we have—our website is ancient. Only Anders knows how to update it, and we haven't put anything on our Facebook page since we posted the closing date last fall."

"I could fix it. It really isn't difficult. And I could teach you how to maintain it."

Einars chewed his food, his eyes moving from Sanna to Isaac and back. Truthfully, Isaac really wanted to redo their website. He had been horrified when he'd come across it while researching the orchard before he took the job. The site was created in FrontPage and completely unusable on a smartphone. When he viewed it from his laptop, half the photos didn't load and most of the links were broken. At least the address and phone number were easy to find, but that was the only positive. On principle, he couldn't let them continue like this.

"I'll do it for free as part of my employment—it won't cost you anything. It pains me that much to let you continue as it is."

A timer dinged before Einars could respond. Isaac noticed the other three had finished eating while he'd been talking business. Isaac looked into Sanna's bold blue eyes and before she could look away, he said, "Please. Please let me do this for you." He paused. "And your dad."

She looked at her plate.

"I think it's a good idea, Pa."

From behind him, Isaac could hear Einars pull the dessert from the oven, flooding the room with the mouthwatering scent of warm cinnamon and apples. Isaac shoveled in the last few bites of potato, then helped Sanna collect the dinner plates, following her into the kitchen.

"Well, then I guess you'll be fixing it—but orchard work needs to come first," Einars said.

"Agreed." Elated, Isaac thrust out his hand to shake on it.

In his pocket, his phone buzzed. Against his better judgment, he looked at it.

CALL ME NOW OR I'M TELLING THE POLICE TO TRACK YOUR PHONE!

He really needed to show his mom how to text without all caps.

"Can you all excuse me for a minute, I need to make a quick call."

"You can use my room," Einars said, pointing to the far right door on the wall.

Which meant Sanna's bedroom was the room on the left. Isaac tried to look in, wondering what her room might reveal about her. Did she have a stuffed bear collection, cover her bed in pillows, or leave her dirty clothes strewn on the floor? He caught a glimpse of green and blue before he had to face forward or risk being obvious. Einars's room was painted a soft gray with a cushy bed. Hand drawings of the orchard hung on the wall, intermingled with photos of Sanna with a tall blond man about the same age—that must be Anders. The room contained a bed, dresser, a side table, and a blue-gray rug covering the plank floors.

Once he closed the door, he made the call he'd been dreading for days.

"It's about damn time," his mom said with a huff.

"Mom, I'm—"

"You can't disappear like that." So it was going to be one of those calls where she talked and he listened. He deserved it. "I've been worried sick about you and Bass. People are asking when the funeral will be, what we should do with the remains? Where they should send memorial checks? We need to pick a cause. There are things that need to be done. Where are you?"

As her words rushed over him, all the distance he'd put between himself and the mess back at home shrunk to nothing. He'd run away, but reality could still find him here. He needed to get off the phone, and quick.

"You don't need to worry. We're fine—"

"How can you be fine? Bass must be devastated." There was only one thing to do when she got like this. Talk louder.

"We're fine and safe. We're going to spend the rest of the summer in Wisconsin."

"What's in Wisconsin?"

"What we need. We'll be back when we get back. Please cremate her. We'll deal with the rest when we get home. I have to go. Love you."

He hung up before she could say anything else. He took a few breaths to ease his nerves. He wanted to find that energized place he had been a few minutes ago, but the moment was gone. Before he had even left the room, his mom texted again.

DON'T HANG UP ON ME. I'D CALL BACK BUT I KNOW YOU WON'T PICK UP. NEXT TIME I WANT REAL ANSWERS. LOVE.

He shoved the phone back in his pocket and returned to the table as they were sitting down to warm plates of dessert.

"Sanna," Einars was saying, "you won't believe who I caught sneaking over the border and taking clippings from our trees early yesterday morning."

Sanna shook her head. "Was it Mrs. Rundstrom? Again?"

Einars chuckled. "I was surprised she could move that fast in her fuzzy slippers and housecoat."

"I'll talk to Thad. They only need to ask."

Isaac wasn't following the conversation, still torn between the responsibilities back home and the bucolic peace he needed here. He took a breath, hoping no one had noticed, but of course Sanna had—her head tilted slightly to the left as she watched him. He forced a smile and hoped she bought it.

"This looks amazing, what is it?"

He was surprised when Bass answered instead of Einars.

"It's caramel apple bread pudding with a cider sauce."

Bass looked at Einars as he spoke and smiled when Einars nodded that he'd gotten it correct, Bass's pride obvious on his glowing face. See? He wouldn't have had this moment in San Jose—this was what they were here for—new experiences and new memories away from the complicated heartache. Some of Isaac's guilt eased the more Bass's smile widened.

"You helped make this?" Isaac said. He scooped up a large bite and his taste buds exploded with joy. Cinnamon apples and custardy bread pudding melded together with the creamy caramel sauce spiked with cider. It might be the perfect dessert. "Good job, Sharky."

Sanna leaned toward Bass across the table and whispered loudly, "You did a better job than my dad normally does."

She didn't smile or wink to undermine the verity of her words or dumb it down, just issued the straight compliment. Isaac's heart melted as Bass sat up taller in his chair. Maybe that wasn't the only reason Isaac's heart melted.

CHAPTER NINE

Eva Drake covered her left ear with her hand and with her right pressed the phone tighter to her head to hear better. Her sensible black Birkin hung in the crook of her elbow, swinging against her torso each time she moved. The wind pulled at her short blond hair. Annoyed, she tucked the longer strands in the front behind her ears as best she could. She looked at the huge sailboats and small yachts that filled the marina around her. She hadn't expected such visible wealth in the middle of nowhere, but as she read the names of the boats, it became clear many were owned by Illinois people. No Wisconsinite would name their boat *Ditka's Dinghy* or *Cubbie #1*. At least that's what her market research had told her. She was in one of the small towns that made up the heart of Door County—Efrom or Eframe or Egads . . . something with an *E*.

"It's under control," she said, her voice tight with frustration. "I've given him all the paperwork and he sees the logic. The other contract will be signed in a few days—they're having their lawyer read it over. They've also given me insight I hadn't expected. We're in a very good position."

"You said that last time."

"Last time I had an inferior partner undermining my decisions. This time that isn't happening."

"That's not the version I heard." He paused to slurp liquid, probably the cold, black coffee that sat on his desk all day. "I don't care how it happens. I expect to have signed papers by the end of the month. Otherwise, I'll send Patrick to take care of it."

The line clicked off, but Eva checked the phone's screen to be sure.

"Dick!" she said. Her dad never said good-bye when he ended a call, so she could never finish telling him everything completely. She'd bet anything that he didn't hang up on her brother like that. But she'd be damned if she allowed Patrick to touch this project after roadblocking her at every turn on their last one. Besides, if and when it succeeded, and she knew it would, he'd just take all the credit—just like he'd been doing since she started at the company a year after he did. It was her idea to bring WWW to this area, and she'd make it a success without Patrick.

Her dad had founded Wild Water Works fifteen years ago, realizing the opportunity—and waterfalls of money—to be made building hotels and water parks together. He hadn't been wrong and they were growing faster than industry predictions. Now, she and her brother jockeyed for who would take it over when he retired. Her father played them against each other, and she hated them all—including herself—for buying into the competition. That's why she'd been scouting territories on her own that hadn't been touched by the water-park craze yet. Door County, with its abundance of family visitors and quiet winters, would definitely benefit from a cold-weather destination like an indoor water park. She could almost smell the over-chlorinated water now.

And she would make it happen.

The person she was negotiating with had said to meet here at two, and it was one forty-five. In Eva's book, fifteen minutes early was nearly late. She stepped with purpose on the wooden dock, careful not to get her four-inch black pumps stuck in a crack. The sun turned her black suit into an oven, forcing a trail of sweat down her spine, so she slipped the tailored coat off her arms and pulled the shirt away from her skin to let the breeze cool her down. Her father insisted she always be the most professionally dressed person in the room—even without her blazer, that wasn't a problem here.

She studied the shoreline, where small galleries and shops fringed the streets as tourists weaved in and out of them. This whole town just looked like a lot of money to be made. Families by the hundreds, according to her research, looked to entertain kids in a safe, controlled environment where they could read a book and sip cocktails. She looked at her hands in the sun and picked at a chip in her French manicure. With any luck, she could have the deal wrapped up in a week, because she really needed a manicure—and it was impossible to find a place in this whole county that made a decent cold-pressed green juice. The continental breakfast from her hotel consisted entirely of carbs and butter.

She meandered her way to the end of the dock, where a bench overlooked the water. The afternoon sun filtered through to the rock-speckled bottom. Instead of a Caribbean blue, the bay waters looked algae green. She'd already been isolated here for a week, and who knew how much longer it would be before she could return to her condo in Chicago. They may share the same lake and time zone, but Door County and Chicago were worlds apart. At home, they'd never leave all this gorgeous real estate for cottages and farms.

Her intuition had her smiling and reaching out a hand, even before her appointment could identify himself. Everything was on track, or would be soon.

CHAPTER TEN

S anna woke before the sun. She slipped on her work clothes and snuck into the barn. Yesterday, she had pulled out of the freezer a few special juices from the Looms that she had frozen last fall and set them in the cooler to thaw. When she had pressed them last October, they hadn't produced as much juice as the apples from younger trees, but even the raw juices by themselves were interesting and complex, layers of apple and honey and something earthier. At the time, she'd decided to save them for inspiration to strike. As she had lain in bed, though, waiting for the first rays of light, a color blossomed. A rosy pink, with a hint of coral, bold and opaque. It didn't have any sharp edges. She knew instantly it required juice from one of the Looms.

She measured and blended, noting each of the juices she used and in what combination. Two parts Rambo, one part Winesap, a half part Britegold. She sipped it, but the color was too red, almost searing. She needed something to mute it. She walked into the large freezer where she had stored some of the frozen juices and even a few bushels of frozen apples she was experimenting with.

She ran her fingers over the giant apple ice cubes in flattened Ziploc bags, closing her eyes and letting the colors emerge—green, periwinkle, sunshine yellow, and a sunset orange. Like the sound of a puzzle piece snapping into place, she knew she had found what was missing. She pulled a bag and set it in the sunlight streaming through the broken window. She didn't need all of it right now, just enough to confirm she was on the right path. While she waited for it to thaw, she flipped open her journal and wrote down the measurements she had established, then pulled out her colored pencils to create the shade emblazoned on her mind. The color spoke of vitality, passion, and strength.

Isaac, she wrote absentmindedly next to the drawing.

Startled at what she'd done, Sanna threw the pencil across the room. One day with him, and he'd already wormed his way under her skin. She didn't want him—or any man—around to complicate her life. All she wanted was to run the orchard and make cider. Her life was uncomplicated, and she preferred it that way: trees, apples, cider. Unfussy. Hardworking. Simple.

"You want to talk about it?" Sanna jumped as her dad's face appeared in the window as he balanced on a ladder to reach the second-story panes.

"No, Pa. I don't."

He studied her through the broken glass, outlined by the sunny morning behind him.

"It's been too long since you had new people in your life. You closet yourself in this barn too much."

"I go out with Thad." She picked at the corner of her journal, folding and unfolding it.

"Don't make me laugh. I don't know why you waste your time. He only wants our land and you very well know it. Plus Mrs. Rundstrom is a nightmare."

Sanna gave a little smile. He wasn't wrong about Mrs. Rundstrom—that woman once complained to a room full of mourners about the poor caliber of casseroles at a post-funeral luncheon, then filled large plastic containers with them, which she shoved into her purse. Last year, Sheriff Dibble found her loading her truck with wood from trees cut down in the state park even though she knew they sold that wood to campers for firewood. Sanna knew for a fact—from Thad Rundstrom, her son—that all of the perennials in her garden, including a rare pink peony, were dug up from various yards and parks around town in the dead of night.

And she didn't really know why she wasted time with Thad, either. He'd become a convenient habit. They had dated during college, but had settled into a friendship when they graduated. Early on, he'd tried to rekindle their romance, but she had no interest. They would see movies, grab dinner, and talk orchards every couple of weeks. She'd assumed he'd eventually find someone new and that would be the end of that, but in the meantime, he was decent company. They each knew where they stood with the other. No expectations, just company. It was simple.

"Why don't you wait for Isaac to help you with that?" she said. "You did hire him to help you around here." She looked down at the drop, and it was higher than she thought. He scowled at her.

"I've been fixing things around here for years without someone watching my back." He tugged at the windowpane to loosen it, needing to get it out to replace the broken glass.

"You just told me you were getting too old to do everything." He kept working and ignored her worry. Sanna picked up the Ziploc of melting cider and turned back to her blending, already drifting off toward that rosy pink she was so drawn to today. If she hurried, she could have it blended before Isaac and Bass arrived. "Fine. If you fall, I won't visit you in the hospital."

"Ow, dammit." Her father's curse broke her concentration, and she was about to scold him for handling broken glass without gloves. At his age, he should know better. But a screech of wood ripped her back to the present. She turned in time to see her dad's arms flailing backward, the ladder sliding off to the left and falling with a clatter so loud it almost muffled the sound of Einars hitting the ground and another awful noise she didn't want to dwell on. Her stomach jolted even harder. The silence after the fall pushed her into action, and she dashed out the barn's side door, down the grassy slope, and around the corner of the building, unable to move fast enough, the air turning to molasses she had to power through. Incapable of looking at her father yet, her eyes moved instead to Isaac tearing out of the trees at a dead sprint straight to where her father lay.

Isaac didn't even glance at Sanna but knelt beside Einars. She finally looked at her dad. His right side had taken the brunt of the fall. His forehead already bled from where it had smacked the gravelly ground, his wrist flopped at an odd angle, but the worst was his leg. As he had fallen, it had gotten trapped in between ladder rungs. Bile rose up her throat at the sight of blood soaking his jeans, which folded as if they were draped across the end of a bed, perfectly normal except there was a leg still inside. At least he seemed to have passed out from the pain, or was he . . . ?

Sanna finally knelt on the side of her dad opposite Isaac and their eyes met.

"Is he?"

"He's breathing." He pointed to the shallow rise and fall of Einars's chest. "Do you have a phone on you?"

Sanna shook her head no.

"Get mine. Back pocket. Right side." Sanna stood to move around to Isaac's rear when Bass appeared, his shorter legs not able to move as fast as his father's longer ones. It had been moments since her father had tumbled to the ground, but it already stretched into hours of torment. She couldn't react fast enough. Bass grabbed the phone from his dad's pocket and did as his father instructed, but Sanna couldn't make sense of anything. All that registered was her strong, always-there father not moving, barely breathing, broken on the ground.

Bass held the phone up to Isaac, who nodded as he listened to the calm voice on the other end. He stripped off his long-sleeve plaid shirt and tore it in two, using one-half and a thick stick to tie a tourniquet on Einars's leg in confident, quick motions. Blood already smeared his hands and jeans.

A tiny part of her acknowledged that his steadfastness soothed her, the part that wasn't shutting down from panic.

She'd never seen her father so pale—his skin had always had a faint pink to it, unable to contain the vitality flowing through his veins. Or so still. A tree always needed trimming, grass mowing, or a windowsill painting. Even at night, he made dinner, dusted knickknacks, straightened pictures. He was a perpetual motion machine when his eyes were open, grace in his long-limbed movements—always strong and capable.

"Sanna, here." Isaac held a folded square of plaid out to her, interrupting her thoughts. "Press this to the cut on his forehead." Detached, she watched her hand grab it and her knees bend—then she didn't know what else to do. Isaac wrapped one of his hands around hers—his long fingers gentle and firm at once while leaving smears of her father's blood on her own pale skin, guiding her to the spot where it trickled down his temple. "Be firm, with the palm of your hand."

He opened her palm one finger at a time, then pressed it to the wound—his hand covering hers. He was so confident, surely this would all be okay. She could do this. Focus on the task at hand.

"Keep it there."

As soon as his hand left hers, her certainty fled with it. She started to rock back on her heels.

"Sanna." More than anything, Isaac's gentle tone pulled her back. She nodded and pressed, only worrying about her part as Isaac barked orders to Bass. In minutes, the sirens of the Door County EMTs pulled into their drive, followed by Sheriff Dibble in his cruiser. Isaac pulled Sanna back to make room for them to do their work. Sheriff Dibble joined them, reaching an arm up to pat Sanna's shoulder.

"He'll be okay, Sanna. Einars is made of tough stuff." Sanna could only nod. When he realized she wasn't going to talk, he reached out his hand to Isaac. "Paul Dibble, but everyone just calls me Sheriff."

"Isaac Banks." Isaac paused, looking at Sanna and the EMTs as they worked. "Are you related to Mrs. Dibble?"

"She's my mom—but half the county is related to her." He nodded in the direction of the EMTs. "I'm going to get some info."

As they carefully put Einars on a board and Sheriff asked a few quick questions, Sanna swayed where she stood. The EMTs loaded him into the truck and Sheriff joined them again. Sanna found her voice.

"Is he going . . ." was all she could get out. Why wasn't she rushing to his side? That's what a good daughter would do. Instead she was useless.

"He'll be okay. Some broken bones, some blood loss, but they're taking him to the hospital. Isaac here will get you cleaned up and follow. Okay?" He switched his eyes to Isaac. "I'll catch up with you there."

He returned to his cruiser, flicked on his lights, and led the ambulance out of the driveway. Isaac guided Sanna by the elbow toward the house but she resisted. Bass stood nearby in silence. "No." She pointed in the direction of the retreating ambulance. Isaac moved in front of her so he could look her in the eye.

"We'll meet them there. I promise."

She believed him and so let him lead her into the house, the blood on her hands tacky. She kept pressing her palms together and pulling them apart, like a child might. Isaac turned on the faucet in the kitchen, letting the water warm before guiding Sanna's hands under the stream. He soaped up his own hands, the white suds turning a rusty brown, then used them to soap up Sanna's, too, gently rubbing off the drying blood with his soft touch, rinsing, and repeating until the suds stayed a clean white.

"Sanna, I need you to help me get to the hospital. Can you do that?"

Sanna blinked. She could hear him speaking and feel the way he carefully handled her, comforted by the contact and concern, but when she blinked, she couldn't stop seeing her father bent in unnatural ways. Her mind couldn't imagine what would happen next. Isaac looked her in the face. He was getting closer and closer, his eyes looking at hers. His lips moved in explanation. Inches from her face the sound finally came back in a roar.

"I need to get to him. I need to get to my dad. Why didn't I go in the ambulance? Why are you just standing there? Let's go."

Isaac took her hands in his. They were both still wet.

"I know. That's where we're going. I need you to tell me how to get there."

Sanna almost insisted she would drive, but knew enough to know that she couldn't.

"There's no time to get to your car, let's take Elliot."

"You trust me to drive him?"

Sanna paused before answering. Remembering his sprint to her dad's side, his control of the situation, the gentle way he washed her hands.

"I do."

Isaac ushered Bass and Sanna out the door, watching for any sign that Sanna would disappear to wherever she had gone before. It had been disconcerting to see someone who, in the short time he knew her, lived life with confidence and strength disappear into uncertainty.

As they walked back to the gravel driveway, Isaac first noticed the shiny, silver pickup truck, then registered the man leaning against the driver's-side door. Everything about him was taupe. Sand-colored hair blended into dusty skin as if he'd rolled around in the dirt like a hog on a hot summer day. His tan and cream plaid shirt topped khaki pants. If he were to lie down on the dirt and gravel parking lot, he'd disappear. Everything about him mumbled dull and predictable. Isaac would have yawned if his adrenaline weren't still pumping.

As they approached, Sanna's gait slowed, her body resisting the forward motion, whereas moments before it had strode with purpose. But it was too late, Mr. Taupe waved to them. They had been spotted. She resumed her pace toward Elliot, both he and Bass rushing to match it.

"This isn't a good time," Sanna said as she approached him. Taupe's face molded into a condescending smile.

"Since you skipped our date last night, I thought I'd see how you're doing," he said, ignoring what she'd said. "Find out why you canceled."

The man's eyes twitched to Isaac and Bass, seeming uncertain of how to take this new development. Isaac watched Sanna for any sign he should get rid of him, which he'd be all too happy to do. She paused long enough to listen and respond to him.

"It's not a good time." Sanna carved each word into the air so there would be no mistaking the meaning the second time. "Pa fell off a ladder, and the ambulance just left. We're going there right now."

To his credit, this man straightened and understood the urgency immediately.

"I'll drive you."

Sanna ignored him and continued toward the barn and truck. Isaac and Bass hustled after her, leaving the man behind to watch them all clamber into the seat. As Isaac pulled Elliot out of the parking lot, the silver truck followed in their wake.

Who was this guy? And why did he need to follow them to the hospital? What did she cancel last night? He wanted to ask Sanna, but now was not the time, and besides, it wasn't his business, was it? He looked over at her, leaning on the door at the far side of the bench seat, Bass sliding between them as the truck veered around corners in response to her terse directions. She rubbed her hands together as if still trying to remove the blood, her forehead against the window so he couldn't read her expression. She only looked forward to point in the direction Isaac needed to turn then resumed her stare.

As they rumbled down the highway, the silver truck tailed him menacingly, nearly rear-ending them at a stoplight. Surely this guy didn't need to follow them so closely. If he was local, he would know the way to the hospital.

"Do you want me to get rid of that guy when we get there?" Isaac said, unable to stay silent.

Sanna looked at him over Bass's crazy curls, her eyes still a million miles away, and shook her head.

"He's been our neighbor since I was little. He and his mom have always lived there. He's known my dad forever. Up here, a tragedy happens to everyone. We'd do the same for them."

She returned to her staring. Bass's and Isaac's eyes met, and Bass's face said it all. He felt bad for her, too, and scared for Einars. His small hand reached out and patted Sanna's leg, doing what Isaac wished he could.

CHAPTER ELEVEN

Compared to the vibrant greens and earthy browns of the orchard, the hospital in Sturgeon Bay was blindingly white as Isaac led their haphazard group into the building. No natural light made it to the corridor as he, Sanna, and Bass hustled to the emergency waiting room with the neighbor close behind them. All signs of Sanna's shock were gone as she stormed through the doors even more no-nonsense than her usual self. He was in awe of her.

Sanna stopped in front of the main desk and even before she could ask, the woman working Registration whispered to them.

"I can't officially tell you anything, but the EMTs said your dad'll be fine. The doctors need to patch him up a bit, he lost a lot of blood, and you're going to probably need to tie him down so he can heal properly. Lord knows that man doesn't know how to sit still."

"Oh, thank God. Thank you, May," Sanna said, unsurprised by this unsolicited influx of information. Isaac assumed that like so many in this small community, they knew each other.

She turned to the area behind them, then back to May. "Where should we wait?"

"There's a room down the hall. I'll make sure the doctors know where to find you."

They had the room to themselves. Maroon cloth chairs and muted green wallpaper were a feeble attempt to seem homey, but the piles of dog-eared magazines and antibacterial sanitizer dispensers hanging on the wall made it impossible to forget where they were. Isaac had moved to sit in one of the chairs when Thad grabbed his arm.

"Who are you?"

Before Isaac could answer, Sanna walked through them and said over her shoulder, "Isaac, Thad. Thad, Isaac." Before the silence stretched into full-blown awkward, Isaac thrust his hand out—he may as well be polite. Thad took it more firmly than necessary—using his flat brown eyes to bore into Isaac's, clearly taking his measure. Isaac added an extra-firm squeeze before disengaging.

"You're the new help? He never hires help this early in the year," Thad said, though it came out as more of an accusation with a small bite on the end, like a harmless dog snapping at an intruder from behind his owner's legs. Thad's eyes roved over him, and Isaac resisted the urge to stretch his height. He didn't need to prove anything to this clown.

"We started yesterday. The Lunds have really welcomed us, almost like family." That last bit might not be entirely true, but he couldn't resist.

Thad visibly bristled. "I've known them all my life. Sanna and I have been dating since college."

"Oh? She hadn't mentioned you." Isaac's chest sank a bit, even as he knew Thad was trying to goad him and it had worked. He glanced to where Sanna sat under a print of a lighthouse and rocky shore, oblivious to their posturing. Bass sat next to her, kicking lazily at the nearest leg on a coffee table. This was the first indication of a man in her life other than Einars, but what did he expect? Of course a woman like her would have a special someone.

"Want something to drink? I saw a machine around the corner," Isaac said to Sanna.

"I'll take a tea if they have it—any kind."

"Can I get hot cocoa?" piped up Bass.

"Sure, Minnow."

Isaac hurried to buy the drinks, not wanting to leave Bass and Sanna alone with Thad for too long. He found the machine tucked into an alcove down the hall. He tapped his foot as he waited for each drink to fill, trying not to fixate on what could be happening back in the waiting room and knowing it wouldn't take Bass long to get bored. As he entered the room, he saw his fear had been justified. Thad filled the chair next to Sanna's, his wide frame overflowing into her space, his arm resting on the back of her seat. Bass stood in front of one of the hand sanitizer dispensers, a large foamy glob filling both his hands.

"Oops." The glob wobbled like a water balloon in an earthquake.

"Here." Sanna stood, held out her arms, and scooped some of the foam with her fingertips, then rubbed it onto her hands.

Bass offered his hand to Thad.

"Want some?"

Thad curled his lip. "No," he said in a disgusted tone.

"Don't be a jerk, Thad. He's a good kid," Sanna said.

"Well, that didn't take long," Isaac said, seeing Bass with the mound of hand sanitizer still resting in his hands. He passed a steaming paper cup to Sanna, scowled at Thad for being a dick to Bass, and set the other two cups on the table. Then he plucked a tissue from a nearby box and handed it to Bass. "Let's keep the chaos to a level three in here, okay?"

Bass nodded and sat back down in the row of seats adjacent to Thad, wiping his hands of the excess foam. Sanna still stood, blowing on her tea. Isaac sat beside Bass and sipped his bitter coffee, wishing hospitals had found a way to have decent beverages for hospital waiting rooms. If they were in the hospital waiting room, loved ones already had enough to worry about without suffering crap drinks.

"Is Mr. Lund going to be okay?" Bass asked him quietly. "That was a lot of blood."

Thad barked a laugh, and Sanna chose not to return to her seat next to him, but moved closer to Isaac.

"Sebastian Banks, that is not appropriate to talk about." Isaac's voice was sharper than usual. He glanced anxiously at Sanna, who didn't need to be reminded of the scene on the gravel below the barn's window. She waved him off.

"It's fine. And it was way too much blood. I never want to see that again and I can't stop thinking about it. But May said he'd be okay, and I trust her. Though I can't understand how it's possible. His leg and arm were going in directions they weren't supposed to go. Will he walk again? Write again? Will he need blood? What about a wheelchair? I need to get back to the orchard. We have to spray the trees, and there are more bottles ready to be filled with cider I started in February. Teal. Should be juicy and satisfying. We need to graft some of the Looms onto new stock just in case they get decimated—but I can't make it work. And the mower needs to be given a tune-up before it's used this season, and it should be done this week or the grass will get too long." Isaac had no idea Sanna even contained this many words, but he didn't dare interrupt.

As Isaac and Bass watched her go—it was like she'd been

saving up all the words since their arrival and now they had broken through the dam in her brain. Thad shifted in his seat and picked up a magazine—either used to this or he didn't care. Either way, Isaac wanted to drag his callous taupeness out of the room. Sanna deserved better.

"I forgot to put the juice I was thawing back in the fridge. I hope it doesn't go bad. Though the weather isn't too warm. We could use a little more rain, but not much. Apples are sweeter when the rain accumulation is low. Did you know that? And where is Anders? He should be here. I texted him while you were getting the coffee, and Green Bay isn't that far away. I wonder if he'll help at the orchard or if—"

"Of course I'll help, Sanna-who." In ambled her brother, an inch or so taller than her, blond hair neatly parted on the side and trimmed. He had their father's high forehead and sharp cheekbones. Every year that he aged, he looked more and more like Pa. Women always thought he was handsome, though she just saw the boy who used to dash through the orchard like Bass did now. He still wore a navy suit and golden tie, so he must have come straight from work in his Green Bay real estate office. He carried on like he sold high-end New York pieds-à-terre, instead of fifties ranches and suburban houses, but he seemed to be making a living if the new mini-palace he built last year was any indication.

Behind him trailed his wife, Julie, the top of her head barely reaching his shoulders, and their girls, Gabby and Sarah. All three of them wore summer dresses with pastel cardigans, like they'd popped off the cover of a Land's End catalog. Julie pointed the girls to a corner and gave them both iPads to keep them distracted. Sanna hoped that meant they'd be unobtrusive.

She bent down to give her sister-in-law the quickest of embraces, never having truly warmed up to her. She was always so tiny and clean, with a perfect manicure and silky brown hair that ended in a precise straight line at her shoulders. Sanna envisioned her measuring it every morning to make sure each strand was the correct length.

The girls were miniature, spoiled versions of Julie. Already, they whispered too loudly about who got the iPad or the iPad mini, both wanting the larger one. Just once, Sanna would love to see them running through the orchard or stomping in a mud puddle, anything that might result in dirty hands and wild hair, anything that would prove them related to her.

Despite being annoyed with all the choices her brother had made in his life that had taken him away from her and Idun's—where he hadn't lived since high school—she loved Anders just as much as she always had. She stood and hugged him, relieved that he could help now with any decisions that needed to be made. He smelled like lavender and vanilla fabric softener, familiar and comforting.

"You made it," she said, holding him by the arms.

"Of course I did."

"You didn't need to bring the crew."

"Julie wanted to come and help."

Sanna would have called bullshit, but she didn't have the energy. For as long as they'd been married, Julie had wanted as little to do with the orchard as possible. She probably came to make sure Anders didn't stay too long.

"How nice."

She introduced everyone, Isaac and Anders meeting each other's level gazes, Julie offering a limp hand, and the girls ignoring the adults entirely. Julie settled into a chair on the edge of her seat with her legs crossed and tucked beneath, like she was having an audience with the queen. Thad gave them both a hug like they were best pals. What was he even still doing here?

"What happened?" Anders asked.

"He was being bullheaded." Having Anders there made her feel more like herself, like it would all be okay again. Like everything would go back to normal again soon.

"What's new?" His ordinary opening salvo.

They settled into their usual polite conversation, which they'd perfected over the years to avoid their family hot-button issues.

"I finally got off the waitlist for Packers season tickets. You'll need to come down for a game."

"Of course I'll come, when the fall winds down. Congrats, how long were you on?"

"I put my name down my last year in college, so fifteen years almost."

"That's not too bad. Sheriff said he was on for twenty-five."

Sanna sipped her tea, searching for something—anything—neutral to discuss.

Apparently also running out of easy topics, Anders got to the point: "So how did it happen?"

"He climbed up a ladder to fix a broken window. I think he sliced his hand on a shard of glass, then lost his balance. There was so much blood. I'd never seen him so pale. He knocked himself out on the fall, thank God. And all this after he hired Isaac, claiming he was too old to do everything himself anymore."

"I wondered about all the extra people. I guess that makes sense, but I doubt Idun's can afford labor this early in the season."

Sanna bristled at the criticism, aware of Isaac's eyes on her, though he was holding a magazine.

"The orchard is fine."

"No, it's not. It hasn't been for years. If you helped with the books, you'd know."

"You don't help with anything, what do you know?"

"I know that we could all retire tomorrow if we sold that land."

Sanna gasped and her hand twitched, ready to smack that ridiculous idea right out of his head. Thad set down his magazine, suddenly rapt.

"Keep your stupid ideas to yourself. We aren't selling."

"Why not get out while we can make some money? Before you two run it into the ground," Anders said.

"You know nothing. You haven't touched a tree in ten years and have no idea what or how we're doing."

"I know you're playing with your cider while a seventy-year-old man is climbing ladders and injuring himself."

Heat burned the tears in her eyes before they could fall. How dare he question how they ran the orchard? He got his annual check of the profits, he should have nothing to complain about. It kept his family in the latest Apple products—the closest the girls came to the family business.

Anders softened his voice and put a hand on Sanna's shoulder.

"I know you love it, but you can't keep going. It makes sense to sell while there is good money on the table."

Sanna pushed his hand off.

"What do you mean good money? What aren't you telling me?"

Anders shook his head and closed his eyes, and Sanna knew he hadn't intended to share that bit of info.

"I've gotten an offer."

"Why did an offer go to you? You don't even live in Door County."

"Wild Water Works had their representative reach out to Dad, and he told them where they could shove the offer." Sanna smiled, enjoying the vision of her familiar, feisty father. "They contacted me in the hopes I could be more convincing."

"How did they even find you?"

"I'm listed on paperwork filed with the county. After that, I'm easy to find—I'm in real estate—my contact number is everywhere."

"You should have told them where to shove it, too."

In the silence that followed that statement, Sanna's ears picked up on what had been going on while the adults had been fighting. In the corner, the girls were giggling and pointing at Bass, who had gone to see what they were playing on their iPads.

"Why is your hair so long?" Gabby asked.

Bass shrugged his shoulders.

"Can you put it up in a ponytail?" Sarah asked.

Sanna's eyes narrowed across the room.

"No." Gabby laughed. "He would look even more like a girl." Bass scowled, and Sanna's blood boiled. She stormed over to the girls and grabbed their iPads.

"Since your mom isn't stopping this behavior, I will. You can't say whatever thought pops into your mind. For example, I don't call you mean, useless twits, even when you're acting like ones."

Their eyes widened, and big fat tears poured out of both sets in an instant. Julie bustled to them, pulling them into her arms and scowling at Sanna. Sanna rolled her eyes, recognizing crocodile tears when she saw them. Bass shuffled over to Isaac, who gave Sanna a grateful nod.

"You can't talk to them like that, Sanna." Anders rubbed his eyes with the palm of his hand. Their whining sniffles rubbed at her already raw nerves. She didn't want to be in this small, fluorescent room with any of these people anymore. She needed the solitude of her barn with its dim lighting and sweet, musty apple scent.

"I'll be back."

She left the room and turned a few corners to find a door leading to a small outdoor patio. Bursting through the doors, she sucked in the warm late-June air. The hospital was close enough to the lake for the air to carry a fishy tang. She breathed deeper. If she couldn't be back at Idun's, this bit of space to herself would have to do. Sanna had endured enough mean girls growing up, she couldn't abide it in her presence. Mean-spirited teasing like that made her skin twitch. She knew she should apologize to her nieces for speaking so harshly, but she couldn't muster the necessary sincerity. For the sake of her dad, she turned to give it her best shot, but Thad stood in her way.

"You okay?" he said.

"Fine."

He put his hands on her shoulders, and she had to tilt her head down to look at him.

"Sanna, I couldn't help hearing what your brother said about the offer and the orchard. I've been meaning to talk to you about it for ages, but now with your dad hurt and apparently so much debt on Idun's . . ."

His monotonous words droned on, mushing together into a dull murmur. When would he stop talking? She needed to get back to the waiting room in case a doctor came to talk to them.

". . . why we should marry."

She moved to go past him, then froze.

"Marry?"

"Yes. It'd be ideal."

Sanna snorted, then realized he wasn't joking. This wasn't

a friendly attempt to cheer her up with absurdity—he really meant it.

"You can't be serious." But his blank expression made it clear he was. "You and me? No. Absolutely not."

He took a deep breath and began to speak as if he were explaining to a toddler for the tenth time why he couldn't eat gum from the sidewalk.

"Sanna. I've known since we were kids that you should be my wife. It's perfect. Our orchards are next to each other. Neither of us would even need to move—not really. Mom always said we'd make a great team and you know how she loves your trees. And now your dad is hurt, so I can help with your land, too. You can let Isaac go, and I'll take care of all the finances. Mom says I'm wonderful at numbers. It makes perfect sense."

Wow. He wasn't proposing to her, he was proposing to her orchard. Sanna had stopped thinking about marriage years ago, but when she did used to dream of finding a good husband, the imaginary proposal always mentioned love and passion—not an actual land merger and her future spouse's mother. Her mouth opened and closed a few times before she could even find words to respond.

"Do you even like me, Thad?"

"You're a little tall for me, but we've known each other a long time, and we're a good fit." When Anders had suggested they sell the orchard, she thought she had heard the craziest thing possible. This, this she couldn't even comprehend, like string theory or why people liked candy corn. She started to speak, but he apparently wasn't done. "Okay, I get it. You want a little romance, a good story."

He took a knee in front of her and clutched her hand in his sweaty palms. He'd always had sweaty hands, even back in college. Sanna tried to pull her hand away to stop this farce from continuing, but he held firm.

"Sanna. Marry me. Your eyes are sparkly like blue diamonds, and your hair is soft. I love how you can handle heavy machinery without the help of a man. Let's get married."

She couldn't listen to any more of this. She yanked her arm out of his grip—without the help of a man, good grief. This was why she'd dismissed dating years ago. She didn't need this kind of frustration complicating her life.

"Thad. Stop. You're being an idiot. I am not marrying you. Ever. Get it out of your head."

She left him gulping air like a fish and pushed through the doors, straight into silver-haired Mrs. Dibble, who had evidently been watching through the window. Great, now all of Door County would know about that proposal disaster before the sun set. Fresh heat rose up her cheeks, rising until her eye twitched in irritation. As she stomped back to the waiting room, attempting to slow her breathing, she reminded herself that all that mattered was her dad getting better. With one more deep breath, she entered the room where Isaac and Bass quietly talked in the corner, Julie and the girls sat in another, and Anders paced.

"We need to seriously talk about this offer, Sanna," Anders said, then realized she was alone. "Where's Thad?"

"Gone."

She could still feel her cheeks flushed with irritation as Isaac studied her face from where he sat. She didn't want to think about what had just happened, let alone explain it to anyone. They would know soon enough. Thankfully, she was saved by a doctor.

"Are you the Lunds?"

Sanna turned to face him as he entered the room.

"Yes," Anders said. He reached out his arm and took the lead in the conversation like he was the one in charge here.

"How is he?" Sanna made sure to stand even at her brother's side and not one centimeter behind.

"He broke his wrist, cracked three ribs, lacerated his hand, and thumped his head pretty hard. The worst of the injuries was a full break of his fibula and tibia. They're finishing up the surgery right now, and he'll be moved to his room when he's awake. At least the break was clean, so it should heal well. We'll need to keep him for a few days and make sure there aren't any other complications. Eventually he'll be able to have a walking cast, but he'll need to take it easy. Something tells me he won't like that very much, so you'll need to keep him in check. Assuming he listens to the instructions, he'll make a full recovery or mostly full recovery. I'll write up the instructions with his discharge papers."

"Can we see him?" Sanna asked, rubbing the wood of her necklace relentlessly.

"After the nurses get him settled. Someone will come get you when he's ready."

Sanna nodded and breathed a sigh of relief. Pa would be okay. All the anger at Anders about the money, irritation at Gabby and Sarah for bullying Bass, the horror at Thad's proposal evaporated. None of it mattered anymore. As soon as he got home, everything could return to normal.

During the doctor's visit, Isaac had pulled Bass into the hallway, giving the family some privacy, but he was still able to hear every word.

"Do you think my hair is too long?" Bass whispered, struggling even to get the question out. Isaac's little boy widened his eyes to dry the tears welling above his lower lashes without wiping them away. If Sanna hadn't told those brats off, Isaac would go back in there and give them a piece of his mind. He tried hard not to judge other people's parenting styles, but sometimes other people just did it wrong. He knelt down in front of Bass so he could look him straight in the face.

"I don't. If you like your hair, then it's perfect."

Bass tucked his face into the top of his shirt to wipe away the extra wetness on his face, and Isaac gave him the moment. When he emerged, it was clear his mind had moved on. The two leaned against the wall. "We should probably head out." Then Isaac remembered they didn't have his car. He had started calculating the miles to walk back to the orchard when Sanna popped out of the room.

"We're going to be here a while. Did you want to head back? You can take Elliot."

"That would be great."

The redness in her cheeks was gone. From the way she'd stormed back into the room, tightly controlled in her movements, he could tell something had happened between her and Thad, but she seemed okay now. Even relieved. Sanna dug in her jean pockets, then patted her back pockets. Her brows scrunched as she turned back to the waiting room. Isaac followed. She looked under all the chairs and poked in the cushions where she had been sitting.

"What are you looking for?" Anders asked.

"My keys."

"What do they look like?"

"Keys." Anders glared at her. "Two keys on a key ring."

Anders joined Isaac, Bass, and Sanna to keep looking. Sanna stood and ran her hands through her hair.

"And you checked all your pockets?" Anders asked.

Sanna sighed but went through the motions of patting herself down, then paused as she hit the pocket on her plaid shirt. She reached in and pulled out the keys.

"And you want to run the orchard by yourself," Anders said, and sat back down by his family. Sanna huffed and clenched her jaw instead of responding. She held the keys out to Isaac.

"Be good to him."

As she set the keys in his hand, her fingertips grazed his palm. He resisted the urge to grasp her hand and not let go. Now wasn't the time. But he could do everything in his power to make sure this woman didn't need to sell her land that was clearly part of her.

CHAPTER TWELVE

Sanna stood in the hospital room doorway, watching her father's chest rise and fall, an IV hooked up next to a blood pressure machine. His leg had metal rods sticking out of it, like an acupuncture practice dummy, and was elevated by a complicated set of pulleys from the ceiling. A faint pink colored his cheeks, so much better than the icy white right after the accident. Without his work clothes on, his body seemed thinner and frailer than normal—the hospital gown didn't add any bulk to his lean frame. He was her only friend and the only person she had. Would he ever be the same again?

"Stop hovering and get in here," Einars said. He opened his eyes.

Sanna slipped into the room and stood in the corner near a window, as far from the contraptions as she could be. Her eyes flitted to the sink and mirror, then the curtain and the laptop on a rolling cart. She read the dry-erase board that recorded the names of Einars's nurses and his current medications. Near the bed were a faux-leather recliner and two more padded chairs, as if people were meant to watch the ill person like a television show. The aroma of hand sanitizer clouded the room as the air chilled her skin. She ran her fingers through her hair—it was getting too long and curled at the ends. Sanna looked everywhere but at her father.

"Sanna-who. Look at me." Her eyes pulled to his, and she swallowed. "I'm fine. Really. Just a few broken parts that'll heal up in no time."

Sanna nodded and resumed her room scanning. Einars studied her.

"Something else happened. What?"

"All you need to know is Thad is an idiot."

"Oh, I already know everything that happened with him. Mrs. Dibble saw me as they were wheeling me in here. She told me all about it."

"How did she get to see you before we did?"

Einars coughed. "No one bothers to stop her, do they?" Sanna scowled. "Come here." He patted the bed next to his good leg, and Sanna sat down. Einars took her hand in his. "Did that fool really propose? Today? At this hospital?"

Sanna focused on his face. If she did that, she could ignore all the machines and pulleys and pins sticking out of his leg.

"He actually used the word *merger*, Pa. As if that's what would convince me. Though I suppose it's better than trying to convince me he loved me." She rolled her eyes.

"He's not the one for you. He could never make you happy."

"Idun's is the one for me. That's all I need."

Einars squeezed her hand.

"Trees and dirt aren't going to make you happy forever, dear one."

"But they can't up and leave me either." She didn't want to have this conversation with her dad right now. Sanna pushed her hair out of her face. "I just want you to get better."

"Things will be back to normal in no time."

"He's not wrong about that, but he's got some work ahead of him," the doctor said as he came into the room. Anders entered behind him and shut the door. "As we talked about earlier, your father took quite a fall, but with some rest, time, and good rehab, he'll be back to himself."

"So, he'll be able to help with the orchard?" Sanna asked.

"It isn't always about the trees," Anders mumbled next to her so only she heard.

"His body is going to need most of its energy for rehab and healing. I've written all the instructions down and I'll print them with his discharge papers in a few days. He needs to heal and he's going to be in a fair amount of pain for a while."

"What's the damage, Doc?" Einars asked.

"You sprained your wrist badly, cracked three ribs, and snapped your shin in two. And you lost a fair amount of blood in the process."

Sanna tried to listen as the doctor talked about X-rays and casts, but instead focused on the reassuring beep of the heart monitor. It was regular, predictable, calming. Beep. Beep. She nodded her head in time with her father's heartbeat. By the time Sanna watched the white coat disappear behind the privacy curtain near the door, she had her purpose back. She and her dad would get through this together, like they did everything. They were a team. Both Anders and Sanna turned toward their dad, but Anders spoke first.

"I'll stay to help get things in order."

Sanna paused as she took in his words.

"Nothing is out of order," Sanna said.

Anders clenched his jaw.

"Fine. Then I'll stay to help keep them in order."

"How would you even know what order around the orchard looks like?"

"Sanna," Einars said, his voice low.

"No, Pa. He hasn't worked Idun's in over fifteen years. He won't know how to do anything."

"Have trees changed how they grow?"

Sanna narrowed her eyes and turned back to her dad.

"Your brother can help with the paperwork and accounting, I'll keep him out of the trees," Einars said. He patted Sanna's back, but he may as well have put a knife in it.

Anders smirked, and Sanna wanted to slap the satisfaction off his face. He had no business in any orchard matters.

"Stay out of the barn."

"I wouldn't dream of upsetting your precious cider hobby."

Sanna faced her dad, widened her eyes, and tilted her head, hoping he'd understand that Anders was going to cause more problems than help, but he closed his eyes and leaned back into the pillow. Sure, the doctor had said he'd be fine, but so many things could go wrong. He could get an infection or a blood clot. He could fall again during rehab and make it worse. She remembered an article somewhere about a stray shard of bone getting in the bloodstream and traveling to the heart, causing instant death—or maybe that was a book. Her quarrels with Anders didn't matter when compared to all the possible complications. She would drop the argument and settle in to watch him tonight.

Anders cleared his throat, and Einars opened his eyes again.

"I heard from Eva Drake again," Anders said.

"She knows what I think," Einars said.

"Who is Eva?"

"No one you need to know about," Anders said at the same time that Einars said, "Some woman from Wild Water Works who I've already told to go away."

Sanna glared at Anders.

"Why are you even bringing that up again? I told you no. Pa told you no. The matter is settled."

"First, I wasn't addressing you, Sanna. Second, Dad should consider the offer, especially after this accident. This hospital visit isn't going to be free."

Sanna stiffened, gave her dad's hand a squeeze, stood, and walked out of the room. As she left, she heard Anders say, "Why do you still let her get whatever she wants?"

She didn't need to hear any more.

Sanna hadn't thought her grand exit through until she had gotten out of the hospital doors. Isaac had taken Elliot home, so she had no ride. Luckily, the upside of being raised in a small community was there was always someone you knew nearby. Before she could even turn around, Mrs. Dibble had walked out the hospital doors and had offered her a ride back to the orchard. In addition to witnessing Thad's bended knee debacle, she had dropped off a care package for Einars with the nurses, containing items he'd need overnight, like a toothbrush and deodorant—something she'd never have thought to do. At least she let Sanna think in silence during the ride home. She may be a gossip, but she knew how to stay quiet when it counted. When they pulled up to the house, Elliot waited in the parking lot.

As she left the car, Mrs. Dibble piped up.

"I'm glad you said no to Thad, dear. That fall couldn't kill your father, but having Mrs. Rundstrom as an in-law might have. Get some rest."

Sanna blinked, mumbled "Thanks," and shut the door. She'd been buffeted by so much today, she'd lost the ability to process. She needed to get to the Looms.

She found the keys to Elliot on the seat complete with a new addition—a green dragon keychain.

She picked up the tiny gift—her heart warmed by Isaac's

thoughtful gesture. It fit neatly in the palm of her hand, and a small button protruded from its back. When she pushed it, a light glowed from its mouth along with a tiny roar. A mini-Elliot for her big Elliot. She climbed in and started up the truck—it jumped to life.

During the car ride with Mrs. Dibble, she had looked up Wild Water Works on her phone. They were a development company from Illinois that paid handsomely for property to build water-park hotels. As of now, there were no such establishments in Door County and even Sanna, who knew next to nothing about business, could see that being the first would be lucrative indeed. All those vacationers who now hiked and biked in the state forests and along the bendy highways would spend their time zooming down giant tubes and sitting in bacteria-infested hot tubs. The Eva Drake woman whom Anders had mentioned was the daughter of the CEO. Her picture on the website tried to make her look dainty and defenseless, with short, blond hair and tasteful makeup on her perky nose and flawless skin. She clearly tried for a conservative look with dark clothing and minimal jewelry, but instead of making her appear professional, it made her look hard. Sanna didn't trust her one bit.

She eased Elliot to a stop when she reached the Looms, killed the engine, and hopped out. From the bed of the truck she pulled a red wool blanket, faded from so many years in the back of her truck and soft from so much use. She spread it under the branches of the sprawling Rambo, sunlight filtering through the gaps. Sanna lay on the blanket, propping her feet against the trunk and tucking her hands behind her head. A fat bumblebee flitted from wildflower to wildflower, and grasshoppers had started their summer song. Her heart rate slowed as her mind calmed down.

How had Anders gotten so distant from the orchard? When they were children, they'd weave through the trees, playing tag until their dad put them back to work trimming the branches for the upcoming season or wrapping tape around a newly grafted tree. They grew up planning which bedrooms their families would take over when they all lived at Idun's together, but then he went to college and everything had changed. He only came home for holidays at first, and then that dwindled to just Christmas after he'd graduated.

And now he cared so little for their land that he wanted to sell it to developers. Cash out. Her heart squeezed tight at the thought of someone else sitting under this tree—or worse. What if they destroyed all her trees to make way for some monstrosity like that hotel? Marrying Thad would almost be worth it if it meant keeping her land. She shuddered at the thought.

She spread her arms wide, past the width of the blanket, and buried her hands in the long grass, stretching her fingertips to the cool dirt. Lying like this, she fancied she could hear the orchard talking to her, telling her about the apples, and what trees should be grafted next. She drifted and envisioned the orchard from above. She could see the scraggly trees where she lay now, and the tiny twigs of the newly grafted Honeycrisp trees on the other side of the orchard, and the precise rows of the eating-apple trees—well groomed and trimmed for easy picking in the fall.

With her eyes closed, a new color spread across the back of her eyelids—a creamy white with a gentle red undertone. Her tongue started to wrap itself around the flavors as she smiled to herself. It would be dry, almost champagne-like, but with a late, sweet lilt of red apple, like a kiss on the nose. It would pair exceptionally with Parmesan, pasta, and a simple salad and it would be the perfect wedding cider, if she knew anyone getting married. She'd add it to her journal to start blending when she returned to the house.

"Hey." Isaac's voice shattered her solitude and she gasped, spinning around on her back like a turtle and rocking up to her knees faster than one would expect for such long limbs. She sat back on her heels.

"Sorry! I was worried I'd startle you, but it looks like I did anyway," he went on. He stepped into the shade with her. She liked that she didn't feel enormous near Isaac. "I saw the truck was gone, so I assumed you were back. I wanted to check in, see if there was anything Bass and I could be doing to help out."

Sanna looked around for Isaac's mini-me.

"Where's Bass?"

"He was a bit off his game after seeing Einars this morning. I let him have his iPad for a few hours." Isaac tilted his head to the side. "How are you? I thought you'd still be at the hospital."

Those warm eyes nearly broke through the dam keeping her emotions in check. She wanted to tell him about how awful today had been, from the fall to the proposal. She wanted to trust that he would listen and say the right things, but she also knew she needed to get through this hurdle on her own. Relying on him would only end badly for both of them.

"It was leave or kill my brother. Too many witnesses and medical professionals at the hospital." Sanna stood and picked up her blanket, ducking out of the branches and away from the urge to ask him to hug her.

"I didn't mean to ruin your quiet time."

"It's okay." She tossed the blanket in the truck. "I need to run to the grocery store. Any interest in joining me?"

While she wouldn't spill her guts to him, she could let herself take comfort in his simple presence. For the first time in a long time, maybe ever, she didn't feel like being alone. So it came as a relief when he responded.

"I'd love to."

CHAPTER THIRTEEN

Bass flattened his hair with the palm of his hand as he walked through the orchard toward the Lunds' house, pulling a fistful down in front of his eyes. He could touch his nostrils with it. Crossing his eyes to focus on the end of his nose, he walked into a low-hanging branch. He rubbed where the rough bark left a scratch on his forehead.

He had written his mom a letter last night and his dad said he would mail it today, but with Mr. Lund getting hurt, he probably hadn't.

He had spent the last hour playing games on his iPad, but without Wi-Fi they were boring. Half the fun was searching for new games to download. And he would have really liked to text his mom.

As Bass walked around the barn, a shiny black car was parked where Miss Lund's truck normally was. He could tell it was a Mercedes by the hood ornament. No one was in the car, but it was still running. He looked around and heard rocks skitter, so he jumped back around the corner and watched a skinny blond lady in high heels totter across the parking lot, her ankles wobbling as she navigated the rocks. Who was she? And why was she by Miss Lund's barn? Before she got in the car, she turned toward the orchard and took photos. He pulled the small notebook from his back pocket and wrote "dark car, high heel lady." He was going to write *Mercedes*, but he didn't know how to spell it.

Behind him, he could hear Miss Lund's old truck rumbling through the orchard, the metal bouncing and creaking. The woman got in her car and zoomed out of the parking lot before the green truck appeared. He stepped out from around the barn's corner, ready to tell Miss Lund about the woman's odd behavior. Maybe she knew the fancy lady and they were friends—but he couldn't really imagine that, and his dad always said he had a great imagination.

But all thought of mentioning the woman evaporated from his mind when his dad opened the passenger's-side door and waved for Bass to join them inside.

"Hop in! We're going to the Pig." Before Bass could say anything, Isaac continued, "I know, sounds awesome, right?"

It did. Of course, everything sounded awesome when stuck on an orchard with no people your own age. He liked Idun's fine, but he missed his friends and baseball and Internet. Bass climbed over his dad and settled on the big bench seat between him and Miss Lund, excited to be going somewhere new and completely forgetting about the high heel lady.

CHAPTER FOURTEEN

As they drove through Sister Bay, one of the many small towns on the bay side of the peninsula, Isaac watched as the passing fields and orchards were replaced by charming houses and quaint shops. Banners announced the upcoming weekend's Fourth of July fireworks and brat frys. Bass leaned forward as much as his seat belt would allow with his head on a swivel, soaking up all the new sights. Isaac noted the location of a baseball field where they could hit a few balls. A few people waved as Sanna drove by but she didn't wave back. Perhaps they were confusing her with someone else. By the time Elliot eased into the parking lot for the Piggly Wiggly, a squat white building, Isaac knew that wasn't the case—too many people had taken notice for it to be coincidental.

"Who are all those people?" he asked.

"What people?" Sanna looked around the parking lot as she pulled to a stop.

"The ones waving at you as you drive by?"

"I didn't see anyone."

"This is not reassuring me about your driving skills."

Sanna shrugged.

"Do you know them?"

"They probably recognize the truck. It used to be Dad's."

As they walked into the store, Bass grabbed a cart and went straight for a display of chips. Isaac noticed as the other patrons reacted to Sanna. Some, clearly tourists, paused as they took in her height, their heads visibly tilting back. She seemed to ignore them, but slouched down a few inches anyway. An older gentleman stocking tomatoes nodded to her in recognition. She nodded back and aimed their trio toward the deli counter.

"Hey, Sanna," the older woman behind the counter said. Her gray curls were tucked under a black hair net and her name tag read *Bev*. "How's your dad?"

Sanna sighed. "Mrs. Dibble told you?"

Bev smiled and nodded. "She was buying him things he'll need in the hospital."

"He'll be fine assuming he doesn't push it." Sanna perused the case and pointed to each item as she spoke. "Can I get a pound of ham, a half pound of cheddar, and a large container of the broccoli salad?"

Bev nodded but gave Isaac and Bass a glance, clearly curious about how they fit into the picture. Perhaps Mrs. Dibble hadn't shared all the gossip. As they waited, Bass drove the cart around one of the nearby islands stocked with local cheese and sausages. Isaac reached out to stop the cart before he crashed into another shopper.

"You know, Mrs. Dibble is the one who gave me your dad's name to contact for a job. I'm assuming she's the same?" Isaac asked.

Sanna nodded. "Thank God there is only one Mrs. Dibble."

Bev handed Sanna her items, plus an extra container of shocking blue fluff: blue raspberry Jell-O mixed with Cool Whip. Bass waggled his eyebrows in excitement.

"That's on me," Bev said when Sanna looked up at her. "Let us know if you need any help, dear."

"Thank you. I'll let Pa know it's from you."

They finished their shopping, filling the cart with frozen dinners and pizzas, jarred sauce and pasta, and hot dogs, plus a box of Pop-Tarts for Bass, who insisted on holding it in one hand as he pushed the cart with the other. As they checked out, the cashier gabbed about local goings-on while Sanna stared out the window.

"I hear the fireworks are going to be the best yet. Bev said some company from Illinois contributed extra money. Looks like the rain they were promising is going to hold off, too. Maybe you can take your visitors? Show them how we do it up for the Fourth."

Even if Sanna didn't seem to embrace them back, it was clear the locals thought of her as one of theirs. Isaac smiled at the man warmly as he took the groceries so Sanna wouldn't have to carry them.

Driving back toward Idun's, Sanna clucked her tongue as she slammed the brakes when a family of four walked into the street, even though there was a crosswalk at the end of the block, then scowled at the construction of a hotel on the outskirts of town.

"Not your favorite time of year?" Isaac asked.

"There's a reason I don't leave the orchard much. Without visitors, we couldn't keep Idun's, but do they have to be so oblivious to the world around them? Most just cross the street without looking, eat at the fancy restaurants, and forget to look outside and see what's right there." She pointed at the rocky harbor and tree-lined shores. "They're missing it."

"So winter is better?"

"It's a lot quieter. Some of the speed limits are bumped up—which is nice. I read a lot more. When there's a blizzard, it can feel like you're the only person left in the world. I miss the trees, but I do get to spend more time with my cider."

This was more like it. Finally, Isaac was getting to know her a little better. She was opening up.

"Do you get so much snow you can't open your door to get outside?" Bass asked.

"Not recently. But I remember a few times when I was little, we would open the door after a big blizzard and it was a sheer wall of snow. The wind had blown just right to create a giant snowdrift. My dad had to climb out a window to get a shovel and dig us out."

"Baller."

Sanna shook her head and smiled at Bass's reaction.

"Baller, indeed."

Isaac wanted to hear more stories from her childhood—he wanted to know why he found her alone in the orchard instead of at the hospital with her dad, what she had ever seen in Thad, and why she so clearly preferred solitude when an entire county of people seemed to care about her. As she turned into the orchard parking lot, he noticed the small dragon keychain dangling from the ignition. So she'd liked it—he wasn't sure she would. Pleasure that a little part of him was now in her life warmed his chest.

Sanna rolled the dingy sheets off the bed in the guest room, careful to keep the dust from jumping off the material. After doing the same with the ones covering the chair, dresser, and lamps, she plugged in the lamp and set the fresh bedding on the end of the mattress.

"Can I help?" Julie stood in the room. Sanna shrugged. They'd known each other twelve years, but if Julie had been paying attention, she'd have known that company was not what

Sanna wanted. Julie grabbed the fitted sheet and fluffed it out so Sanna could grab the other end, both tucking in their corners. "Thanks for getting the rooms ready."

Sanna shrugged. "Anders doesn't know where anything is anyway."

Julie's jaw twitched, but she stayed silent as Sanna tossed her the flat sheet.

"He's a good man."

Sanna stopped straightening her half of the sheet and stared at Julie. Julie looked down at the bed and fidgeted with the edge she held in her hands.

"I wouldn't know. He left. Just like the Donor."

She knew Julie would know who she was talking about. At least Anders would have clued her in about that. She finished tucking her end and jammed pillows into their cases, tossing a few at Julie. They finished spreading the comforter in silence.

Sanna scooped up the cloths, holding her breath to keep from inhaling the dust, and dumped them in the basket waiting in the common area. There were four such areas in this part of the house—a center room surrounded by three bedrooms and a bathroom, then a hallway that led to the neighboring common area. A set of stairs led to a similar floor plan on the second story. This arrangement allowed for each family to have some privacy and unity, while being able to join together in the great rooms. When she was little, her grandparents lived down the hall and she lived here, with Anders, her dad, and the Donor. This was where she had lived until Anders moved to Green Bay.

Growing up, she'd always envisioned her and Anders each getting married and taking over their own pods, filling up the house with laughing children. She'd hoped to have four little ones, at least. Maybe she and her husband would take over the second story because they had so many children. All those plans, already damaged by the Donor's departure, cracked completely when Anders didn't return after graduation. The cracks spread, then broke into nothingness by the time she came home from college, no longer the whimsical wood sprite her father had once called her as a child.

Sanna picked up a second pile of bedding and went into the next room, the room that had once been hers. A faded poster of the four Hogwarts houses still hung on the wall next to a framed picture of her and Anders hanging upside down from one of the Looms by their legs. She used to love that picture and hadn't seen it in years. Julie had started to carefully pull off the sheets and drop them into the basket outside the door.

"I'm sorry about your dad. I know how close you are with him."

Sanna refrained from sighing—I guess they were going to make small talk. Her favorite.

"Thanks." She tucked the fitted sheet around the mattress on her side, while Julie finished her side. "The girls are getting big."

"Like weeds. I'm already getting flickers of what they'll be like as teenagers. It's scary. They've always been okay with sharing, but now they insist on having their own everything. Good thing the new house has extra bedrooms."

Why did Julie think Sanna wanted to know this?

"The girls will need to share. I'm not making up more rooms," Sanna said.

Julie nodded.

"That's fine. They'd prefer that in a strange house."

Sanna's nostrils flared.

"It wouldn't be strange if you ever visited."

Julie's face darkened.

"Not everyone wants to be trapped here." Julie exited the

room, leaving those loaded words echoing. Sanna finished making the bed by herself, focusing on the repetitive motions so she could ignore the memories of the last time someone had said that to her.

She heard Anders's heavy footsteps before she saw him.

"What did you do? Julie looked really upset."

Julie hadn't told him the details of their conversation. Yet. She straightened the duvet, smoothing out the wrinkles that were no longer there.

"You can yell at me all you like. Do not upset my wife and daughters. Ever."

Sanna nodded. She couldn't fault him for defending his family, no matter what she thought of him and his choices. At least he had that right. She took the photo of them off the wall. Pressure built behind her eyes and swallowing became harder.

"Remember when we were little and we used to stay in the trees past dark?" Her voice cracked from holding back her sadness, so Anders finished her thought.

"Pa would bring us dinner so we wouldn't need to come in until the last possible minute." He smiled at the memory.

"Why didn't you want your girls to have that, too?"

Anders took the picture from her, glanced at it, and set it on the dresser. His eyes looked sad.

"Your whole life is built on changes. Seasons changing, apples changing from juice to cider, trees changing. Why has this change always been so hard for you?"

"It doesn't count when I know the change is coming. The changes I don't plan for are the ones that I hate. Like today." Her lip trembled so she bit it.

Anders pulled her into a hug, and Sanna rested her chin on his shoulder. It was nice to be close to him. He used to be her best friend in everything and now she barely knew him.

"You don't have to go through anything alone. I'm here."

"Until you go back to Green Bay." A few minutes ago, those words would have had a sharp edge, but now they were merely sad.

"You and Pa could come visit when he's better. You might just like it."

She rolled her eyes at him.

"I should get back to the hospital, see how Pa's doing. If we leave him there alone too long, Mrs. Dibble will start pestering him."

"Pa's not getting any younger, Sanna, whether you like it or not. Just meet with Eva. She has a lot to offer. It's only coffee."

Sanna wanted to say no. She wanted to refuse. She wanted to, but she didn't.

"I don't drink coffee."

Anders chuckled. He knew he had won.

"You can have tea." He pulled away and looked at her. "Just hear what she has to say."

She took a deep breath, proud of herself for not letting any tears fall. Too much had happened in one day. When she woke up that morning, the thought of selling Idun's had never crossed her mind, and now . . .

"Fine, set it up. Let me know where and when."

CHAPTER FIFTEEN

Eva intentionally stood and waited for the Lunds to arrive, enjoying the way her high heels pinched her toes. The slight pain reminded her she was stronger and tougher than all those around her. The door opened and in walked two gloriously tall, obviously related people, a man and woman with similar short pale hair and striking blue eyes. Strong cheekbones and jawlines carved from stone. They moved with grace—what she wouldn't do with that height. The woman wore unflattering jeans and work boots. She hadn't even bothered with lip gloss. The man, at least, had on khaki pants and a neat dress shirt with a button-down collar. Even in her heels, she didn't reach their shoulders. They must be the Lunds, Anders and Sanna. She'd heard from her source that they were tall.

They would need to sit.

The two were already talking about something and didn't realize she was their appointment. She stepped a little closer to hear them better.

"Please keep your mind open," Anders said, his face even stonier. "You aren't the only one in this family."

He stood close to the woman so they didn't have to speak loudly, but it was clear from their stiff bodies they were fighting.

"Dad doesn't want to leave the orchard. We spoke last night when I went back to the hospital."

Anders huffed out of his nose.

"Dad is on a lot of pain meds. When he comes home, he'll realize he can't jump back into work."

"That doesn't mean he'll want to leave Idun's." Sanna played with her necklace, rubbing her fingers on the medallion. "Why are you so against the orchard? Julie commented last night that 'not everyone wants to be trapped here.' Did you feel trapped?"

Anders's mouth froze into a grim line.

"She's not talking about me."

"Then what was she talking about?"

"I'm not getting into it right now." He looked around the coffee shop and his eyes settled on Eva. Sanna hadn't noticed her yet.

"How am I supposed to believe anything you say when you won't tell me the truth?"

Eva could use that infighting to her advantage.

"I'm not lying to you. Withholding information is not the same thing as lying. You'd be wise to remember that." He held out his hand to her and spoke in a louder voice. "You must be Eva."

She pulled out her most friendly and innocent smile.

"Yes. I knew who you were right away. You must be the tallest people in the county. Who knew Finns were so tall?"

Anders smiled at her right away—getting men to smile at her was never difficult. Sanna was another story—definitely not charmed. The tall woman snorted and rolled her eyes.

"We're Swedes, not Finns."

Eva blinked. That mistake would cost her, she'd have to appeal to Sanna with a different strategy.

"Well, now I know." She cleared her throat. "I'll grab us a table while you get your drinks."

Eva left them to it while she settled into a tiny table in a corner. The shorter chairs would bring them down to her height. She set her binder of documents on the table. It shouldn't take long to convince them that the money was definitely worth it. Her offer was well over market for their land. In a few minutes, they were all settled.

"Eva, why don't you start with what you plan to do with the property?" Anders began.

Eva paused. Most people didn't care what WWW planned to do with the land. They just wanted the money. But easy enough to change her pitch on the fly. She pulled out another binder and opened it to a rendering of the proposed hotel and water park.

"Here is the initial sketch. It always changes during the project, but you can see this is the road, the parking lot, water park, hotel." She pointed to one end. "This will be an adults-only pool. We find some of our patrons prefer a quieter atmosphere." She winked at them, grinning. Anders smiled. Sanna just stared at the image.

"Where are the trees?" Sanna asked.

"The trees?"

"You're buying an apple orchard. In Door County. You've even named it The Orchard." She pointed to the top of the image. And it's true, they were planning to name the complex The Orchard, or at least something tied into a Door County theme. Her designers were still working on final interior plans.

"I guess we'll plant a few along the edges after construction is done. See, you're already seeing how plans can change." Eva smiled, giving it her best "I'm with you" look.

"You're going to cut down all the existing trees to build this." Sanna pointed at the picture. "Then plant some new apple trees."

"In my experience, it's easier for construction to remove any existing physical obstacles, then bring those elements back as newer or updated." Eva didn't understand what was so complicated about this. "Let's move on to the financi—"

As she spoke, Sanna stood and walked out of the coffee shop with no warning and no explanation. How unprofessional. Anders rubbed his forehead with one of his huge hands.

"Is she coming back?" Eva asked.

"No." Anders looked at her. "Let me be frank. I think it makes sense to sell. I think your offer is a good start. But if you want any chance of making this deal happen, you either need to find a way that she won't care about those trees being cut down or build the water park around them. Call when you have something new."

He stood and followed his sister out.

Save the fucking trees? Who cared about trees? You can always plant more trees. But Eva's mind already started churning out ideas. Her brother would have strong-armed the sellers into an agreement using more money as his blunt tool, but Eva could tell money alone didn't matter to Sanna. This was what her dad and brother never understood about women, about people, really. There was usually more to any deal than dollars alone. She needed to win Sanna over, earn her trust, find a way to save those trees, and then her deal would be done.

CHAPTER SIXTEEN

It was barely light out when Sanna snuck out of the house, leaving a fresh pot of coffee brewing. She used her dad's truck so Elliot's loud engine wouldn't wake her brother—she'd see him soon enough at the hospital, where, after five days of eating bland hospital food supplemented by containers of Mrs. Dibble's home cooking, her father was waiting to come home. Before she left, she stopped at the mobile home and knocked softly on the door. No response. She waited a few moments, then knocked again more firmly. She admired the trailer's recent improvements. The grass had been edged neatly around the base of the building and mowed a few yards out, creating a small yard. Terra-cotta clay pots of geraniums flanked the steps, the red popping against the surrounding emerald. It looked homey.

She raised her hand to knock again when she heard steps on the other side of the door, and in moments she stood face-to-face with Isaac. A shirtless Isaac. A shirtless, rumple-haired Isaac, who rubbed his eyes and waited for Sanna to say something. He wore gray loose-fitting shorts, and that was it—a light smattering of hair highlighted rather than covered his toned chest and stomach. The man needed more dessert. Fuzzy tan lines blended the dark tone of his forearms into much paler skin on his upper arms and shoulders. She'd never had the urge to trace a farmer's tan, but at the moment, she needed to stuff her hands in her pockets to avoid it.

"Is everything okay?" Isaac asked. He scratched his beard while waiting for her to speak.

"Uh . . . yes. I'm bringing my dad home from the hospital. Today."

Sanna returned to blinking. She could feel the warmth of sleep radiating off him.

"Good." He paused. "Is that it?"

"No. Sorry." Sanna scrambled for an excuse. "I didn't get much sleep last night. Take the day off since we won't be doing any work. I wanted to let you know so you could do something fun with Bass if you wanted."

Isaac smiled, and she resisted the urge to lean into him. Instead she took a step away and stumbled down the few steps, barely keeping her balance and knocking over one of the pots. Isaac stepped out onto the tiny landing where Sanna had just stood.

"Are you all right?"

"I'm so sorry." Sanna shoved the loose dirt back into the pot and righted it. When she straightened, she was looking directly at his navel. Being around him left her unmoored, like one of those candy-colored kayaks pulled off the beach by an incoming storm, bobbing around on the waves at the mercy of the current. She couldn't tell if he was the storm or the rescue boat. The closer she was to him, the more she tossed about, except the few times they touched. Then calmness and security took over, and she knew no harm would come to her. Was he her safe harbor or a fierce storm? Or perhaps it was best to stay well away from him entirely? She didn't like the idea of him affecting her at all.

"What would you recommend we do?" Isaac asked softly.

Sanna rubbed her thumb and forefinger on the wood of her necklace, trying to come up with why he wanted recommendations, but the past few moments had scrambled her thoughts completely. Heat spread from her cheeks to her ears to her neck. Could she make a bigger ass of herself? She'd come here with a clear purpose and now she couldn't even follow their conversation.

"Bass and I . . . You said we had the day off." He was biting his lower lip to keep from laughing. She looked up at the sky to pull herself together and aimed for a coherent response.

"The weather looks nice today. There's good hiking and a tower you can climb at Peninsula State Park, on the bay side, that gives a great view of Green Bay. And then I'd take him to Al Johnson's in Sister Bay. Goats live on the roof, and kids seem to like that. You could also head down 57 to the quiet side, to Baileys Harbor. There's a lot less traffic and amazing views of Lake Michigan."

"Those all sound like perfect suggestions."

His smile was so genuine and kind. She wanted to stay there and not face her broken father at the hospital or Anders's irritation when he realized she left without him. She was mostly sure her wanting to stay had nothing to do with his missing shirt.

"See you tomorrow," she said.

She left Isaac standing in his pajama bottoms, giving in to one last glance as she walked away.

Sanna sat in the reclining chair next to her dad's empty hospital bed. He was hobbling up and down the hallway per the physical therapist's instructions, though she suspected he only listened to the PT's suggestions because her warm smile turned into a laugh at all his ridiculous jokes. Dad probably thought she was flirting with him. Sanna rolled her eyes to herself and stared out the window. She could almost see the bay and then looked northeast, wondering if Isaac and Bass had made it to the top of the state park's tower, or were they already watching the goats? She wished she'd thought to tell them about the swimming spot she and her brother had discovered when they were little. It was the perfect place to jump into the water on a warm day.

Speaking of her brother, he had finally made it to the hospital. "What took you so long?"

A lock of hair had fallen from his precise style. Sanna liked it better that way, it reminded her of the boy she used to know. Not the brother who wanted to negotiate with that woman.

"Thanks for leaving me to finish the meeting yesterday—like grown-ups do. You can't walk out like a toddler having a tantrum. And then leaving so early this morning that I had to bring a separate car. Super mature, Sanna."

"She didn't have anything to say that I wanted to hear. There was no reason to stay."

"It's not just about you. Think about Dad. About how this treatment is getting paid for. About how he has no savings."

"He doesn't want to sell either."

"He'd change his mind if you did."

"I'm not letting anyone cut down our trees. And you shouldn't either."

Sanna burned from head to toe. He would always treat her like the dumb little sister. She didn't want to fight with him, but she didn't want him to succeed in convincing their dad to sell, either. The sooner he went back to Green Bay, the better.

"What is all the tussle about in here, you two?" Einars hobbled into the room with crutches, his left leg encased in a thigh-high bright blue cast while his right arm wore one to match. After a few days in the hospital, he already moved better. A younger woman with a high ponytail followed him into the hospital room and watched as he lowered himself onto the bed and hoisted his leg onto the mattress. She tucked a pillow under his heel and turned to face Anders.

"I have a list of things he can and can't do and exercises he'll need to do at home. We already have some appointments scheduled for PT."

When she paused, Sanna stepped in.

"I'll be taking care of him."

"Oh, okay. Then you and I will need to go over everything. I'll get it all together and come back."

The therapist asked Einars a few more questions, then left with another promise to be back with instructions for Sanna.

"When are you heading back home?" Sanna asked Anders. He had slumped against the wall, taking up space like a lopsided coatrack, all lean limbs going in different directions.

"I'm not heading back."

"Surely the girls don't want to stay."

"Julie took the girls shopping, but they'll be driving back later."

"But you're staying?"

Sanna's shoulders tightened at this news.

"Yep. I picked up some cherry pastries for all of us. The girls were sick of apples and oatmeal." He spoke casually, studying the information on the whiteboard.

Sanna threw her arms in the air. Everything he said and did proved her point that he didn't understand her or their dad—that he was wrong about selling the orchard.

"How can they get tired of apples? It's in their blood, and they know nothing about it."

Anders covered his face with his hands. "When are you going to get it? There's nothing magic about that place. It's not a crime to want more out of life. Try it, you might even find you like it." He looked at Einars. "Dad, can you help me out here?"

Anders looked between the two other Lunds and raised his eyebrows, asking his dad for support. Einars sighed.

"Sanna, you can't complain he's never here, then insist he leave when he offers to stay. Who knows? Maybe a longer visit is what he needs to be reminded about how much he loves it here."

Anders snorted, but kept silent as Sanna glowered at the floor, biting her tongue. She'd lost that battle, but she would win this war. They'd sell the orchard the day Sanna no longer had breath to protest.

CHAPTER SEVENTEEN

Isaac watched Bass as he surfed his hand on the breeze out his open car window. They needed a day for just the two of them, but he couldn't drop the feeling that Sanna would make a good addition to their outing, and not just because she knew all the best places in Door County. He didn't know how to read her, not really. Sometimes it felt like she couldn't wait to get away from him, and other times, like this morning, he was pretty sure she was checking him out. It might have been a while since he'd caught a woman admiring him, but even rusty, he could still recognize it.

He was happy to have been there to help when Einars fell, liked that she allowed him to help her, but he wanted more. He wanted to know how those long arms would feel wrapped around his neck, if there were hidden speckles in her blue eyes. He wanted to know the story behind the necklace she touched when worried or scared, drawing his eyes to her throat. But he couldn't have that. His life—Bass, Paige, the inevitable truth coming out—was complicated, and he wouldn't draw her into that.

But today was about spending time with Bass. Driving through

Peninsula State Park was a whole different pace than what they'd seen of the area so far. If most of Door County was lined with rows of apple and cherry trees or else corn and summer crops, then the state park was its wild core, a hidden pocket free from the tiny gift shops and trendy eateries that lined the small towns up and down Highway 42. Lush forests edged the road, revealing orange-domed tents and cream pop-up trailers between the many tree trunks and shorter shrubs. A few campers still sat around fires, enjoying the last sips of fire-brewed coffee before going about their days, bedding slung over ropes tied between tree trunks.

As Isaac drove through the park, he and the handful of other drivers slowed for the abundant cyclists cruising the well-shaded byways. He looked at the map he had gotten at the ranger station and pulled into the parking lot for the Eagle Tower. The wooden tower rose four stories above the parking lot overlooking the water below, with three viewing platforms; halfway up, three-quarters of the way up, and at the top. After their early start, this seemed the right place to begin the day. Campfire and damp earth mingled on the breeze as Bass and Isaac stepped out of the car. Isaac double-checked that his backpack contained their water bottles, phone, and the poorly refolded map. He sprayed them both with sunscreen and topped their floppy curls with matching tan wide-brimmed hats. He'd taken Sanna's advice and gotten them both decent ones for working in the orchard.

"You ready for this, Perch?"

"I own this."

Isaac checked to make sure his backpack was secure and that there weren't many people on the stairs before shouting, "Go!"

Isaac dominated the first two landings, his longer, stronger legs taking the worn wooden steps two at a time. He was a full seven steps ahead of Bass when they reached the halfway point, when gravity and age started working against him. Since Isaac and Bass had begun their road trip, he'd stopped his daily runs, never wanting to be even one mile from his son. Now he paid the price. His lungs burned and he had to start taking the stairs one at a time. He heard Bass's quick, light steps gaining behind him as he dodged around a family of four.

"Watch out for the family," he shouted between ragged breaths as Bass bounced off the railing to narrowly avoid a mom holding the hand of a toddler.

As they rounded the last flight, Bass pulled ahead, his lighter body and younger lungs unaffected by the rapid climb.

"Burn!" Bass screamed, and the handful of other people on the observation deck looked on with good-natured smiles, especially when they noticed Isaac gasping for breath as Bass completed his victory dance, complete with the Dab and a booty shake.

"Okay, okay. You've made your point. I'm old."

Isaac went to stand at the railing, and Bass joined him. A stitch had formed at his side, but his breathing slowed after a few moments' rest. The tower stood near the edge of a cliff overlooking Green Bay. He hadn't even known there was a real Green Bay besides the football team before coming here, and now he was looking at it. White boats crisscrossed the green-tinged waves. They were a million miles from everything they knew. Isaac let the remoteness wrap around them as he pulled Bass in for a hug.

These moments were why he ran away with Bass. The laughter, the racing, just him being a kid. When Isaac finally did tell him about his mom—and he would, soon, he swore it—this innocence would evaporate. They would need to talk about drugs, overdosing, addiction, and why Paige couldn't get better.

Isaac would never forget the day he gave up hope she would beat her addiction—the day he knew their marriage was over.

Bass had been finishing up kindergarten, and Paige still worked nights at a nursing home. Little did he know that's where she was getting her supply. The nursing home kept a stock of fentanyl lollipops and patches for the patients who used it to manage their pain. He had known for months something was off—she'd been losing weight and sometimes at night her breathing almost stopped. When they would lie in their bed, she would curl into a ball while he curved around her, close but not touching. He'd count the seconds between breaths and some nights it would stretch to seventy or eighty seconds. A few times he nudged her to prompt an inhale. But it was never bad enough that he confronted her about her changed behavior, and he'd always regret that.

One day he came home from work early, hoping to meet Bass as he got off the bus. He'd pulled into the driveway as the bus turned the corner, just missing it. Bass and Paige would already be back to the house. He had wanted them all to drive to the coast as a family for dinner, maybe watch the sunset over the Pacific with a picnic. He quietly opened the door into their kitchen, planning his surprise. If he was lucky, he could execute the tickle attack that always sent Bass into cascading giggles—Isaac's favorite sound in the world.

He poked his head around the corner into the living room, where what he saw made his excitement crack off like a calving glacier into an icy ocean. His wife, Paige, lay on the couch, her eyes closed and sweat covering her face. On the table in front of her were open packets and a handful of lollipops. Bass stood next to her, barely taller than the back of the couch, still wearing his Yoda backpack. He wasn't looking at his passed-out mom but at the candy. He already held one in his hand and was reaching for a second.

Isaac didn't remember crossing the small living room or picking up Bass. He couldn't remember if he shouted or scolded or said anything at all. He only remembered seeing the lollipop, then holding a screaming Bass, who was angry his daddy had taken the candy from him.

He settled Bass down on his bed with a bowl of ice cream and *Return of the Jedi* so he could wake up Paige and have a real discussion about what was going on, finally. He checked her breathing—she was asleep, not passed out—covered her with a blanket, then gathered all the lollipops and pills. He didn't know what to do with them, only that he needed to get them away from Paige. He sat on the coffee table with the bag of drugs in his lap, wondering what to do next.

Isaac stared at this shadow of a woman he once loved. She'd always been prone to anxiety and depression, even mania sometimes, and medicine seemed to help. After having Bass, it had gotten worse. She was so miserable. Isaac had offered her anything to make her happier—counseling, moving, whatever she needed. When she began working at the nursing home, things got better. She was content, calmer. They were happy for a few years again—their little family. Now her skin clung to her bones, gray and bruised in places. Her hair stuck to her head with sweat and her eyes fluttered behind her lids. The thoughtful, delicate woman he married was broken, his marriage was over, and he couldn't fix it or her.

She started to stir. Her high had worn off. It took several seconds for her to move into an upright position, and Isaac didn't offer to help.

"Am I dreaming?" she said at last.

"No," he said. "This is all real."

Her eyes saw the drugs in his lap, then scanned the room.

"Did he?" At least she asked the right question, a question a mother would ask, but her words were flat and distant. A mere echo of what the real danger warranted.

"No. I stopped him in time."

She nodded her head, an uncontrolled movement, as if the muscles could no longer fight gravity.

"You're going to rehab, then you're finding somewhere else to live. This can't ever happen again. I'll help you, Paige, but you can't live with us anymore."

She didn't even argue.

She'd been in and out of rehab ever since. This last stint had seemed the most promising—except she had found someone to supply her. Too late, the doctors found out she was sucking fentanyl patches she had stashed in her mattress. That, combined with her anxiety drugs, stopped her breathing for good.

Isaac sucked in the fresh air at the top of the tower and gave Bass one last squeeze. He and Paige may not be married anymore, but the loss still hurt, compounded by his guilt for not being able to help her, and guilt at his attraction to Sanna. But none of that mattered. This summer was about Bass. He was so grateful they had each other and hoped that would be enough once Bass learned the truth.

"Time to go down. Let's get some hiking in. Then we can see the goats."

Bass gave one last look at the view.

"Race you?" he said, then dashed for the stairs before waiting for Isaac to accept.

The waitress set their hot cocoa mugs in front of them, and Bass's face was in the whipped cream before she could turn to her next table. The frothy white blob doubled the height of the mug and had already started to melt into the steaming liquid. They'd stopped for lunch at the famous Al Johnson's restaurant in Sister Bay. The food was good, but it was made all the more fun by goats roaming the restaurant's grass roof. Inside, diners could buy assorted Swedish goodies and goat paraphernalia from the gift shop, and the staff wore wooden clogs that looked uncomfortable—though their waitress assured Bass they weren't bad.

They ended the meal with hot cocoas once Bass had seen a mug delivered to a neighboring table. He took it as a chance to get as much whipped cream on his face as possible. It was even in his eyebrows. Isaac handed him extra napkins. Once Bass had devoured all of his, Isaac switched their mugs.

"Try not to inhale it this time."

"We should come here with Miss Lund and Mr. Lund."

"I'm sure they've come here enough. They live here."

"Do you think she gets hot cocoa? I bet Mr. Lund does. He seems like a hot cocoa kind of guy."

"What's a hot cocoa guy like? Am I a hot cocoa guy?"

"You do have one in front of you, but you gave up the whipped cream too easily. Mr. Lund wouldn't give up his whipped cream. Instead, he would sweet-talk the waitress into getting me more."

Isaac laughed.

"Sweet talk! What do you know about sweet talking?"

"It's when you say nice things to someone to get what you want, but in a real way. Not an evil genius way, but in an 'I just want to get what I want' kind of way."

"Sweet talking is a good life skill. Especially when you find someone you really like. But I think you're on the young side to be mastering it."

Bass scowled, then brightened.

"Did you sweet-talk Mom?"

Isaac swallowed a sip of hot cocoa, buying time, and it settled in his stomach like a rock.

"Why would I need to sweet-talk your mom?"

"To get her to go to the hospital and get better."

And here was a disaster Isaac couldn't stop from happening, he could only delay.

"I didn't need to sweet-talk her. She wanted to get better."

"Have you heard from her? How is she?"

"Let me check, Guppy."

Isaac pulled out his phone, his hand quivering. Was this the moment? His chance to be honest? He had one e-mail from the hospital asking him to call and several text messages from his mom.

IT'S BEEN A WEEK! HOW IS BASS?

I FOUND THESE ARTICLES ABOUT CHILDREN AND GRIEVING.

READ THEM!!!!

CALL ME!!!

His hand holding the phone began to shake more violently. He turned the phone off and set it on the table. He would delete them later.

"Nope, nothing."

Bass's whipped cream–crusted eyebrows scrunched together.

"When will we hear something?"

"I know you miss her, but sometimes people need time before they are ready to get back to normal. Sometimes they are never ready, and we need to accept that things change. Does that make sense?"

The whipped cream was gone, and Bass slurped the cooling hot cocoa.

"Do you think the Lunds will need some time?"

Lucky, a topic change.

"I do. Mr. Lund was hurt pretty badly and won't be able to do all the things he could do before. At least not for a while."

"We should help them."

And just like that Isaac's heart switched from constraint to nearly bursting with pride. This kid always surprised him. One minute he'd be a maniac, and the next he'd say the sweetest thing.

"Maybe that's why we ended up here. They needed some help, and here we are: two strapping lads ready to do whatever's needed."

Bass made muscle arms.

"I'm ready."

They both were.

CHAPTER EIGHTEEN

The next day, Isaac and Bass approached the farmhouse ready to help the Lunds however they could. Bass trailed behind him as Isaac saw Einars ease himself into the ATV, trying to get his injured leg into the vehicle. Isaac shifted into a jog to get there faster.

"Are you supposed to be out here?" Isaac said.

Einars waved his hand in the air as Isaac and Bass stopped beside him.

"I'm perfectly capable of moving, it just hurts a bit more than before." His lower leg was wrapped in a large blue cast, and he wore sweatpants with one leg cut off. Sanna stormed out of the house, letting the screen door slam behind her.

"Busted," said Einars, his shoulders slumping as he scrunched the hat in his hands.

"I can't even pee now without you escaping. You are supposed to be resting with your leg elevated—not cruising over bumpy ground with your leg dangling from a moving vehicle like a broken muffler." She turned to Isaac and Bass with a small smile. "Morning."

"I have worked every day since I can remember. I am not stopping now that I'm home," Einars said, setting his hat firmly on his head. "Besides, Isaac is driving me around. I'm teaching him to prune."

"Pa, how many painkillers did you take this morning?" Sanna asked. Isaac's eyes darted to Einars, searching for the signs he knew too well. His muscles relaxed when he didn't find any. "I will get Isaac and Anders to help me carry you in the house if I have to—but you are going back inside. I can't get any work done if I'm worrying about you. Then we'll all be immobile. Right, Isaac?"

"I'll help, too," Bass added. Sanna gave a crisp nod and towered over her dad. She could be intimidating when she wanted to be, and Isaac didn't mind at all.

"Bass," she started, but never finished, as a silver truck pulled into the parking lot. It stopped and Thad emerged, a foil-wrapped pan in his hands. Sanna's shoulders stiffened as he walked toward them. Isaac wanted to block him from approaching, but judging by Sanna's stern face, he thought that might irritate her more.

"Hi, Einars, Sanna." Thad nodded at them both, yet ignored Isaac and Bass. Dick. "My mom asked me to bring this over for you. It's her Friday Night Goulash." He held up the pan as if they couldn't see he carried something and handed it to Sanna, who held it carefully away from her body. A waft of air brought its aroma to Isaac, and he resisted the urge to gag. Pungent overcooked cabbage and sharp undercooked onions mixed with something not quite right. Tuna, perhaps?

"You'll need to thank her for us. That was very thoughtful of her," Einars said, watching the aluminum foil for any sudden movements. "Sanna will take care of it for us. You know where to put it, right?"

Her lips turned up ever so slightly.

"Sure, Pa." She moved to leave when Thad reached out for her arm.

"Are we still on for this week?"

Sanna let out a small bark of laughter, then pulled her features back into her resting stern expression.

"You serious?" she said.

"Nothing's changed for me." He rubbed her elbow, and Isaac hoped she'd dump the stinky pan over his head.

Bass had grown bored with the grown-ups and poked a stick at small rocks stuck in the ATV's tires, occasionally releasing one to skitter across the gravel. He moved to the tire closest to Sanna and Thad while Isaac and Einars watched the conversation carefully for any sign they needed to jump in, though they knew that Sanna rarely needed help.

"I can't. I'll be taking my dad to the doctor that day. In fact, that reminds me. Bass." Bass's head shot up, not wanting to miss his part in the conversation even though he was practically on their feet. "I'll leave you a note in the barn on what to do that day, okay? That way you can still help out."

Isaac didn't know if that was true. It sounded more like she meant she'd be "washing her hair" than an actual obligation, but Bass would be happy to help with a ruse.

"Won't that be during the day? We can push our evening back so it won't interfere," Thad said.

Sanna exhaled slowly out her nose and pulled away from where his hand touched her.

"I will be busy." She headed toward the house, and the three men watched her until the door slammed shut. Isaac didn't even try to stop his smile. Thad clenched his jaw until a muscle jumped near his temple. Einars just looked tired. They needed to get him inside to rest.

Thad turned to Einars.

"She makes her own choices," Einars said, giving a weak wave with his hand.

Bass was still poking at the stones stuck in the tires when one flicked out and hit Thad's cheek.

"What the hell? Watch what you're doing, kid." He kicked gravel at him.

Bass scuttled to the other side of the vehicle, and Einars started to rise from his seat, wincing at the pain from the sudden movement.

"Hey now. He didn't mean anything by it," Isaac said, moving directly in front of Thad and holding a hand toward his chest. It took all his restraint to not grab his face and give him a much closer look at the gravel, but that wouldn't send the right message to Bass on how adults were supposed to act. "Accidents happen."

Thad narrowed his eyes, taking Isaac's measure, and stepped back.

"Yes, they do. But you still have to deal with the consequences." He looked at Einars. "Tell Sanna I'll be in touch."

They watched him drive away, dust trailing down the road.

"That's just sad," Bass said when the sound of the truck disappeared completely. Einars and Isaac laughed.

"Yeah, it is," Isaac said. "Some guys can't take rejection so they go after the smallest person to make themselves feel bigger."

Before they could talk more, Sanna emerged carrying a small white trash bag and dumped it into the cans near the barn, then returned to where they stood.

"I saw the scuffle from the window." She looked at Bass. "You okay?" He nodded, and she nodded back. "We still need to return the dish, but the worst of the smell is out of the kitchen. I lit some matches."

Einars shuddered. "I can't believe that woman is still sending that out into the world."

"Dare I ask?" Isaac said.

"Imagine every bad school cafeteria casserole, then mix them together. Nothing is as it should be. That's all you need to know," Sanna said, looking down at her father. "Time to get you back inside."

He nodded.

"I can stay with him. Why don't you and Bass get some work done?"

Sanna looked from Isaac to Einars. Would she trust him to care for her dad? Isaac felt like he was being tested but never saw the questions.

"Make sure he takes it easy," Sanna finally said. "He's a stubborn fool."

"Fear not, fair maiden, your father is safe from all hideous casseroles and dangerous orchard chores while I'm around."

Sanna scrunched her face at him, a smile peeking through her confusion, then walked away toward the barn with Bass.

"Let's get going before you're tempted to say anything else," Einars said.

Isaac eased him to standing and maneuvered the crutches into the correct position. His silly words might be pathetic, but he was pretty sure he saw a twinkle just for him in Sanna's eye, and he'd say all the ridiculous things he could just to see it again.

CHAPTER NINETEEN

After a long day thinning out the growing apples, Bass proved himself to be an eager helper and a mostly quiet companion. They worked until their shoulders ached, pausing long enough to drink water and eat peanut butter and jelly sandwiches in the shade of the truck. Ready for dinner and a shower, they walked into the kitchen, where Isaac and Einars already sat at the long table, laughing with Mrs. Dibble. Einars held his normal spot at the head with Isaac to his right and Mrs. Dibble to his left. Her straight gray hair was twisted at the back of her head with a large clip, but a few strands fell onto her face, making her appear girlish as she tapped Einars's hand at something he'd said. She wore comfortable khaki Capri pants and a simple blue button-down shirt that brought out the silver in her hair. Sanna almost turned back around, but it was too late.

"Sanna, dear. Come here. Your father was just telling me all about the day he fell."

Mrs. Dibble pulled out the chair next to her and patted it; her rosy cheeks and welcoming smile already had Sanna self-conscious about what they'd been discussing. She could imagine the details her dad was sharing, and none of them had to do with the fall, but everything to do with the story she had told him about Thad's ill-fated proposal. Isaac waved Bass to his side and spoke softly to him, then pointed to the loft.

Immediately the large, airy room seemed full of more people and more noise. Bass looked to the loft and giggled. When a red ball bounced in front of Sanna, she followed its path to the source—two more boys around the same size as Bass leaned over the railing with arms outstretched, waiting for the ball's return. They looked vaguely familiar, and she remembered Mrs. Dibble had grandsons. Children were multiplying, and none of the other adults in the house seemed concerned about flying balls and possible broken objects.

"I need to shower." She held up her hands as evidence.

As she walked behind the counter, keeping her distance, Isaac's eyes followed her and Mrs. Dibble's followed his. Great. More fuel for the gossip train.

"Then you can join us when you're done. Dinner will be finished by then. And I brought cherry strudel for dessert. I made it this morning from the first fresh cherries."

Sanna may avoid Mrs. Dibble at every possible turn, but her cooking was legendary, the antithesis to Thad's mother's pan of indigestion. She wouldn't say no to that strudel, even if the price was a little gossip.

The echoing noise of the boys on the stairs reminded her of her own childhood, before they'd closed off the bedroom wing and before the Donor left. Sanna only had a few memories of her, fuzzy with time. The Donor wasn't from Door County, but a small town in northern Wisconsin. She was always happiest when they took trips to Green Bay, or all the way to Milwaukee for a special Christmas shopping trip at the big malls. Sanna remembered being overwhelmed by the traffic and people, but the Donor loved the bustle.

They would put the Christmas tree in the corner, near the staircase. Her dad would climb the steps and lean over the railing to put the star at the top, and the floor would be covered with presents. She and Anders would spend the day playing with the toys while the grown-ups talked and something delicious baked in the kitchen. She couldn't imagine a more perfect place and now it was so close she could reach out and touch it, and she hated it and yearned for it at the same time.

With the promise of such a tasty dinner, she set her memories and solitude aside after her shower and slipped into a simple blue maxi dress, though it barely covered her calves. She wrapped herself in a light sweater and emerged from the steamy room, hair still damp, but the smell of garlic and tomato sauce made up for the chaos.

Anders now sat at the other end of the great table surrounded by papers, his forehead lined with deep creases, oblivious to the noise. Being a parent must have taught him to tune out the clamor that had somehow gotten louder during her shower.

"Sanna, you look refreshed. You can help me finish dinner," Mrs. Dibble said.

Mrs. Dibble may have looked tiny in their kitchen designed for Sanna's tall family, yet she had no problem telling Sanna exactly what to do.

"We need eight forks, plates, and glasses. Get them out and the boys can set the table." She raised her voice to be heard above the racket. "Boys, in the kitchen now." Like a herd of elephants, they trampled down the stairs and stood at the end of the counter like soldiers reporting for duty. "Set the table. You boys can sit in the middle while the adults are at the end closest to Mr. Lund." She turned back to Sanna. "Can you dress the salad? And I'll get the lasagna and bread out."

Sanna listened, because what else could she do when faced with such confident commands? In minutes, they were all gathered around the table—even Anders had joined. He took the seat next to Mrs. Dibble, leaving Sanna the seat next to Isaac as the boys took their plates at the middle of the table to snort and make fart jokes. Sanna girded herself for the interrogation about to commence, but it was softened by the feast on the table. Einars always made simple and filling meals for the two of them. They were fine, but they weren't this. This was a celebration. The lasagna filled a huge roasting pan, covered in thick browned cheese that was crispy in the corners.

"Get me a corner piece, and I'll owe you one," Sanna whispered to Isaac, who sat closer to the pan.

"I'll hold you to that." He scooped the darkest corner onto her plate with a wink that caused Sanna's heart to skip. She wished she could come up with a pithy response, but instead she turned her attention to the food, unable to find her words.

The garlic bread was made from a local bakery's signature item, the giant Corsica loaf. It was slathered in sesame seeds and baked in olive oil so the bottom was crispy yet dripping. Mrs. Dibble had carved huge slices, coated each with garlic butter, then warmed it until the butter soaked in. The salad rounded it out, something light to balance all the heavy food so you could keep nibbling on lettuce to stretch the time at the table.

"Sanna, why don't you pull out a few bottles of cider for dinner?" Einars said.

Glad for the distraction, Sanna brought out three large bottles she had in the fridge, all from the same batch—toasty brown. Not the most appetizing color, but it was the best match to go with a dinner like this one. It was a nearly still, unfiltered scrumpy style that was layered and complex, but not sweet and not dry. It wasn't acidic, so it didn't compete with the tomato sauce, and the subtle apple notes didn't confuse the palate with too many conflicting flavors. It was refreshing and smooth, a dark amber in color with bits of sediment floating around. She poured it into stemless glasses for each of the adults and enjoyed how the evening light got trapped, making the liquid glow when she held it up in a beam of evening summer sunlight.

She set the remaining open bottles on the table and tried to catch her brother's eye. Anders shoveled his food in without a word, still flipping through papers, tut-tutting as he discovered a new bill.

"Anders, put that away. We're eating," Einars said.

"We need to talk about these," Anders said.

"Later. Now is the time for eating and conversation. We all worked hard today and deserve some good food and better company, which is saying much given Mrs. Dibble's exceptional culinary talents."

Mrs. Dibble blushed and seemed to flutter her eyelashes at Einars, then filled his plate so he could eat with his one working arm. They all started eating, and Isaac sipped his cider, looking immediately to Sanna.

"You brewed this?"

Sanna cringed at the term *brew*, but didn't feel like going into the difference between brewing and fermenting—so she nodded and focused on her food. That way, she couldn't pay attention to how his long fingers held the glass in his hands as he studied the color. He may as well have been studying her. She felt exposed and naked as he took another sip. Did he like it? Hate it? Not everyone liked cider, and normally she didn't care. She didn't want to care now. Instead, she built the perfect forkful of Parmesan, lettuce, and crouton rather than watch him—but that didn't stop her from hearing the clink of glass on his teeth as he took a much longer sip.

"That's astounding," he said. "It goes so much better with the meal than any red wine I've ever had." He smacked his lips and took another sip. "It really lets the food shine."

Sanna had to respond. She couldn't ignore him no matter how much she wanted to. She couldn't keep eating, then escape with a plate of dessert to the loft as she usually did. She couldn't rewind time to the beginning of the summer when she only thought about the next cider she wanted to blend. Or ignore that the memory of him washing her hands after her dad's accident had played through her mind before she'd fallen asleep every night that week.

"Thank you." That's all she could muster and hoped it would be enough. She could feel her father watching her, and Mrs. Dibble half listening to their very one-sided conversation. She sipped her own cider and enjoyed the burst of soothing rich brown that rushed her senses. Toasty really wasn't the right term. It was lush and alive, like peat or a balanced dark chocolate.

"Sanna, this is amazing." His voice was soft and rumbling as he tried to keep the conversation from prying ears and eyes. When did their chairs become so close? They had an entire table. His voice in her ear was rich, just like the cider was in her throat. She couldn't help but look at him, and his face was so close. Everything about him was rich and balanced. He was the physical embodiment of this cider. Would she discover more layers the longer she knew him? He was close enough that the flecks of gold in his eyes sparkled at her like the cider's missing effervescence. He was close enough for her to smell the cider on his breath, the color of it making her light-headed and giddy. She'd never experienced her cider that way. Would it be even more potent if they kissed? She leaned away to capture her runaway thoughts.

"It's my favorite of the current batches."

"Batches? You have different types?" He took another long drink. "Anytime you want a sampler, I'm here for you." Sanna's mouth curved. He had no idea how little she needed a sampler. She always knew exactly how it would taste before she tried it. "I mean it." Then he set his hand on her arm, the fingers warm through the thin cotton of her sweater, and the room turned upside down. Her nerves exploded and then calmed to a simmer instantly.

"I'll remember that," Sanna whispered, and pulled her eyes away from him and back toward the food that hadn't changed, but her appetite had. This was too much for her—all the new emotions and interactions overwhelmed her order and she couldn't sort out what was what. Did she want to know Isaac better? Being near him could calm her, at least when it wasn't scattering her nerves like shards of glass on a sidewalk. She swayed toward him, then caught herself and pulled back.

Her hand traced a circular stain on the table the diameter of a mug and remembered the day the Donor left. She and Anders had been building snow forts in the orchard. Their dad had plowed snow into a huge mound earlier in the day so they could carve tunnels in it like prairie dogs. The sun had disappeared even though it wasn't even five o'clock. Their noses and cheeks were flushed—or blooming with snow roses, as their father used to say. They clomped up the wooden steps, snow coating their clothes like an extra sheet of insulation, and stopped at the top to remove all the layers, then carried them to the rack set next to the fire for the purpose of drying out their snowy coats and snow pants.

Their parents weren't anywhere.

"Pa?" Sanna called. She wanted hot cocoa, and her mom didn't like it when they made a mess. "Mom?" Taking charge, Anders filled two mugs with milk, warmed them in the micro-wave, and Sanna mixed in lots of hot cocoa powder, careful to wipe up any that fell on the counter. They had carried their steaming mugs to the table and set them down when a sound came from the loft.

Anders raced up the steps before Sanna. He was always beating her at things. Sanna followed him, but before she could reach the top, Anders spoke.

"Sanna, stay downstairs."

She didn't listen. When she reached the top, she saw Anders crouched over a lump on the floor. As she got closer, she knew the lump was her dad. His body shook, and sobs tore the painful silence.

"I told you to stay downstairs."

"What's wrong?" She crossed the loft to them. "Is he hurt?"

"Go, Sanna."

But her dad shook his head as he straightened. When Sanna's eyes met his, she ran to him and wrapped her arms around him. He hugged her back, the tears on his face wetting the top of her head, her hot cocoa forgotten.

He pulled back and opened his arms to include Anders.

"Mom is gone. She's not coming back. Ever."

And she hadn't.

They lost twenty acres of the Looms that summer. Those rows of the orchard still stood empty.

She never wanted that to happen to her. Especially when she had other things—like everything—to worry about. She stopped tracing the circle on the table and stood, Isaac's hand falling off her arm.

"I forgot something in the barn I need to do."

Sanna heard the gravel crunch before the door to the barn opened and knew who it would be. She picked up the pencil to at least pretend she was taking notes instead of staring out the still-broken window like she had been doing.

"I brought you some dessert," Isaac said, that rich voice walking up her spine.

"Just set it down there, thank you. I'll eat it when I'm done here."

The plate made a dull clink on the stainless steel counter, but he didn't leave. He stood a few inches from her.

"Did I do something to offend you?"

"No."

"Because you left right after I—"

"You didn't do anything to offend me. I just needed to get this done before I forgot." She pointed at the notebook with only a few words written on the page and a lot of loopy doodles.

"I can see that." The laughter she heard in his voice poked at her pride, and, hotheaded, she stood to face him. She always forgot he was as tall as she was, and it startled her that they were so close. Again.

"Thank you for bringing dessert, but you can return to the others. I'm sure Pa will be pulling out the aquavit soon. If you're not around, he'll probably give it to Bass."

Isaac's eyes searched her face, and Sanna worried he could see the confusion inside her. He exhaled.

"Look. I get the sense you don't really like me. Shocking as it may be, you wouldn't be the first. But Bass and I are staying through the season, and now that your dad is hurt, I think we'll be working with each other more. You don't have to like me, but I'd like to make working with me less difficult for you. Just tell me what to do, and I'll do it. But I'm not going anywhere."

Sanna watched him say these words, giving her permission to set the rules—yet she could really only focus on his soft pink lips and how she wanted a cider that was precisely that color. It would be sweet and crisp and bubbly. Something you could drink and drink and never get enough of—each sip would reveal a different shade to the flavor, from a lush rose to a pale blush.

She had to know what lips that color tasted like, so she leaned forward and kissed him. Barely a whisper, the briefest of touches on his fascinating lips, with a hint of the toasty cider they'd had with dinner. Her senses lit up like Christmas lights. She pulled back even faster than she'd leaned in. The surprise she saw on his face matched her own.

"I don't know why I . . ." Her voice trailed off. Colors still crackled around her.

Isaac moved an inch closer, leaning in to inhale near her ear, but he didn't touch her, didn't push her any further. His face was so close she could count the silver flecks in his beard.

"I'm glad you did. I like you. You're interesting, smell unexpectedly like roses, and are obviously gifted." He waved a hand at the cidery as he took a shaky breath. "The few times I've made you laugh have made my days, and I hope to succeed at it again. If that will be a problem, let me know. And, Sanna, I give you permission to kiss me whenever you want." He pointed to the plate and stepped back a few inches. "You better eat that before Mrs. Dibble comes out to supervise you herself. That woman is a tsunami in grandma's clothing."

Sanna finally smiled. Something safe they could agree on.

"And a gossip to match her delicious food. You'll no longer be anonymous in Door County," she said. "She'll tell everyone about the handsome man and his son at the Lund orchard. I wouldn't be surprised if there were a line of single ladies here in the morning."

Isaac smiled, his eyes crinkling, and Sanna's chest thumped. What did she say to cause that smile?

"You think I'm handsome."

"I'm not blind. Any fool can see you're attractive."

"And you're no fool."

"No, I am not. Fools take actions without understanding the consequences. That's no way to make a decision."

"Not even for love?"

"Especially not for love."

Isaac studied her face in silence, long enough for Sanna to want to adjust her position, but she refused to move. She wouldn't let anyone see her squirm.

"What happened to you, Sanna Lund?" His face clouded over and his direct question caught her off guard.

"You'd better get out of here. Mrs. Dibble is probably spreading some insane tale of an illicit relationship between the two of us. The tales that woman spins are better than any soap opera."

"Is it really that outlandish? Two attractive people working side by side in the hot weather, isolated. All of it starting with an impulsive kiss. It's like a romance story."

Sanna smiled again, but this time not so warmly. She appreciated his charm, but she wouldn't make the same mistake twice.

"There are no happily-ever-afters." She finally took a bite of the cherry strudel. "Except maybe strudel."

CHAPTER TWENTY

Sanna dumped the ingredients into the casserole dish. If she could get this made now, then she'd only need to put it in the oven after her dad's physical therapy appointment this afternoon, but before changing the sheets on both their beds. Anders could change his own sheets. She added the water too quickly, sloshing some onto the counter. She reached for the paper towels but only found air.

"Pa, where are the paper towels?" Sanna said after looking in all the usual spots in the kitchen.

Einars sat at the table next to Anders, going over the paperwork he'd refused to look at last night.

"I stopped buying them. Just use a regular towel. Silly to waste all that paper when a towel works just fine."

She grabbed the washcloth and wiped it up, rinsing the rag and hanging it to dry. Using a spatula, she stirred the dish, then covered it with plastic wrap and set it in the fridge. She gave the counter one last wipe.

"I'm going to the store later, where's the credit card? It's not in the usual spot."

He pulled out his wallet and handed her three twenties.

"Here, use this instead."

Sanna took the cash, confused. They rarely used cash.

"I can get cash from the ATM." She tried to hand it back.

"Just use this."

She shrugged and stuffed it in her jeans pocket as Isaac and Bass entered the kitchen.

"Great, right on time." She pulled out a stack of papers and handed one to each person. "These are your schedules. I've mapped out everything I need you to do and how much time you have to accomplish it."

Yesterday had been her first full day in charge, and they hadn't gotten nearly enough work done. Due to her dad's accident, they were behind on everything. Yesterday, they needed to thin the eating apples, spray the late-harvest apples, and mow the orchard, but they only finished half the mowing and a third of the thinning, and didn't get to the spraying. Never mind she had two batches of cider that needed bottling. From now on, she'd be more on top of everyone's job list to make sure everything was accomplished.

"Mine just says 'Whatever,'" Anders said, holding up his paper.

"I don't know what you do, so you can keep doing that." Anders crumpled the paper, then picked up his stack of papers. "I'll be in my room if you need me, Pa."

"When do we pee?" Bass asked.

"When you need to," Isaac said, rubbing his hair. "But seriously, I don't see lunch on here. I'm okay with eating as I work, but Bass needs breaks."

Sanna looked at her master list.

"Damn it."

She collected all their schedules and laid them out on the counter. Isaac stood behind her shoulder and pointed.

"Here. If I take Einars to his PT, he and I can eat something in the car. Then you and Bass can have a lunch. Would that work?"

Sanna nodded, not trusting herself to be pleasant. She should have seen that error. She needed everything to go perfectly today. If she hadn't let her dad climb that ladder, then this never would have happened. If she hadn't kissed Isaac, she wouldn't find herself so distracted when he was around. It was the main reason she had assigned him jobs on the opposite side of the orchard. She couldn't let any more mistakes happen. She had to prove it to Anders. She had to prove it to herself.

She scribbled the changes on the schedules and handed them back to everyone.

"Okay, I'll get Isaac started and meet Bass in the barn."

Sanna led Isaac to the orchard, where the ATV sat next to the sprayer.

"You're going to be giving the late-harvest apples their last spray."

She pointed to the sprayer, but Isaac already started to hook it up without waiting for her instructions.

"How do you, an office worker guy, know how to work a sprayer?"

"First, I'm an independent contractor in the tech industry, so it's a bit more involved than office worker guy. Second—my grandparents had a small farm south of San Jose when I was growing up. They had a sprayer just like this and they taught me to use it. As a sixteen-year-old, it was still fun to drive a tractor around. I'm not completely clueless."

"I didn't say that." The words were as clipped as all her nerves.

"Hey, it's okay. You're doing great."

He rubbed her arm from elbow to shoulder, and Sanna

instantly calmed. How did he do that? She breathed deeply, focusing on the smell of summer grass and sun-warmed apples.

"I'm not. But I will."

"That's why I know you're doing great. I've led enough teams of people. Half the battle is wanting to do it well." Sanna checked her watch. She needed to meet up with Bass, then check on her dad or she'd already be behind. "Though you might want to rethink the strict schedule. Micromanagement never ends well."

Sanna nodded, her mind already three steps ahead.

"I'll take that under advisement."

Isaac's fingers flew over the keys on his laptop as if it hadn't been almost five weeks since he'd coded.

"You really know what you're doing on that thing?" Einars said. He sat next to him with his leg propped on the adjacent chair.

That made two Lunds who doubted his ability today—like father, like daughter. After he'd finished spraying the trees, Isaac had joined Einars in the house. They sat at the kitchen table while Sanna and Bass worked in the orchard. He'd been copying the bits of usable information off their old site into a file. Their entire website made him itchy and it needed to be fixed. He could have a bare-bones site up in half an hour, and something more robust by the end of the night. It would take him a few more weeks to get everything set up the way he wanted. Once that was done, he would create Instagram, Facebook, and Twitter accounts.

"This is what I do. Big companies pay me a lot of money to make over their online presence. Customers use the Internet to find everything, so having a well-crafted website should bring more people here. That's the goal of a website, to get people to either buy something or go somewhere, hopefully do both. Once they're here, then they'll buy apples or cider. Then those happy customers can mention you on their social media accounts, sending more people to your website. It all works together."

He was already thinking of favors he could call in for graphic design work. He'd started scribbling lists of what information he'd need for the website—like apple varieties, harvest dates, cider flavors. As he took notes, Einars got up from the table.

"Hey, what are you doing? I'm supposed to keep you off your feet."

"I need to take my meds and then make the dessert for to-night."

"I can do that. You sit and make a list of all the apples you grow and when they are available for purchase. Where are your meds?"

He shoved the paper and pen at Einars, who huffed, but sat back down as Isaac moved into the kitchen.

"They're by the sink."

Isaac found the bottle and his stomach dropped. Fentanyl.

"You're leaving these out on the counter where anyone could grab them?" Where Bass could grab them? Or Sanna after a stressed-out day? It was like seeing a cobra in a baby's crib—unpredictable and deadly.

"Of course. It's right next to the water, so I can get my pills and water in the same place."

"You can't keep them out in the open like this. I'll keep track of it for you. You let me know when you need it, and I'll give you the right dose."

Isaac's breathing grew shallow and fast. Einars crossed his arms and studied him. Isaac knew he wasn't making sense and he didn't know how to explain without telling him about Bass's mom.

"There something you want to tell me about?"

Isaac's hands shook as he opened the bottle and took out one pill. He gave it to Einars with a cup of water, the bottle still clutched in his hand. The older man took the pill and water, then set his fingers on the bottle, but Isaac didn't let it go. Letting it go would be the same as putting that cobra in the crib—he'd be responsible if Einars took too many. If he kept them, he'd be in control and no one could get hurt.

"I knew someone . . . It didn't end well."

"I don't know about your someone, but I don't like taking the damn things. They make me sleepy, but if I don't take them, then the pain keeps me awake and the doc says I have to sleep. I need to be in charge of my own medication, but how about you keep count of how many I take and I promise to keep them somewhere safer?" Isaac nodded and let the bottle go. "I'm sorry about your someone."

Isaac took a few deep breaths to get control of the fear. Einars swallowed his pill and slid the bottle into his shirt pocket. Isaac took the empty glass back to the kitchen, then stared—unsure what to do next.

"Do you even know how to bake? I think I should do it," Einars said.

The question brought Isaac back to the present, knowing that he needed to keep Einars with his leg up or Sanna would not be pleased.

"How do you think I've been keeping Bass alive? Of course I can cook."

Einars seemed to understand he'd put his past back where it belonged.

"Cooking is not the same as baking."

Isaac chuckled, feeling more like himself.

"Fair enough, but I'm very good at following instructions." He picked up the recipe and read the instructions for the salted caramel apple pie. "Maybe you have a simpler option I could make?"

Einars snorted.

"We'll do a lazy-person's apple pie. Which is basically cooked cinnamon and sugar apples over ice cream with a hunk of piecrust. I even have the crust in the fridge—you only need to roll it out and bake."

As Isaac worked, Anders joined them with the papers and his omnipresent frown. Since Isaac had first met him, he and Anders had rarely spoken. He knew there was a lot of tension between Anders and Sanna, but there seemed to be more beneath the surface he didn't know about.

"Dad, I need to talk to you. I've finally made it through all the books." He looked at Isaac in the kitchen. "I'll help you into your room so we have privacy."

"We can talk here."

"I don't think Isaac needs to hear all the finances."

"I know what's in those books and I'm not fussed about him hearing. He runs a business, he might have a few ideas."

Isaac gave a thumbs-up with flour-covered hands and continued rolling out the pie dough. "I'm happy to help, but I'm also happy to forget it all."

"Fine." Anders sat next to his dad and pulled out papers, then lined them in front of Einars. "How could you let this happen? You've borrowed so much money there's no way you can make the monthly interest payments."

"I've barely touched what the land is worth. It'll only be tight until Sanna gets the cider up and running. She's so happy when she's making cider, I know it will take off."

Anders rolled his eyes.

"Assuming that ever happens, you still can't pay the bank the interest until that money materializes, no matter how happy Sanna is. You don't have any cash on hand. Where do you think it will come from?"

"I've been taking care of the money for years. It was time to take this kind of risk. With only the two of us, the land is struggling. Cider is Idun's future."

Isaac really didn't want to be here for this, but he had to finish baking the pie dough while the apples cooked. Maybe he could hide in the bathroom.

"Isaac, what do you think?" Einars asked.

Too late. He couldn't very well ignore the question, but he felt Einars knew exactly what he had done and had a bigger plan that Anders and he didn't understand.

"Well." He walked to the table and looked at the papers spread out. "Anders is right. Usually agriculture is land-rich and cash-poor, so that can be a big problem if you borrow more than you can pay back with cash reserves. If these numbers are accurate, you need enough to get you through to the cider being profitable because your normal orchard profits won't be enough. You won't be able to make the payments by the end of the fall."

Anders nodded along in agreement as Einars rubbed his chin in thought.

"I'm not ready to sell. Idun's needs more time. There has to be another option."

Isaac was saved by the buzzer. He pulled the crust from the oven as Sanna and Bass bounded up the stairs. Anders collected the papers and stuffed them away, clearly frustrated that nothing had been solved but unwilling to push the issue.

While he had only lived on the orchard for a•short time,

Isaac understood Einars's stubbornness. This place was too special for the Lunds to lose. All he could do, really, was finish the website. The sooner people learned about this amazing place and Sanna's amazing cider, the sooner the Lunds could stop worrying, the sooner Sanna could relax, and the sooner she might kiss him again.

CHAPTER TWENTY-ONE

Two weeks after Einars's fall, Sanna finally had some time to herself. This was the first time in weeks that she was alone in the cidery, and her unsettled nerves tried to find the routine she had abandoned and missed. Each day was a scramble to keep pace with the orchard and get her dad to all his PT and follow-up doctor's appointments. Her journal was covered in sticky notes to herself about tasks that needed to be done, making every day different from the last, no predictable pattern other than the daily chaos of chasing the problems. She picked up one sticky note with GARBAGE scrawled in her tired handwriting with a green colored pencil.

She had written it last night, right after Anders had finally gone home. He'd come to the loft where she'd been planning what needed to be done the next day, deciding what Isaac could handle, and what she'd need to help him do. If it required her assistance, she'd find a way to accomplish it with Bass rather than spend more time alone with Isaac. With Bass she could keep busy and avoid conversation. She only needed to show him something once and he could do it, and when his attention

166 • AMY E. REICHERT

strayed, she let him play on her phone or wander the orchard. With Isaac, she didn't trust herself.

When Anders had sat down next to her, she stifled the disappointment that he wasn't Isaac. But when she saw his stack of papers topped with a WWW brochure, her disappointment turned to irritation.

"We need to go over the finances," Anders said.

"Why? Dad's already feeling better, he can take them back. Adding in one more person to the process will just confuse matters."

"You can't keep ignoring me or the truth. The orchard is wildly in debt, mostly because of all your new cider equipment." He flipped through the papers, pulling out one covered in numbers. Sanna looked out the window. Every day since her dad surprised her with the trailer full of new equipment, guilt had weaseled into her thoughts. Before then, cider had been about pleasure, making what inspired her—now all that expensive equipment waited unused. She didn't know if she could make such large batches, if they would still be good, and if she failed, they would lose it all. Avoidance was the only coping strategy she had left.

"Why are you always against us? You can't come in here and tell Dad he's doing it wrong when you are never here. He has a plan and has been running Idun's fine without you. Stick to real estate."

Anders sighed and looked at her the way only an older brother could, full of exasperation and love. Or at least tolerance.

"I'm not against you. I've never been against you, but I am a realist and selling the orchard is real estate . . . so if anything, I'm more of an expert than you are." He held out the sheet with all the numbers Sanna was not looking at. "Dad hasn't been doing okay. He's making decisions based on your turning a profit with the cider, but you aren't selling the stock you do have."

"I sell it."

"Mrs. Dibble and Thad do not count as a thriving business, and I'm pretty sure you lost Thad as a customer."

"I sell more than that." Sanna crossed her legs and arms. Sanna knew it was petty, but he brought out the worst in her. She didn't know where to begin, who to ask, or the first thing about selling. She only knew about making.

He waved the paper for her to take, then gave up and set it back on top of his pile.

"If you claim you want what is best, you'll consider the offer. Do you really want Dad to have to work until the day he dies? Shouldn't he be able to enjoy some form of retirement?" he asked. Sanna just stared at him. "If we sold the orchard, he would never have to worry about anything."

"But what about me? What would I do?"

Anders set the WWW brochure on her lap.

"Everything isn't about you, Sanna."

She ignored the itch at the back of her mind created by Anders's words, worried that if she scratched it, they'd be true. Dad believed in the orchard, in her, in family. So she would, too.

Anders had packed up his car and left the orchard. Sanna had unfolded the WWW brochure, looking at the frothy water slides and tacky cartoon wave that was the company's logo. Out the window, she tried to imagine a hotel and whining children in inflatable water wings and distracted parents, the scent of chlorinated water replacing ripening apples and summer sun— warmed grass. She couldn't imagine their beautiful orchard destroyed for this type of monstrosity.

As she had stared out the window, lights flickered at the edge of the orchard. Kids sometimes snuck in with blankets on warm summer nights—the dancing fireflies made a romantic background for frenzied teenage romps. She could certainly understand the allure—it would have been her first choice, too. She made a note to check the area tomorrow for any garbage they might leave behind and stuck it on her journal.

This morning, Sanna peeled that note off her journal and decided to check it out before Isaac and Bass arrived. Elliot trundled over the ground as she recited the list of chores she needed to accomplish. Spray the Looms, mow the grass near the new trees, take dad to PT and doctor, and check on the early harvests. If time permitted, they could start organizing the farm stand.

She stopped the truck a few trees away from where she had seen the lights. The apples here were starting to blush a pale pink. From experience, she knew these Galas would be entirely red in a few weeks. Sanna trailed her fingers over them, their perfect skin evidence that she could run the orchard. She'd been in charge and making the decisions and everything was going well. Anders didn't know what he was talking about.

Her eyes scanned the ground for empty cans or stray condom wrappers—it wouldn't be the first time, and she certainly didn't want Bass to find those. One of the kids must have left a tennis ball, odd. She bent to pick up the green orb before her, hard like a baseball, and then her stomach dropped.

All around her, the ground was covered with little green apples. At first her eyes didn't register what she saw, her mind rejecting the possibility. She glanced at the trees down the row and a carpet of unripe apples speckled the ground. If it had been a few weeks from now, she could have gathered them up and let them sweeten, but it was too early for that. They were lost.

Her stomach churned. Who would intentionally pick and discard apples? That was a lot of work to handpick them. She looked above and only a few apples on the tallest branches remained. Why would horny teens do this? She'd never given them a hard time about sneaking onto her property. If anything, she was more tolerant than the other neighboring farms.

The sick feeling in her stomach turned to rage at the unknown saboteur. Were they even a big enough operation for another orchard to sabotage? How dare someone do this to her trees? Adding insult to injury, the culprits had yanked the apples off too far up the stem, meaning there would be no buds next year. Only four trees lost their apples, but that was two years' worth of crops, and what if they came back tonight to do more damage? Her body grew more exhausted with each new question. The last thing she needed was a sleepless night keeping watch for punk kids. By the time she got back to the barn, her blood was on a steady simmer. Einars and Isaac had already left in the ATV, leaving her alone with Bass. She had hoped to talk it over with her dad alone first.

"Hey, Miss Lund, how ya doing?"

She nodded. "Hi, Bass. I'll be with you in a second."

She was still adjusting her schedule for the day as she entered the barn to get her journal and list of to-dos. Bass followed her in, tossing a baseball from one hand to the next. She picked up her journal and turned to see Bass throw the ball high in the air and take a couple of steps back to catch it. She saw the crash unfold in slow motion and before she could say a word, he backed into the tower of crates. Each crate was full of empty bottles waiting for cider, cider she hadn't had time to bottle because she'd been too busy caring for her father and running the orchard. She watched Bass bump them and the stack wobbled once, then twice, like a tower of blocks assembled by a toddler. It reminded her of a swaying tree in a windstorm, except that there were no roots to keep the crates safely planted, and the tower toppled in a thunder of smashed wood and shattered glass.

Bass tried to stop it by grabbing a crate halfway up the pile, but the top's momentum was already too much. He froze as it toppled and turned his little face up at Sanna for reassurance that it would be okay, but she had no reassurance to give him today.

A part of her brain knew it wasn't a big deal—that most of the bottles would survive. Even if they all smashed, bottles were easy to replace, not even that expensive. But today that part of her brain had no hope of winning. It was a Little League team against the New York Yankees, or a baby seal swimming in shark-infested waters, or a kite in a tornado. Today, logic and levelheadedness had no place, so even as the words left her mouth and her face scrunched into an angry expression, that corner of her mind regretted it. The rest of her wanted to light the world on fire.

"Out," Sanna said. She didn't shout. It was barely a whisper. But it was hard and cold, and Bass's eyes widened with something too close to fear and he ran.

CHAPTER TWENTY-TWO

Bass knew that look. It was the look his mom had given him a few times when he'd dropped a cup of milk or spilled his goldfish crackers or left his Legos lying on the ground. Mom would give him the look and he'd run to his room until Dad came home from work. His dad would come to his room, bring him dinner on his special *Cars* tray, and read him stories until bed.

Bass didn't know where to find his dad in the orchard, so he ran in the direction he and Mr. Lund had headed and found himself in the Looms. He ducked under the branches. This tree was older and shaggy looking. The long, arching branches looked like enormous spider legs, drooping toward the ground under the weight of the growing fruit. Hiding in a giant tree-spider seemed safe, until he could find his dad.

He hadn't meant to knock over the bottles. It was an accident. And he would have helped clean it up and even work it off, but that look was scary and he didn't want to know what would happen next.

Under the arching branches, the tree made a tent, cutting him off from the world like a safe cocoon. He leaned his back against the tree trunk, pulling his knees to his chin, and he finally let his tears fall. Miss Lund had become his friend, and he really liked her. He wished he had Snarf with him right now. When he was alone, he liked to read the notes hidden in the secret pockets. They reminded him of when he was in a family.

He scrubbed the tears off his face with the palm of his hand and listened for sounds of the ATV or Elliot, expecting Miss Lund would follow him. That's what most adults did when kids were upset, they followed you to make sure you were safe. But he only heard the insects buzzing. The air was getting stuffy because the breeze couldn't reach him.

Bass didn't know when he'd leave, or if someone would find him first. His mouth got dry from thirst, and his stomach rumbled. He'd left his bag of snacks in the barn with his water bottle and hat. After watching a spider scurry up the tree bark and spin a web, he worried no one would ever come look for him. Maybe he'd have to spend the night out here.

He heard footsteps approaching along with the voice of a man and a woman. The only woman he knew was Sanna, so he stayed hidden. The voices stopped outside the tree and he could see their legs between the bottom of the branches and the ground. He stayed still in the dark shadows of the branches. The man wore brown pants and work boots, and the woman wore a dark skirt with tan, black, and red plaid rain boots.

"These are the trees?" the woman said.

"Yeah. They call them the Looms. Losing them would devastate her."

"How do I tell them apart from the non-Looms?"

Bass heard a clicking sound, like a camera, and the boots turned in a circle.

"They're bigger and more spread out."

"Excellent. Thank you, that's exactly the information I needed." They walked to the next tree.

"When will we get our payment?" the man asked.

"We've been over this. There . . ."

The two walked out of earshot the way they came, and Bass breathed deeply. Why were they in the orchard? He'd have to tell Miss Lund—then he remembered he didn't like her anymore. He wrapped his arms around his knees and set his head down. He tried counting seconds, but lost count at 578. From the distance he heard the thrum of the ATV, and it stopped not far from Bass.

"Bass? You out here?" It was his dad. He did come to find him. "Bass." His voice trailed out the vowels like he was calling a pig and the sound needed to carry a long distance. It wrapped around Bass almost better than a hug. He gave his face one more swipe to make sure there were no more tears on it and duck-walked out from under the branches.

"Here, Dad."

Isaac ran in his direction and pulled him in tight while Bass wrapped his arms around his neck, letting his dad pick him up and hold him tight. He didn't normally like being picked up like a little kid—unless they were wrestling—but Bass wanted to be as close to his dad as possible.

Isaac carried him to the vehicle, then set him in the passenger seat, bending so he could look him straight in the eyes. His dad's forehead looked like the dunes they played on in California before heading east, all deep, curvy lines.

"You okay?"

Bass nodded.

"When you weren't with Sanna and she didn't know where you had gone and what had happened . . . I was so worried. You are too young to go running off by yourself without telling anyone where you are. You can't run away, Minnow."

"I didn't. I was trying to find you, but then I couldn't so I hid until you found me. Like I always did when Mom would get angry."

Isaac kissed his forehead.

"Yeah, that's what you did. You want to tell me what happened?"

Bass looked down. Up until today, he had liked Miss Lund, especially since she didn't treat him like a kid. He didn't want to tattle.

"I already know what happened. I just want to know from your side. You won't get in trouble, and Miss Lund and Einars have left for the doctor."

"I was playing with my baseball inside and I was being careful but I knocked over a stack of crates on accident. I was going to clean it up. But . . ."

His dad's lips pressed together, almost disappearing into his beard, and his eyes pinched at the corners.

"But what?" he said.

Bass swallowed and finished.

"Then she looked at me like Mom used to and told me 'Out,' so I ran. I know I should have stayed anyway and helped, but I just couldn't."

His dad pulled him in tight again and being close eased some of his worry. Dad couldn't be that mad if he was hugging him so much.

"You did the right thing. You don't ever have to let a grown-up make you feel afraid. I wish you would have found me or gone back to the trailer, but if you liked it here, then that's okay, too."

"Do I have to keep working with Miss Lund?"

"No." They got in the ATV and headed back toward the house. "How would you like a sleepover with the Dibble boys? I can call Mrs. Dibble and see if that would work out."

Aaron and Zach were awesome and they had told Bass that Mrs. Dibble let them sneak cookies from the cookie jar whenever they wanted. That sounded like a lot of fun.

"Can I bring my iPad?" Maybe they had Wi-Fi he could use.

His dad's forehead got all wrinkly again.

"No. But maybe we can pick up a cool outside game you can bring."

Visions of flying balls replaced shattered glass and Bass already looked forward to a night of fart jokes and never-ending cookies, thoughts of the mysterious people disappearing along with his tears.

CHAPTER TWENTY-THREE

Sanna put the rest of the dinner dishes away, staring at the barn wistfully. It had been so long since she'd blended a new cider, the colors were piling up inside her imagination, muddling to a flat brown. And she hadn't followed Bass after he ran away. She had cleaned up the fallen boxes and found the baseball in the wreckage. The damage hadn't even been as bad as she'd initially thought. She knew she'd overreacted, but still, he shouldn't have been playing ball inside.

Sanna sighed. Even she knew that was weak, or "sad," as Bass would say, and her stomach twisted with regret as she remembered the scared look on his face. She never wanted to cause a look like that again. First the ruined apples, now her overreacting at a harmless mistake. All the evidence that she had no right being in charge kept stacking up against her. All her life, her dad made it look so easy, and now she couldn't even keep from snapping at a little kid over a few broken bottles.

Her dad emerged from the bathroom. He'd been quiet since they'd left for his PT. Sanna assumed he was making his disappointment in her failure clear. The tactic was effective.

After she had scolded Bass, Isaac and her dad had driven up in the ATV, laughing, as she had stepped out of the barn ready to drive him to the appointment. Isaac had looked around.

"Where's Bass?"

"He ran into the orchard."

All humor disappeared from his face.

"What do you mean he ran into the orchard? Did something happen?"

Sanna swallowed. She had told herself she didn't do anything wrong. He had made a mistake and she just told him to leave, she hadn't even punished him. But the look on Isaac's face told her there was no right answer she could give him, and those rationalizations wouldn't help.

"He knocked over a tower of crates and bottles because he was playing with his baseball inside. I told him to get out of the barn. He did."

Isaac flared his nostrils and turned to the ATV. Einars was already sliding out of the passenger seat and hobbling out of the way with his crutches.

"Try the Looms. Kids are always drawn out there," Einars said.

Isaac had given her one last look of hurt and anger, like she had broken some unspoken vow. Her dad's eyes spoke of disappointment.

"I told you I don't even like kids." She had walked to the house to clean up, but the words soured her mouth. During the entire drive to the appointment, during the appointment, during the drive back home, and all through dinner, her dad had kept his silence. Normally Sanna would love the reprieve from his endless prattle, but it felt like a punishment for a crime she didn't fully grasp or, maybe, chose to not fully grasp.

When Einars emerged from his postdinner shower, after insisting he could do it all himself and didn't need her help, his skin was pale and his face drooped. Every movement required visible effort. Sanna moved toward him.

"Let me help, Pa." She reached for his good arm to loop around her neck. He pushed away.

"I don't want your help."

With the effort of pushing her away, he lost his balance. It was like watching King Kong fall in slow motion—first his legs crumbled, then his body landed, at last his head bumped the side of his bedside table, knocking it hard enough to send the stack of papers on it flying. For the second time today, she watched, too slow to stop the fall.

She flashed back to him tumbling backward off the ladder and she froze, but this time Isaac wasn't there to shake her out of it.

"Goddamn it," Einars said. "Help me up, Sanna."

He was speaking, he was okay. She moved into action, looping her arms under his armpits and maneuvering him near the bed, where she used her legs to get him upright enough that he could slide onto the mattress. She looked him in the face, but only a small red mark indicated where he'd smacked the table.

"I'll get some ice."

"I'm fine. My skull is thick, maybe too thick."

The tone of his voice was serious, too serious. Sanna didn't like it. Serious meant change, and she didn't want more change. She looked around for something to distract them from this conversation and knelt on the floor to pick up all the papers that scattered. These were the same papers Anders had tried to give her the night before. This time she didn't avoid looking at them, instead she studied them in silence. Columns added up all their monthly expenses, including the loan for remodeling the barn and the cider equipment. The number was enormous.

The next column, a much shorter one, listed their much smaller monthly income.

"Are these figures correct?"

Sanna knew they were, but Einars nodded and confirmed the fears her denial had allowed her to ignore for almost a year.

"I had a plan. It had seemed possible, but now I realize that was just me being stubborn. I love this orchard, this place with every fiber of my being. If I had a soul mate, this orchard would be it. Idun's has whispered to me for years, filling me with dreams. And you seemed to share a similar dream, but we can't do it alone. I thought Isaac and Bass might be the last puzzle piece in the plan, but I can see now that's not the case. I should have known better. You are who you are." He rubbed his hands over his face, trying to scrub away the sadness. He maneuvered himself under the covers and turned off his bedside light. "Anders is right. We should sell the land and cut our losses."

In the sudden darkness, Sanna clutched her stomach as if the words were punches. She gasped for air her lungs couldn't find and backed out of the room, still holding the papers. She couldn't unsee the stack of bills. Anders had been right about everything. The thought made her mouth pucker and her eyes pinch.

Everything was falling apart and she couldn't separate herself from it. Everything was her fault, she thought as she walked back to the kitchen. Her dad spent all that money for her to make cider, which she hadn't been able to sell. She had been so busy and selfish making cider that he had to hire help for the orchard, which resulted in Bass breaking the window. And then again, she was too busy with cider making to help him fix the window, which caused him to fall. Now, while he was trying to heal, she couldn't even keep the orchard running smoothly without being mean to a child. She was a failure.

On the counter before her was an enormous loaf of bread,

left earlier in the day by Mrs. Dibble. If she weren't so angry and heartbroken, she'd tease her dad about how he was being courted with food. She unwrapped the six-pound beast and set it on the cutting board, where it spilled over the edges while littering the counter around it with errant sesame seeds.

She wrapped her hand around the bread knife, her knuckles turning white as she squeezed the worn wood handle. She wasn't ready to give up on this place. Staying here was the one balm to the deep, lingering hurt she'd nursed since college.

It was her freshman year at UW–Green Bay, her first time away from home. She settled into her dorm, which she shared with a girl who was rarely there. That suited Sanna just fine. Thad would often visit on the weekends, and they'd watch reruns on her little dorm TV or awkwardly make out. She'd made a few friends on her floor, and Anders wasn't far away at another college, so they would meet occasionally for lunch at Kroll's to feast on butter burgers and cheese curds. And then everything changed.

It was a Thursday. She'd finished her first biology exam and picked up her mail. She often had a card or package from her dad, but that day she found a pale blue envelope. It was addressed to her in a handwriting she didn't recognize. She ripped it open and pulled out a cream card with pink embossed letters spelling out THINKING OF YOU. The thick paper didn't waffle in the late fall breeze, it stood stiff as she opened it and read the words inside.

Dear Sanna,

I know you're probably shocked to have this letter from me. Why wouldn't you be? Now that you're in college, I had hoped

we could reconnect. I can never make up for the years you had
without a mother, but I'd like to explain my side and get to know
the amazing woman I'm sure you've become.

I can drive up from Milwaukee anytime you'd like to meet.
My number is below.

All my love,
Mom

Sanna stopped in the middle of the sidewalk, her world tilt-ing sideways. This was the woman who had left her father. This was the woman who broke Sanna's childhood in half and taught her never to get too close. This was the woman who kissed her six-year-old daughter on the head, then sent her out to play in the snow without another word. In her fuzzy memories, her mom was petite, with light brown hair and thin lips in a downward crescent. She had big, watery brown eyes, but Sanna understood now they were tears. Her mom had stayed in the house or ran errands at the local shops, but never worked in the orchard. She never ate apples.

This little piece of stiff paper confused her. She wanted to tear it, burn it, flush the ashes into the toilet in her dorm room, then forget it ever existed. Just holding it felt like a betrayal to her father. But the six-year-old in her wondered what a hug from her mother might feel like, and she held the paper to her nose, hoping to smell a hint of her mom's perfume, a hint at what her life was like. She was rewarded with a waft of spice.

There was no address on the envelope, but it was post-marked from Whitefish Bay, a suburb near Milwaukee. Was that where her mom lived now? What did she do? Were her eyes still watery?

Sanna didn't call her but kept the card for weeks, taking it out, sniffing it, then hiding it again. She didn't tell her brother during their lunches. She didn't mention it to her father when she went home for her first Christmas break. She didn't tell Thad, because why would she?

After Christmas, she returned to school and on her birthday received another card, this time a pale yellow envelope, postmarked again from Whitefish Bay. The front of the card said HAPPY BIRTHDAY in different-colored letters. Inside it read,

> Dear Sanna,
>
> I assume because you didn't respond to my first note that you have no interest in reconnecting. I understand. But now that you're no longer with your father, I couldn't let your birthday pass again without sending this card. If you ever change your mind, I can be up there in a few hours. I promise.
>
> Always in Love,
> Mom

She had added her phone number again. Right at the bottom. All ten digits starting with a 414—the Milwaukee area code. It seemed foreign. She only ever called numbers in her own area code—920. She picked up her new cell phone, the one her dad had given her for emergencies. Without thinking it through, she called and held her breath as the phone rang.

"Hello."

Sanna swallowed.

"Mom?"

There was a pause, and Sanna almost hung up.

"Sanna? Is that you?"

"I got the birthday card you sent. And the other one."

"I'm so happy you called. Can I see you? Can we meet?"

Sanna stared at the posters on her walls, the ones she'd bought in the bookstore to make the room look less bare. Everything was new and didn't have a history, so she had hung post-ers of Calvin and Hobbes and a map of the Shire—she liked hobbits. Her roommate's side had one calendar—the kind that arrived free when you gave to a charity—stuck to the wall with a tack, still open to September's panda.

"I have some tests to study for this week."

"Oh, well, maybe another—"

"But this weekend is open."

"Wonderful! Where should I pick you up?"

She gave her mom directions to her dorm and wrote down the time on Saturday. Should she tell her dad about it? Anders? But she knew she wouldn't. It was her secret, and she wanted to know how everything would turn out before she explained it to anyone. For the rest of the week she had envisioned the meeting. Her mom would hug her and apologize and tell her exactly the right things to make her understand why she left. She would realize her mistakes and come home to Idun's. She knew it was a childish fantasy that her parents would reunite, but she couldn't help it. When it came to her mom, she still felt like a child.

She had wanted to wear a dress, but the below-zero tem-perature meant jeans and a sweater. She waited outside, peer-ing inside every car and wondering if she'd recognize her. At last a cream-colored car with gold trim pulled up to the curb. Out stepped a tiny woman. She only came up to Sanna's shoulder.

"I would have recognized you in a crowd—you've grown as tall as Einars."

She hugged Sanna, but Sanna could barely feel her mother's tiny arms through her puffy winter coat.

"Get in. It's too cold to stand outside long."

Sanna folded into the seat, her knees almost to her nose, and fumbled for the seat adjustment. At last she found a button on the side. The seat moved like magic, silent and smooth, until it had gone as far as it could. She still couldn't stretch out her legs, but at least they weren't in her face anymore. The bauble on her hat kept bumping the ceiling of the car so she took it off. Her mom looked over.

"I guess I should have brought my SUV. Sorry."

"It's okay."

"I thought we could have lunch. I know a great Italian place."

Sanna nodded.

When they arrived, the restaurant was dark, with white tablecloths and napkins folded into fans. Wineglasses already sat on the table waiting to be filled, along with three different forks. Sanna shifted uncomfortably in the chair, but her mom looked at ease.

"The gnocchi is to die for. Would you like to get an appetizer? The calamari is good, too."

Sanna looked at the menu, conscious of her worn jeans and the stray thread from her sweater that refused to stay tucked in her cuff.

"No. I'll have the spaghetti."

They gave their orders to the waiter.

Sanna's mom looked at her as Sanna straightened the fork she'd knocked crooked with the menu and sipped from the water goblet. Her brown eyes were no longer watery and her formerly light brown hair was now a rich milk chocolate. Huge diamond studs sparkled at her ears, and another hung around her neck. No one would ever guess they were even related. Sanna's eyes grazed her perfect pale pink manicure and stopped at the additional sparkles on her finger. Her ring finger. The diamond there was as big as a cherry pit. Pieces of her familial reunion fantasy disappeared with an explosion—in huge fiery chunks and all at once.

"You're married?"

Her mom touched her hand.

"Right . . . you wouldn't have known. I am. I remarried about eleven years ago."

Sanna did the math, and her body stiffened.

"That would have been about a year after you left us."

Her mom's shoulders sagged.

"You're right. But I met a wonderful man who was perfect for me."

"You never came back. You never visited. You never called. You never wrote."

"About that. There's something you should know—"

"Why did you leave us?"

"I couldn't stay there. I begged your father to move. I was so isolated at Idun's. I didn't realize how empty Door County was in the winter. When we married, I had only known it in the summer with all the tourists, but the summer is when all the work needed to be done. I hated it. I hated everything about it."

"You hated us?"

"You need to understand, Sanna. I can't even look at a map of Door County without a black hole swallowing me up. That was a very dark time for me."

A waiter placed their food in front of them, but Sanna couldn't look at her spaghetti. Her mom studied her with her fork poised above her plate.

"Eat. It's the best food in the area."

Her mom had just admitted she had hated her as a child, or at least didn't deny it, and now she was telling her what to do. She shouldn't have come here. This was all wrong. This woman didn't deserve to know her. She needed to leave. Right now.

Sanna stood.

"This was a mistake."

"Sanna, don't be ridiculous. Eat and we'll talk more. I want to know about you and I want you to know about me."

"No. Don't contact me again." She wrapped her scarf around her head and swung her coat around her shoulders.

"At least let me drive you back. It's freezing out."

Sanna crammed her hat on her head.

"I'm tough."

She walked into the arctic temperatures, letting the cold freeze out any remaining thought of her mother. By the time she'd arrived back at the dorm, her heart was as numb as her toes. After she graduated, she would return to the orchard and not leave—finally able to breathe deeply again for the first time in four years. Idun's was safe and peaceful and predictable. Idun's was home.

Except it might not be much longer.

Isaac knocked on the door to the Lunds' house and waited. Nothing. He could hear a hard thudding from inside and knocked again. No response, so he opened the door. He needed to talk to Sanna about Bass, and it wasn't going to wait until morning when he could hear that she was inside. He reached the top of the steps and saw her standing at the counter, hacking an enormous loaf of bread into uneven chunks with a bread knife, wielding it like a machete. Red blotches marked her cheeks and throat, and her hair shook with each thud. His initial response was to help her, but then he remembered why he was there.

"Sanna. Do you have a few minutes?"

She paused her bakery abuse and looked at him, though it took a few moments before she pulled back into the present, the journey from wherever her mind had taken her lasting a few moments. She set the knife down.

"Of course."

He joined her at the counter. Sesame seeds were scattered everywhere like sand, including on her shirt, her hands, and even her cheek. He longed to wipe off the seeds for her, cup her chin in his hand, but he ignored that impulse and continued.

"It's about Bass. He hid in the orchard after you yelled at him. That's not okay. He's a little boy who has been through a lot, and he doesn't deserve to be scared by you. If you ever speak to him that way—"

"Scared? He was afraid of me?" Her forehead wrinkled in confusion.

"Yes. You're almost twice his height and not the warmest person. To a ten-year-old, that can be terrifying. I know you aren't a big fan of kids, but if you do it again, we'll leave."

Sanna blinked at him, then swallowed. She brushed the seeds off her hands and shirt, scattering them on the ground, and then tears fell down her face, washing away the one seed stuck to her cheek. Isaac didn't know what to do. He came here to yell at her and make sure she understood that her treatment of Bass wasn't acceptable, but he didn't mean to make her cry.

So he did what any kind person would do in these circumstances—he hugged her.

They stood in the kitchen, his arms around her, and her head fell to his shoulder. He could feel her body shake, and it kicked something inside him. He pulled her closer and smoothed her hair with his right hand. A few more seeds found their freedom. He wasn't sure how long they stood there. It seemed like forever, yet when she finally pulled away it was too soon.

She plucked a fresh towel from a nearby drawer and wiped the tears off her face.

"There is no acceptable excuse for how I behaved toward him. I'll apologize immediately."

That, right there, was his favorite thing about Sanna. She saw straight to the center of the issue and addressed it. She didn't equivocate or make excuses. She always told the truth, even if it meant admitting she'd made a mistake.

"You'll have to wait until tomorrow, he's at the Dibbles' for an overnight."

She nodded and wiped at some remaining wetness. Now that the weight of Isaac's task was lifted, he wanted to help Sanna, too.

"So, do you want to tell me about the unacceptable reason you did it? I'm a great listener."

Sanna smiled and wiped absently at the counter. After a few moments she spoke.

"I think we'll need some drinks."

She pulled two bottles from the fridge and popped them open.

Isaac took a long swig from the unmarked bottle. He'd tasted her cider before, but this bottle was completely different, yet just as wonderful. The apple was more prominent, yet not sweet, almost funky but in a good, blue-cheese way. He held the bottle up to the light and could see the sediment swirling in the bottom.

"This is amazing—so different from the other one."

Sanna grinned.

"You really like Olive? I wasn't sure when I blended it. Not everyone likes the murkiness."

"Olive?"

Sanna leaned against the counter, putting her weight on her wrist as she studied him for a long moment, her eyes squinting. She took a long drink from her own bottle.

"I see colors when I make ciders. I can't explain it. Each juice has its own hue. That's what those paintings represent."

She pointed at the watercolors over the fireplace. "A new color comes to me, and I blend the juices until I can re-create it in the flavor. And this one is Olive."

"You color-code your ciders?" He struggled to understand what she was telling him.

"No." She reached across the counter and pulled her journal toward her. She opened it and handed it to Isaac. As she sipped her cider, he studied the page, then the next page, then the next. On each was a swatch of layered color, all wildly different from one another—reds, greens, teals, colors he didn't really have names for. Next to the colors were measurements, apple varieties, percentages, and flavor notes. Scribbles filled the margins and equations contained both numbers and words. Things like sugars and acidity were measured and tested. It was part recipe book, part coloring book, and part wine label, with a hint of spell book. Looking at it was like opening a tiny door into the back of her head. She saw things that no one else did, an imaginary world of cider only she could see.

"You can see the color in your head?"

"It's the easiest way to explain it. A color pops into my head, and I know what it will taste like. When I blend the different raw ciders together, I know I have it right when it matches what I've imagined." She pulled her journal back toward her, then finished off her cider. Isaac did the same. She pulled two more bottles out of the fridge and popped the caps with steady movements. She moved the way tree branches sway in a breeze, slow and graceful, but full of power.

"Do you have a whole rainbow in there?"

"There are a few rainbows in there. That's part of the problem. All stock, no sales. Here's Chartreuse."

Sanna walked around to the stools on the other side of the

counter, pulling a hunk of bread with her. She ripped it in two and gave half to Isaac, oil dripping off her fingers.

"Why no sales? Anyone who likes cider would snap this up." He stuffed the sopping bread in his mouth, the soft middle giving way as he bit into the crispy, oil-drenched bottom. It was just what he needed, as the cider had gone straight to his head.

"I have no idea what to do or where to start. We sell them at the stand, but there's not enough traffic there to make the sales we'd need to justify the equipment Pa bought."

"The website and social media can help a bit there." He took a drink of his fresh bottle. This cider sang of crisp apples, fresh and green, not too sweet, not too tart—refreshing and easy drinking. He took another gulp, then ate more bread as he settled onto a stool next to this remarkable woman. She licked the olive oil and clinging sesame seeds off her fingers. "Ready to tell me why you decimated this scrumptious bread?"

Sanna spun her bottle in her hands and pursed her lips.

"I think my brother is right." She closed her eyes as she spoke, and Isaac noticed how her pale eyelashes disappeared into her cheeks, then slowly darkened as they let a few new tears escape. When she opened her eyes again, wiping the tears and pushing her lashes into soggy clumps, she stared at him directly, not shying away from what she had to say. "My father mortgaged everything for the cider-making equipment, and I don't even have labels for the bottles. This place is my sanctuary, but where can I go when we sell my safe place? Or when they knock it down?"

Isaac nodded to let her know he was listening to every word. Even though he had heard similar things from Anders and Einars, he wanted her to continue. He wanted to hear what she had to say about it.

"Growing up tall and rural wasn't always easy. I didn't have a mom to walk me through the changes. I towered over the boys, so they never wanted to dance with me, not even Thad, and he was my best friend in middle school." Isaac's fist clenched automatically. Another reason not to like that jerk. Sanna continued. "But no matter how gangly and awkward dances and high school clubs made me feel, I could always come home and feel safe, climb the trees, eat our apples, stare at the sky between swaying branches. Thinking about leaving makes my lungs stop working." She held a hand to her chest. "To answer your question about the bread—it had the misfortune of being in the wrong place at the wrong time."

"What can I do?" He meant it. Every word. He wanted to help her keep her home, the one she deserved. He understood the importance of needing a safe space.

"See us through the season, then get your boy back to his mom. It seems like he misses her."

Isaac swallowed the last of his cider, hoping it would drown the guilt bubbling up from the mention of Bass's mom. He ignored it and focused on Sanna, a plan already forming to help the Lunds keep Idun's.

CHAPTER TWENTY-FOUR

Sanna took a deep breath, though her chest still tightened from all she had learned last night. And all she had said. She'd never shared her family gift with anyone but her dad. She never even spoke to Anders about it, though he, at least, knew the family legends. Isaac hadn't thought she was crazy. He'd looked at her like he was intrigued. She wanted to tell him more about it, more about her, listen to his reassurances of help. But first she had one very important apology to make.

She looked out the kitchen window to see Isaac and Bass standing in the shade of the barn. She stuffed the last of her breakfast into her mouth, grabbed her hat from the peg, and avoided looking at her dad. She still hadn't spoken to him about the bills and she still couldn't wrap her head around how she wanted to approach him. While last night she'd felt as defeated as he did, the morning promised new possibilities. There had to be another way—they just weren't looking at the problem from the right angle.

As Sanna approached them, Bass stepped closer to his father's side. That was okay. She had made him afraid of her and she accepted that she had earned the guilty feeling in her stomach.

"Bass, can I talk to you for a minute?"

He looked up at his dad, who nodded to him and winked at Sanna. Her heart eased. At least this she could make okay. She knelt on the ground so she could look him in the eye but was careful not to crowd him. Isaac stayed behind him so he felt safe, and she felt safer, too. Bass's big brown eyes looked everywhere but into her face as his hands twisted together.

"I should not have yelled at you yesterday. Knocking over the crates was an accident, one I've made myself. I wasn't angry with you. I haven't been doing a good job and I was angry with myself. Sometimes adults do stupid things—and I took my frustration out on you, which isn't right. I'm sorry. You don't have to forgive me, but I sure hope you can." Bass nodded at each of her words, and even met her eyes as she finished speaking.

It wasn't even eight in the morning, and he already had a smudge of dirt on his cheek. Sanna wanted to pull her bandana from her pocket and wipe it off, but she hadn't earned that right. The tender urge surprised her. This little boy had come to matter to her, against her best judgment. She stood.

"How about some cookies as a shameless attempt to get you to like me again?"

Bass smiled broadly before he remembered to be cautious. He looked up at his dad, who nodded.

"Okay," Bass said.

Sanna headed back toward the house with Bass behind her, even though every cell of her being shouted it was time to work, not to go back to the house. She ignored it, this was her time to make it right, not hide in the cidery. Her dad hobbled through the door as they approached. Over the past few weeks, he'd gotten quite skilled at moving with his crutches, though he still needed to rest regularly. He gave a small smile to Bass, then continued on to meet Isaac, who had the ATV ready to go.

In the kitchen, she pointed Bass toward the table, then poured two glasses of cold milk and carried them over with a package of Oreos—the classic kind, no creative flavors in this house. Bass settled into her dad's spot and the sight gave her pause. She'd never seen anyone else sit in that chair during her entire life, yet there was young Bass with his floppy hair and cautious eyes locked on the cookies.

She set a few in front of him and left the package open in case he wanted more.

"Aren't you having any?" Bass asked.

"I don't eat cookies in the morning."

"Why not? You're a grown-up. You can have cookies anytime you want. I'd eat cookies all day if I was a grown-up."

Sanna sipped her cold, boring milk and thought on his question. Habit had kept her going for years without her realizing what was really happening around her. She didn't eat cookies in the morning, she ate a cold lunch in the field every day, and she never thought to check her father's paperwork. It was time to break habit.

She pulled an Oreo from the package and twisted it, licking out the cream the way she'd been doing since she was a child. Bass smiled and did the same, then dipped his cookies in his milk.

"I like your style." Sanna copied him, giving the milk a moment to soften the cookie before popping it into her mouth. Bass gave her a cookie-dusted smile and reached for another one.

"You grew up here, right?"

"I did. I've never lived anywhere else."

"What did you do when you were bored when you were a kid?"

Sanna finished chewing her cookie as she thought.

"I don't ever remember being totally bored because there was always so much to do. We helped our dad in the orchard, took turns practicing the perfect swinging dismount from the trees, and caught fireflies." One memory made her smile widen. "When Anders and I had a free afternoon, which didn't happen often once we were teenagers, we'd run to this secret path across the road from the north corner of the orchard. There's a huge oak and a lot of smaller trees. There's a small path there that leads to a cliff where you can jump into the water. On a hot summer day, it was better than flying."

Bass twitched with excitement.

"Can we go? That sounds awesome."

"Not a chance. Your dad would kill me. Anders and I were a lot older than you, and we knew exactly where to jump so we didn't hit the rocks." His shoulders melted in disappointment. "Sorry, Bass."

He shrugged and they twisted and crunched in silence as they pulled more cookies from the package until an entire row was gone.

"How was your sleepover?" she asked as they finished their milk with crumbs at the bottom.

Sanna set their glasses in the sink and led them outside. Breaking habit or no, they still had work to get done. Bass bounced a bit as he answered, clearly excited to talk about the fun.

"We named our butts. Mine is Gary. Theirs are Harvey and Waldorf."

Bass giggled as he said the names. He still had a ring of Oreo dust around his lips.

"You named your butts?"

Bass nodded and snorted. Boys were weird, but Sanna wanted to keep his good mood going.

"Should we name mine? Or is this only for boys?"

"Yes, name it."

They climbed into Elliot and she wiggled in her seat, trying to think of the right name for her backside.

"Marge. Marge seems like the right name. What do you think?"

"Perfect."

Bass and Sanna kept the joke going as they worked all day in the warm sun. Sanna hadn't giggled like this since the last time Anders and she had spent the night in the orchard catching fireflies. As the sun started to set, she texted her father and Isaac that they'd be a little late for dinner.

She parked Elliot in the Looms, and Sanna turned the headlights off on the truck.

"When the car lights went dark in the movie we watched last night, it did not end well for the people. Should I be making a run for it?" Bass asked.

"You're safe—and you shouldn't be watching scary movies. You won't be able to enjoy moments like this." Sanna opened her door. "Let's climb in the back."

They stood on the bed of the truck and leaned against the cab.

"What am I looking for?"

"Hold on to Gary and watch."

In a few moments, pale yellow-green dots flashed all around them. The longer they waited, the more dots appeared, little stars twinkling just for them.

"Are these fireflies?"

Sanna nodded. "There are always more of them here than in any other part of the orchard. It's better than fireworks."

"We don't have fireflies in California."

Sanna looked around her and gently cupped her hands around a bug that had flown close to them.

"Look inside." She held her hands out to Bass, who peeked between her fingers at the creature who flashed in her make-shift cage.

"Can I try?"

"I insist. We can't go back until you catch your first firefly."

Sanna let hers go and it flew straight for Bass's white T-shirt. He gently cupped it and peeked inside. Watching his eyes widen in amazement, Sanna understood something she'd always missed. While kids were messy, distracting, and obviously a ton of work, they also opened a path to the past. Through Bass's wonder, she felt ten years old again—catching her first fireflies and discovering the magic of the Looms.

"I did it." His voice softened in wonder, his eyebrows scrunched in the darkness. "They don't bite, do they?"

"In thirty-two years of catching, I've never been bitten. I've been kissed a few times, but no bites."

"They kiss?"

"On nights like tonight there are so many, they can't help but bump into you as you're walking. My dad called it firefly kisses when I was little so I wouldn't be afraid of bugs bumping into me."

"Your dad is cool."

Sanna agreed.

"So is yours." She pulled out some old jars from a basket in the truck bed and handed one to Bass. "Now let's bring the fun to them."

Isaac looked out the window again. Full dark had fallen, and Sanna and Bass hadn't returned. Even though he now knew Sanna a little better, it was a big step of trust to let her take Bass all day again. He'd smiled when they'd driven off into the orchard with Bass laughing in the passenger seat of the truck, but still, he worried.

"They'll be back. She texted to say they'd be late. Stop worrying," Einars said from his spot at the table.

After a quick check on the early-harvest apples, they'd spent the day inside. After Einars's fall last night, it seemed wise for him to take it easy, which gave Isaac time to work on a gift for Sanna, which had included a trip into town to Everything Office—which was surprisingly true to its name. While he was out, he'd picked up takeout pizza for dinner. Somewhere in their second week here, Bass and he started dining every day with Einars and Sanna. The routine worked well, which made Sanna and Bass's absence all the more unsettling.

Einars pulled a pill bottle from his pocket and held it up for Isaac to see. Isaac's neck tensed. "I wanted you to know that I'm done using these and I'll be getting rid of the rest. Sheriff Dibble lets people turn them in to the police station for safe disposal and will stop by when he gets a chance to collect them. There are still ten pills left. I thought you'd appreciate the update."

"I do appreciate it. Thank you." And he did. He had checked in with Einars a few times during their days together, and Einars had always been very understanding. He knew he had no right to monitor it, but Einars seemed to understand that Isaac needed this reassurance.

Lights flashed along the wall and every muscle in his shoulders relaxed. In moments, Bass's feet pounded on the steps, making ten times the noise a person his size should.

"Dad, look." His eyes sparkled and his cheeks flushed with his mad dash to get inside. In front of him he held a mason jar full of sparkles that were dim when compared to Bass's joy. "My first firefly hunt was an epic success."

"I see that. We'll need to let them go later."

"I know. Miss Lund says they'll die if we keep them longer than a few hours, even with the holes in the lid. But I thought we could eat dinner by firefly light."

Over Bass's head, Sanna reached the top of the stairs and held up two more jars twinkling with fireflies.

"I have backup. We should be able to see our food," she said, her voice full of amusement. A new lightness graced her movements, too.

In a few quick moments, the pizza, plates, napkins, and fireflies were on the table with all the lights out. It took a moment to adjust to the odd yellow light—but then it became better than candles and more like fairy light. Bass shared the excitement of their hunt. While he spoke, Sanna listened to him with soft eyes. Isaac watched her. The light hid the worries of last night and the stress of managing the orchard mostly by herself. It hid the lingering pain of never being asked to dance, and the isolation of her life. This moment was perfect. While they weren't a true family, this feeling, this contentment, this connection was what had been missing from their lives. He knew it couldn't last, and guilt twinged at him again at the secret he was keeping, but he hoped it would fill him and Bass up. Sanna finally looked up at him and smiled—a real, relaxed, happy smile.

"Who knew bugs made such romantic light?" Einars said.

"Everyone knows that, Pa. That's why teenagers sneak into the orchard every summer."

Isaac couldn't blame them. That's where he'd take Sanna, too, given the chance.

"Why do teenagers sneak in?" Bass asked.

Sanna and Einars stifled laughs and pointedly looked at Isaac for his response.

"You brought up teenagers. You explain," Isaac said. Sanna rose to the challenge.

"You know how sometimes couples like to kiss?" she said.

Bass nodded. "Like on TV."

"Yes, like on TV. Well, teenagers sometimes like to sneak around to do that. That's half the fun—and the orchard at night gives them a lot of privacy."

"Gross."

Isaac thought that was a pretty good explanation. True, minus a few specifics. Sanna covered her mouth to hide her laughter, but Isaac could see her shoulders shaking.

"Miss Lund, did you sneak into the orchard when you were a teenager?"

Isaac lifted an eyebrow, curious to hear the answer, too. She cleared her throat.

"I don't need to sneak into my own orchard."

She smiled, knowing she hadn't really answered the question, finished her pizza, and wiped her hands on a gingham napkin. She stood and cleared the empty plates and used napkins, moving the nearly empty pizza box to the counter. Isaac didn't even try to hide his staring.

"Everyone have room for dessert?" Einars asked. "I put an apple pie in the oven to warm. It should be perfect."

Isaac got up to join Sanna on the kitchen side of the counter while Einars and Bass discussed firefly-catching techniques.

"Can I help?" he asked.

"Sure, grab the plates and forks." She set ice cream on the counter, pulled the pie out of the oven, and set it on a blue and white ceramic trivet. As she cut and served the dessert, still bubbling from the oven, a dollop of filling plopped onto her hand. She made the faintest of squeaks, not enough to disturb Einars and Bass, but Isaac noticed. Hell, he felt it. Without a word, he doused a towel in cold water and took her arm. He rubbed the spot to make sure the filling was washed off completely, then held the cool towel over the burn. He kept his eyes on the pale skin, luminescent in the firefly light, not wanting to make eye contact with her—afraid he wouldn't see his own feelings reflected in her face. Instead he focused on the smoothness of her skin, and the rose scent wafting and twining with the cinnamon. In the dim light, it was all too easy to forget they weren't alone.

But he could never forget that they should never be alone, at least not like that. He'd thought a lot about her kiss—and where that whisper of a touch could lead. He'd probably thought too much about it. Each time it led to the same wall. He and Bass couldn't stay here forever. Eventually, they had to return to California, and when they left, he didn't want to hurt her. He had to keep his focus on helping the orchard. That must be his focal point, not his longing to feel her eyes on him.

At last he met her eyes. Her pupils were saucers in the darkness, taking over the blue. She stared at him. He only needed to step forward a few inches, and they would be touching from head to toe.

"Better?" His voice crackled as the word emerged.

She nodded, but didn't move. Isaac braced himself for at least a mild rebuke for manhandling her around the kitchen.

"Yes, thank you."

Isaac wiped the dampness from the dish towel off his hands by rubbing them on his thighs, but couldn't erase the memory of her skin under his.

"I burn myself all the time in the kitchen. If it still stings, hold an ice cube on it."

"It feels fine." She rubbed the spot where his fingers had just been.

"Let's dish this up before the ice cream melts."

She quickly served up two slices topped with ice cream that Isaac delivered to the table. When he returned, Sanna handed him his plate, then headed to the table with her own.

"Wait. I have something I want to give you," Isaac said.

"Better than first aid?" She returned to his side, her eyes smiling.

He pulled the stack of sticker-labels from his back pocket.

"I made these today . . . when you mentioned none of your cider bottles had labels . . ." He spread them out on the counter like a stack of cards. They were four-by-four-inch stickers, ranging in colors from a vibrant aqua to a rusty red, colors taken from her journal. On the side in a bold font read IDUN'S ORCHARD. Underneath, in tiny letters, the address. He'd spent a few hours designing them and a few more hours imagining the delight on Sanna's face when she saw them. He wasn't disappointed. Sanna trailed her fingers over them, finally pulling one out to examine it.

"How did you do this?"

"They didn't take long."

"They're beautiful. No one has ever . . ." And then she hugged him, pulling him in tight, her rose scent enmeshing his carefully constructed, logical wall and tumbling it down. He let his lips graze the silky skin on the side of her neck, relishing Sanna's quick intake of breath. He didn't care if all the ice cream in the world melted—he wasn't pulling away first.

CHAPTER TWENTY-FIVE

"Pa, you ready to go?"

Isaac couldn't stop his head from turning instantly toward the sound of Sanna's voice. She strode from the side of the barn toward the ATV, where Einars sat next to him. Bass followed behind, carrying a crate of bottles. Her floppy hat kept her face in shadow, but he didn't need to see it to know there were light pink roses on her cheeks from a day of working or that her sharp blue eyes took in his every motion before turning away.

After last night's hug and covert neck kissing—which wasn't really a kiss, but it wasn't not a kiss either—he had decided the best way to handle this attraction was to embrace it. Resisting would only prolong the emotions. If he let it run its course, the sooner it would evaporate, and he'd stop feeling like a teenager ogling the girl next door.

"Where you headed? I can take him," Isaac offered.

Sanna stopped in front of him. She wet a bandana from her water bottle and wrapped it around her neck—stray drips escaped to trace a path down her chest and disappear into the tank top she wore under a long-sleeve denim shirt.

"It's haircut day."

Typical Sanna, only giving the barest of information. This woman was driving him crazy.

"What Sanna isn't explaining," Einars chimed in, "is that we normally cut each other's hair, but I can't cut hers with my arm cast, so we have to go to Mrs. Dibble's salon."

Mrs. Dibble had a salon? Sanna must have noticed his confused expression.

"She owns a hair salon. She rarely cuts hair anymore, but she still goes there almost every day. It's the best place to hear the latest local dirt." Sanna rolled her eyes. "Maybe I'll grow my hair out."

"I can cut it," Isaac said. "I've been trimming Bass's for years. And you look good, right, Tuna?" Bass had climbed between Isaac's legs in the ATV and pretended to drive.

"Sure, Dad." He smiled, glad to be included in the conversation, then pretended to push some buttons—most likely destroying the Death Star or flying a fighter jet.

"That won't be necessary. I'll bring the truck around." Sanna sniffed.

"That's probably for the best. Now that it's August, I'm sure Mrs. Dibble can't wait to get the full story about how it's going with Bass and Isaac," Einars added, smiling when Sanna crossed her arms.

Isaac could see her calculating which was the worse option. Exposing herself to an hour of Mrs. Dibble's meddling, which would fuel the Door County gossip train, or letting him touch her hair. He held his breath, unable to guess which would be the lesser of two evils and hoping it was him.

Sanna eyed Bass's head as if trying to determine the quality.

"Let's do it before dinner. You can cut Pa's hair, but first let me get in a shower." She nodded decisively, then disappeared into the house.

"I can't believe she said yes," Isaac said.

"You have no idea how nosy Mrs. Dibble can be on her own turf. She'd probably let a blindfolded Bass cut her hair." Einars looked at Isaac. "You sure you can do this?"

Isaac thought of all the times he'd trimmed the hair on Bass's wiggly toddler head bribing him to stay still just two more minutes.

"I've got this. I'll go get my kit from the trailer, and we'll be back in a few." He got out of the ATV after nudging Bass to get off him. "Can you get inside okay?"

"Don't worry about me. It's like these crutches are a part of me now. Take the ATV."

Isaac nodded and zoomed off with Bass in the passenger seat, veering down the rows that would get him to the trailer the quickest, knowing exactly where to cut across so he'd arrive exactly at the steps, where the geraniums were still blooming. It had been almost six weeks since they arrived, and this little trailer felt more like home than San Jose had for the past five years. Between his business, Bass's school, and managing Paige's latest crisis, he rarely had the chance to enjoy quality time with Bass when they lived in California. He'd spent more time with him this summer than he had since Bass's first day of school. In San Jose, he would work late most nights, pausing only to make dinner and put Bass to bed. Here, once the orchard work was done, they were together. With only Bass to focus on, he had learned to slow down and appreciate each day. He was grateful.

It didn't take long to return to the farmhouse. Sanna had already finished her shower, hair damp and pushed back off her forehead, the ends curling from the humidity. She puttered in the kitchen, peeling potatoes at the high countertop. She used the peeler to point him toward the bathroom, but gave no other acknowledgment that he was present. Was she distracted with thoughts of the orchard? Or, he could hope, distracted with thoughts of him?

It didn't take long to trim Einars's thinning hair or even to wrangle Bass for a quick taming of his wild curls. Isaac used the broom to sweep the hair into a small pile in the corner. When he turned, Sanna stood in the doorway. The previously spacious and airy white bathroom shrunk by half as she took a step toward him. He pointed to the stool he had pulled in earlier from the kitchen and she sat, her long legs stretched out in front of her, distracting him. His mind blanked as he searched for something to talk about.

Focus on the hair.

He used the black barber-style comb to smooth out her nearly dry locks—it slid easily through the blushing strands, but he was careful not to pull when it hit a knot. He cleared his throat.

"Okay, miss. How do you like it?"

"Excuse me?" Sanna said, looking horrified in the mirror.

"Your hair. How do you like it cut?"

"Oh, right, yeah, the same length as my earlobe."

At present, her hair brushed the middle of her pale neck. Up close, he could see uneven lines where Einars had cut it previously and was relieved he didn't have sky-high standards to meet. He took a lock next to her face between his two fingers and lifted it so the end brushed the bottom of her ear. She jumped, then settled into place, but he could see the thrum of her heartbeat in her white throat. Its pace matched his own.

"Is this about right?"

"Yes," she said, her voice softer than he had ever heard it before, like she had just woken up and the fog of sleep hadn't quite lifted.

Though the door was open, Isaac couldn't see Einars or Bass, he could only hear Einars telling Bass to grab plates and forks for dinner, then the sound of a baseball game on the TV. They had privacy for the first time since she'd kissed him in the barn. In fact, he suspected Einars was keeping Bass distracted so he and Sanna wouldn't be interrupted. Sanna sat on the stool facing the large mirror over the sink and counter. When he gathered the top layer of her hair on top of her head in some clips that had come with the haircutting kit, she closed her eyes. She seemed to relax into the moment. In silence, he snipped, the hair falling like golden snow on the fluffy blue towel she had wrapped around her shoulders.

As he bent close to inspect his precision along her nape, the subtle scent of roses and something less common filled his lungs and went straight to his heart. He held in a groan, but couldn't help letting a small sigh whisper across the back of her neck. Sanna inhaled quickly, but didn't move away. Goose bumps arose where his breath had touched.

Satisfied the bottom half was even, he released the top half, combing it again, taking longer than was strictly necessary. He liked watching her when her eyes were closed. He had never seen her this relaxed, like a cat after you'd found its preferred spot for scratching. He began snipping again, pulling each silky section between his fingers. To make sure the sides were even, he stood directly in front of her and pulled a strand from each side of her face, bending inches from her, the subtle rose scent torturing him in a horribly pleasant way. Each strand traced a path through his fingertips, shooting jolts up his arms that stopped his lungs and sent his heart racing.

He could no longer deny he cared for her. The way her direct gaze and honest turn of phrase challenged him only drew him in. He wanted to break through and understand what made her smile and laugh and why she carefully guarded each word, as though using them too frequently would cheapen their worth. Watching her teach Bass how to sanitize her equipment and about the balance of flavors warmed his heart, and he realized that despite her vocal dislike of children, Bass had wormed his way into her heart. He was fascinated by how she could fix anything at the orchard from Elliot to a sick tree. And that kiss, brief though it was, would forever haunt his dreams.

He had never imagined he'd find someone who challenged him this way. Paige had always needed a protector, a guardian. Without him, even after they had divorced, she required his assistance with paying bills, getting to work when her car broke down, and even keeping food in the fridge. She was helpless. Sanna needed no one. If she spent time with him, it was because she chose to be there, no other reason. He wanted to be by her side, living in her passion for Idun's, helping her in whatever way he could. If that meant spraying trees, or hauling crates of bottles, or cutting her hair in a much too small bathroom, he wanted to be there for her—not because she needed him to be, but because she wanted him to be.

But even with all his wishes and wants, he knew nothing could come of this feeling. He grinned a bit at the thought of her deciding whether he was worth her time. Instead, he'd do whatever she needed of him before the season ended. He'd leave her and the orchard in a better place than he'd found them and it would be enough.

With his face inches from hers, her eyes popped open.

"Is something funny?"

He should pull back, but her perfume or shampoo or lotion or whatever the source was kept him there. He tried to swallow, but his mouth was dry. Her breath picked up, her eyes on his, and he couldn't find any words to speak. He inched closer, his newly formed resolve crumbling. Who knew he was so weak?

Sanna's eyes flicked to his lips as his fingers let the strands of hair drop from his fingers, and he moved his hands toward her face. She tilted her chin up to meet him.

"Are you done yet? Dinner's ready," Bass said, his body appearing in the doorway.

Isaac froze, then let his fingers run through her hair one last time before standing straight again.

"Just making sure it's even." His voice cracked. "We'll be there in a minute, Minnow."

Bass disappeared, and Sanna's eyes followed Isaac in the mirror as he slowly removed the towel from her shoulders, using a corner to wipe a few errant hairs off her neck. The skin on her nape pinkened where he had touched her. He set the towel on the counter and stood behind her, gazing at her steadily in the mirror.

"All done." He took a step back, escaping the pull of her.

Sanna moved her head back and forth, looking at the new cut from all sides. She stood and turned, the stool between them.

"It's the best haircut I've ever had. Don't tell my dad."

She smiled at him. A real, full smile. The tension eased now that he didn't have his hands on her. If he could maintain some physical distance, then maybe he could stick to his resolution not to complicate the growing friendship between them.

"At your service, madam." He bowed his head. "Your secret is safe with me."

"Thank you." She left, and Isaac could hear Einars making a fuss about her haircut.

Isaac picked up the towel and shook the strawberry-blond trimmings to the ground, where he carefully swept them into a dustpan and then into the trash. It was simple. He couldn't be that close to her again or he'd have to kiss her, and not the peck she'd given him, a real, long, slow kiss. He shoved the towel into the clothes hamper and took a deep breath, letting his nerves relax. He could hear the chairs scraping at the table as the small group sat down. Before leaving the bathroom, he brought his fingertips to his nose. They still held the scent of Sanna. Just like that, the pull toward her felt even tighter than before.

CHAPTER TWENTY-SIX

Einars hobbled down the stairs in his new, below-the-knee fluorescent green cast, though he still wore a pair of his sweatpants cut for the long leg cast, exposing several inches of pasty-white thigh. His right arm was newly cast-free.

At the bottom of the steps, Sanna held the door open for him with one hand and carried a glass of lemonade in the other. "Pa, you look ridiculous. Why didn't you wear a pair of shorts?"

"These have plenty of wear left in them." He pulled the material on the right leg to above that knee to match the cutoff left side. "There, is that better?" He winked at her. He was getting sassier—that must mean he felt good.

He gingerly walked to where Sanna had set up a lawn chair on their patio, where the August afternoon sun was still bright. He settled himself into it, stretching his long legs in front of him.

"Not really."

Sanna set down the lemonade on a side table next to the latest mystery her dad was reading.

"Bass and Isaac will be here any minute. If you don't go with them to the fish boil, I'm calling Mrs. Dibble to come over and make dinner," Einars said.

"But—" Sanna said.

"Dammit, Sanna. The three of you have been working your butts off for the orchard, while I can barely outrace a snail. I want to do something nice for you and celebrate the sun and fresh air on my upper thigh and arm for the first time in seven weeks . . . by myself. Besides, they've never been, and you can't come to Door County without going to one. And don't pretend you don't enjoy spending time with him. I have a broken leg, I'm not blind. There's money on the counter."

"I'm not leaving you alone for an entire night. What if you fall and no one is here to help?"

Einars picked up his phone.

"I have her on speed dial."

"Ugh. I'm starting to think you did more damage than we thought when you hit your head. Don't think I don't know what you're doing."

She stomped inside to grab her keys and the hundred-dollar bill he'd set aside, and flew down the steps, letting the screen door slam for emphasis. That man . . . She'd seen him watching her and Isaac when Isaac was cooling off her burn, and when they came out of the bathroom after her haircut. And then the labels. She couldn't stop herself from hugging him, thankful the darkness had hid her deep blush when his lips traced the curve of her neck. She didn't know what made her happier, the discreet caress or the labels. No one had ever done anything so special for her before. She'd always intended to make her own labels, but the ones he'd designed were more beautiful than she had ever imagined. Her face blushed just thinking about the haircut.

Outside, Isaac and Bass pulled up in Isaac's tiny car. She'd never fit in that thing, but before he could try anything stupid like opening her door, she got in and regretted it immediately. Her knees were tucked against her chest, exposing the backs of her thighs to the air before she could tuck her dress behind her knees. Her head bumped the soft top of the roof.

"Bass, I told you to move the seat back," Isaac said. "The controls are on the side." He turned to give his son a look as Bass giggled in the backseat. Sanna fiddled with the controls until her head separated from the ceiling and her knees didn't bump the dashboard. Then she turned to give Bass her best stern expression.

"Hell hath no fury like woman stuffed into a tiny car." Then she gave him a quick wink. "Let's hit the road before I get a leg cramp."

Isaac smiled. He'd been doing that more lately. At the first intersection, Sanna pointed the direction they needed to go, but he was already turning confidently toward the restaurant.

"You're starting to know your way around. Soon you'll be swearing about tourist drivers like the rest of us."

"Oh, he's already doing that," Bass volunteered. Sanna and Isaac shared a glance and burst into laughter.

Her mind automatically wandered to all the things she needed to do at Idun's, but she stopped herself. Tonight was about enjoying their hard work, from the tree maintenance to the cider making. She planned to bottle another batch of cider soon and had counted the bottles they'd labeled in preparation. She should have waited, but she was so eager to see the beautiful labels on her bottles.

"Bass, I meant to ask, when you moved the cases, did you take out any of the bottles? A few of them were missing when I checked today."

"Nope. I didn't open them. I just moved them where you told me to."

Huh? That was odd. She must have not been paying attention—considering all she had on her plate these past few weeks, that wasn't much of a surprise. She pushed thoughts of work from her mind and enjoyed the back-road scenery, suddenly so glad she had conceded to come on this outing. Well, glad that Einars had insisted.

"I haven't been to a fish boil in years," she said as she unfolded her limbs from that tiny car.

"Why do they call it a fish boil? That sounds gross," Bass said as they walked around the building to the patio where all the action would take place. Isaac stopped at the outdoor bar to get them both something to drink, leaving Sanna to explain. Smoky air wafted from the large fire in the center of a short brick wall circle. A large pot hung over the blaze with a woodpile stacked neatly at the edge of the circle. Huge hostas with leaves the size of watermelons edged the cozy courtyard, mingling with flowering day lilies. Black metal tables covered by festive red umbrellas dotted the large flagstone pavers, with a door leading to a snug dining room decorated like a bed-and-breakfast with a Swedish flare.

"It's a tradition started by the Scandinavian settlers. It was a practical way to cook a lot of food for a lot of people at the same time, plus it makes an awesome fire."

Bass bounced on the balls of his feet while he took in all the details.

"Cool. It's a bonfire with food."

Isaac returned with wineglasses and set a kiddie cocktail in front of Bass, who immediately devoured the cherries. Sanna took a sip, expecting a white wine, and looked up in surprise. It was cider—a lovely, dry cider.

"It's from a local cidery. What color?" Isaac asked.

"Nothing. I don't see anything when I drink other ciders,

THE SIMPLICITY OF CIDER • 215

only mine. I think it's because the apples come from our or-chard. I've never tried to make cider with anyone else's fruit."

She took another sip. The taste was pleasant enough, but without the color it may as well be water. People filled the tables around them—mostly small families with kids, older couples. Everyone watched the older gentleman wearing a smeared white apron who did all the cooking. It was Mr. Smoot, a longtime friend of her dad's. He gave her a nod of recognition right before he dumped an entire bucket of red potatoes into the boiling cauldron of water, then added a huge scoop of salt.

"What's the white stuff?" Bass asked.

"That's the salt. The fish boil here is just four ingredients: water, salt, potatoes, and whitefish from Lake Michigan. Some places add in corn on the cob or onions, but I like their simple approach best."

"So what happens?"

"In a little while, they'll add another basket that's full of whitefish and more salt. As the fish cooks, the oil will rise to the top. They have a special trick for removing it you aren't going to want to miss. It's the best part. Then we go inside, fill a plate, then pour warm melted butter and lemon over it and eat until we're stuffed." Sanna's stomach growled. She'd forgotten how much she enjoyed fish boils here. Rustic and delicious.

As they waited for the fish to cook, she answered Bass's and Isaac's questions, but saved the best part as a secret. When everyone began to gather around the cooking pit, Sanna maneu-vered Bass to the front so he could have a perfect view for the grand finale with her and Isaac behind him. When Mr. Smoot splashed the kerosene on the fire, it caused the fish oil to boil over the edge of the pot into the fire, making a huge flare—like a fireball. Bass jumped and the crowed oohed as one. Isaac slid his hand around hers during the commotion. The heat from the intense fire singed her skin, but that didn't explain the searing where his hand touched hers.

"That was baller!" Bass said, and turned to look at her and Isaac when the flames died down a few moments later. Isaac released her hand, but the warmth where they had touched lingered.

"Were you two holding hands?"

"I can hold Sanna's hand if she says it's okay, right?" His eyes flicked to hers and she knew he hoped she'd play along.

"Absolutely, and I said it was okay." And it was. Like every time he touched her, holding his hand tortured and soothed her senses. The crowd shuffled around them, and they merged with its tide into the dining room to load their plates with potatoes and whitefish and drench it all in melted butter and lemon. She showed the boys how to remove most of the bones at once by carefully lifting off the top fillet of fish, then peeling out the spine, which—when you did it right—brought all the smaller fish bones with it. The meal ended as it should, with a slice of Door County cherry pie and ice cream.

"Mrs. Dibble's pie is way better," Bass said, though he shoveled it in with no problems, even helping Sanna with hers while he thought she wasn't looking.

The waitresses rushed from table to table, hustling to get the dining room ready for the next wave of patrons already congregating outside on the patio. She knew most of them by sight, having seen them at the Pig, or Shopko, or even at Idun's buying apples.

Stuffed with the good food, all three of them reclined in their chairs to patiently await the bill as the tables around them emptied. Isaac and Bass rubbed their bellies and compared whose was bigger, taking turns "ho-hoing" like Santa to see whose impression was better. She loved how Isaac played with Bass without acting like he was playing. They just had fun being themselves.

A shadow crossed the table, and Sanna looked up to see Thad towering over them. She did her best to not vocalize the *ugh* she thought, but she couldn't stop her smile from sliding off her face. Thad was a mud puddle when compared to Isaac's dazzling rainbow. It wasn't that she disliked him or wanted him to cease existing, she just didn't feel anything much for him—only that ditching him had made her life cleaner.

"You're dating him now?" Thad asked without even the common courtesy of a hello, his jaw clenched and eyes pinched. She'd known him her whole life, and he'd never been boorish before—boring, yes, but not rude like this. Of course, she'd never spent time with another man who she wasn't related to. Was he jealous? She looked up at him as if he were a worm squashed on the bottom of her boot. How could she get rid of him without this turning into a scene?

"You're making assumptions. The three of us are having a fun night out, my dad arranged it for us." Thad's eyes pinched more.

"So your dad set you up? He's your pimp now?"

How dare he say something so nasty! Sanna stood, causing the table to rock and a little cup of melted butter to spill, leaving a greasy trail across the tablecloth. Thad's eyes widened as he was forced to look up a few inches to maintain eye contact. "Never, ever speak to me like that again, Thad Rundstrom."

For a moment she thought he would slink away, properly intimidated. Instead he straightened as tall as he could and smirked in her face.

"People are talking all over town about you and him. Mrs. Dibble has you all but married."

"Everyone knows Mrs. Dibble exaggerates to make a story."

"People are laughing at me, Sanna. They all know I proposed to you. How do you think this looks?"

He grabbed her upper arm for emphasis, squeezing it tighter than necessary. Isaac flew to his feet, knocking the table, sloshing water onto the already spilled butter. Sanna held her free hand up to hold Isaac back, then used it to remove Thad's hand from her. She resisted the urge to bend his fingers backward. To think she had once dated this fool.

"I don't care how it looks. After this, I almost hope people laugh at you. I have always considered you a good friend and a good neighbor. There was even a soft spot in my heart for you as my first boyfriend, but I clearly never knew you. You're spiteful and mean when you don't get your way. Don't ever talk to me again."

She pulled a bill from her pocket and set it on the table deliberately.

"And your mom's casseroles are disgusting."

With that, she strode toward the exit. Given the amount of chair shuffling she heard, she knew Bass and Isaac were right behind her. That last comment was beneath her, but it had felt good.

Mr. Smoot stood near the exit, getting ready to cook for the next round of diners. As she passed him, he caught her eye and whispered, "Good call."

Outside the door, Sanna paused to let Bass and Isaac catch up to her. Without breaking stride, Isaac gently took her hand, and they walked to the car side by side.

CHAPTER TWENTY-SEVEN

E va unrolled the new plans across her hotel room bed, the tube they'd arrived in rolling across the floor. She picked it up and set it on the bed, which took up most of the small room. Even though she had lived in this room for the last few months, it still looked pristine. She kept her clothes and suitcase put away, her computer was precisely in the center of the desk, even her toiletries were kept in a neat case she tucked in one of the corners. Everything in its proper place.

Using the pillows, she anchored the paper so she could free her hands and study the new drawings. She'd asked the WWW planners to design a new layout incorporating her ideas, something she'd never done before. Normally, her father made all those calls, but she wasn't sure he'd approve the changes, so she went around him. She knew that if she had asked his permission, his response would be to send her Patrick. And this was going to get the deal done.

She breathed a sigh of relief. The plans were perfect.

According to Thad Rundstrom's intel, the Looms were the key to getting Sanna to agree to sell—and she was the lynchpin.

If Eva could win her over, the dad would be a piece of cake. These new renderings left many of the older trees intact, building the property's condos around them. She'd even decided to call them Loom Homes. The hotel proper and water park would be on the Rundstrom property, where they had no annoying qualms about razing their orchard.

Her phone buzzed. Patrick.

"Yes," she said.

"I know what you did."

Eva kicked off her heels and walked to the counter where she had placed the ice bucket. She pulled a bottle of Grey Goose from the icy minifridge she kept on its lowest setting and poured two inches into a clean tumbler, then added two cubes.

"Am I supposed to guess what you're referring to, or are you going to tell me?"

This should be good. Her brother was always digging, so let's hear what he found. She knocked back half the liquid in one gulp, searing down her throat. She'd stopped caring what Patrick thought three years ago when he'd gone behind her back on a deal they were both rushing to finalize and pointed out a silly error she had made in the contract to both the seller and her father, humiliating her. Rather than let her fix it, her father had yanked her from the project entirely. She had never been sloppy again. Let him waste his time reading her contracts—he wouldn't find any mistakes.

"You changed the plans for the Door County deal without Dad's permission."

Shit. That wasn't a mistake—it was something she was doing intentionally. She brushed her hands across the drawings. She was proud of this strategy. She'd listened to the concerns of the seller and altered the plan to persuade—not threaten, her dad's and Patrick's favorite business tactic.

"Dad instructed me to get the deal done, no matter what was necessary. I'm just following orders."

She swirled her glass, the shrinking ice cubes clinking together. She'd been doing this job, and doing it well, for five years—when would they stop looking over her shoulder?

"You know he would never accept changes like this. I saw the new rendering. You'll be lucky if he ever lets you head up another deal."

"Did you call for a reason, or just to be a dick?"

"I wanted you to know, so when you screw this up—which you will—and I have to come fix it for you—which Dad will make me do—you'll owe me for not telling Dad about your little idea."

This is what she hated most. Instead of working together, they always fought to outwit each other. Why couldn't they be brother and sister rather than corporate rivals?

"I owe you nothing. I remember when you forgot to get permits for new construction in Indiana. If I hadn't caught it and fixed it by sweet-talking the right people, you still would be staring at an empty field. And I didn't ask you for any favors for keeping my mouth shut—because I'm your sister and I had your back."

She could hear ice cubes clinking over the phone. What did it say about their fractured family that they both needed booze to get through a phone call with each other? She finished off her glass.

"Since you don't have a witty comeback, I'm going. I have a deal to close. Bye, Patrick."

She tossed the phone onto the bed and returned to her drawings. When Patrick wasn't a complete asshole, he could be a brilliant businessman. She wished she could ask him for advice on how to best approach the Lunds with these changes—her heart hurt that she couldn't. It had been exciting to problem-solve with the designer. Sure, she'd hit a roadblock with Sanna's affection for the Looms, but with a bit of creativity, she had found a possible solution. And even if it didn't work, at least this would be her own failure, not her brother's or her father's.

She picked up the phone to call Anders with the new proposal.

CHAPTER TWENTY-EIGHT

Bass searched the trees for wormy apples, ones that couldn't be used in ciders, let alone be pretty enough for the apple stand. He liked that Sanna trusted him enough now to decide which ones had to go. She worked on the other side of the same apple tree, thinning the branches that he couldn't reach. He knew she was double-checking his work, but he hadn't missed one yet.

He picked an apple so rotten that parts of it were mushy and threw it to the ground where Sanna had told him to. He wiped his hand on his shirt and continued to search.

It was almost the end of August and he hadn't spoken to his mom in more than two months. He had written her letters and given them to his dad to send. The last one was still in the notebook Sanna had given him.

Dear Mom,

I hope you're feeling better. I miss you.

We've been spending a lot more time with the Lunds. Miss

*Lund, or Sanna, cause she lets me call her that now, is nice. I
like her. I hope that's okay. We ate Oreos in the morning and I
taught her how to dunk the cookies after the cream is gone, just
like you taught me. She thought that was awesome.*

 *I think she and Dad might like each other. Is that weird? I
would be okay with it if you are. Are you okay with it?*

 Write to me when you can.

 I love you!

Bass

He really hoped his mom was okay with Dad and Sanna liking each other, because he was.

"Let's move to the next tree," Sanna said. "This one's
a Rambo. It's one of the first trees my great-great-great-
grandpa grafted when he moved to this country and bought
this land."

They were in the Looms, the best part of the orchard in
his mind. The air gave him goose bumps, like it was whispering on his skin, but in a good way, not a creepy way. Like the
sounds of grown-ups whispering when he fell asleep on a
couch in a new place. It made him feel safe to hear people
nearby. The Looms made him feel the same way, safe and like
everything was okay.

"Sanna, what's wrong with the trunk?" he asked, pointing to
where the tree's trunk looked funny, different from the other
trees they'd been working on today.

Sanna bent to look at the trunk, then her entire body went
stiff.

"No. No, no, no, no, no. No." She knelt and pushed aside

the long grass around the tree trunk and Bass leaned over her shoulder. Her hand traced a band as tall as one of her fingers that went all the way around the trunk, like someone had tied a wide, pale yellow ribbon around it, except instead of a ribbon, it was missing bark. She wrapped her arms around the gap, hugging the tree and leaning her head against it, whispering words he couldn't understand.

"How did the bark come off?" Bass tried to keep his voice quiet because it seemed like that kind of moment.

She turned her head toward him but left her hand on the tree trunk, her eyes sparkling with tears.

"This is very serious. Someone scraped off the bark on purpose, and it can kill the entire tree. I need you to get my toolbox out of Elliot, then start checking trees. We need to check every tree in the orchard. If this happened last night, we don't have much time before the trees that have been girdled can't be saved. Can you do that? Can you do that fast?"

"I've got this." He dashed to the truck and jumped over the side, just to prove he could be that fast. He knew right where the toolbox was because he had seen it that night they caught fireflies. He lifted it and had to readjust his grip. It was heavier than he thought, so he moved it to the end of the truck and opened up the tailgate to slide it out instead of lift it over the side. Using both hands, he carried it to Sanna, who had released the tree and was scanning its branches.

"Set it there." She pointed near the trunk. "Start checking this row. Go down and come up the next. I've texted your dad and mine, and they're on their way to help. This is really important. You can't miss even one. If you find one that's been girdled, one with bark missing in a ring around the middle, you need to tie a flag on it so we can find it again. Got it?" She handed him flags out of her toolbox, and he was off.

He ran from tree to tree as fast as he could, then slowly checked each trunk, making sure he didn't miss looking at even an inch of bark from the ground to the first line of branches. With each new ruined trunk he discovered, his heart felt heavier and heavier, pushing him to run faster to the next tree.

CHAPTER TWENTY-NINE

Fourteen trees had been girdled. All Looms. After the wasted Galas a few weeks ago, this was no coincidence. Someone was sabotaging Idun's and it was personal.

Sanna stepped into the shower, letting the hot water soothe the tense muscles on her neck and the aches in her fingers from the hours of delicate work.

She'd spent last night and today doing her best to repair the damage. Elliot had kept her company, giving her enough light to see by and some music to keep her awake when her eyes had drooped. She had carefully cut bark from some thicker branches and used it to create a bridge over the exposed trunk, tucking it under the tree's existing bark. Then she wrapped the area to keep in as much moisture as possible. If she could keep the trees alive long enough to merge with the new bark, they might survive. Isaac and Einars had wanted to help, but one was too inexperienced and the other too weak—besides, she needed to do this alone. This had happened on her watch. She needed to make it right.

What she really wanted was to girdle the one responsible,

but laws still applied in Door County, even if the sheriff was a family friend.

After being awake for thirty-six hours—over half of them spent meticulously repairing the trees—she couldn't wait to crawl into bed after dinner. When she turned off the shower, she heard a knock on the door.

"Sanna, Isaac and Bass are here for dinner. Don't come out naked."

She couldn't even muster an eye roll. She pulled her comfy summer dress, which was almost better than pajamas, over her head and emerged. She gave them a wave and yawn in greeting as she walked into the kitchen to help with dinner.

"Don't even think about it. Sit down at the table and we'll bring your dinner to you." Isaac had even shooed Einars out of the kitchen, where he'd been clumping around on his cast. In minutes a plate of scrambled eggs, bacon, and toast slid in front of her. He set an apple tart on the counter to cool for dessert.

During dinner, Sanna kept herself awake by counting Bass's giggles. So far it was twenty-three, but she was so sleepy she had no clue what caused them. The kid was extra-wiggly tonight. He kept peeking at his dad, who'd give him a scowl, then he'd look into his lap and snicker. She scraped the last bite of apple tart off her plate and carried her dish to the kitchen, planning to put it in the dishwasher and head to bed.

To her surprise, Isaac took it from her and put both of their dishes in the machine.

"I know you're exhausted, but I was hoping I could show you something. Out in the orchard. It won't take long." He held out his hand, tan and strong. Before logic stopped her, Sanna set her own hand in his. Unlike the calming sensation of their previous contact, this one rejuvenated her like rain and sunshine.

Her wilted energy rallied with curiosity and something else that awakened lower in her stomach.

"I'll get a sweater."

She pulled on a thin blue cardigan, just enough to keep the late-August night chill off her skin. Slipping into her outdoor clogs, she followed Isaac down the steps.

"We're going to the Looms, do you want to take the ATV or walk?"

Above them stars sparkled in the indigo expanse, still holding on to the sunset in the far west. Ripening apples scented the air with their fruity aroma, and crickets lazily sang to one another. A faint breeze whispered in her hair, more a reminder that she was outside than a discomfort. A few lingering fireflies blinked in the darkness. If ever there was a perfect night for walking the orchards, this was it. And, if she was being honest with herself, this was the perfect night to walk the orchards with Isaac.

"Walk, definitely walk."

They headed into the trees.

"I have a flashlight if you want." He held it out toward her, but she gently pushed it back to him.

"Not on a night like this. It would make it harder to see."

"You aren't a little creeped out by the dark?"

"Are you implying you are?"

"Not at all. I'm saying I'm a grown man and I like to know what's out there."

Sanna smiled.

"I know exactly what's out there. Using a flashlight only helps if you have it pointed in the right direction. You're better off letting your eyes adjust to the starlight and using your other senses. Not that there's anything to worry about. The most dangerous critters out here are the raccoons looking to steal my apples—and they're too fat to move fast."

"Raccoons? Sounds dangerous."

"Only if you trip over one. And they'll waddle off to the next tree before we even know they're there."

They walked for a few minutes in silence, each enjoying the night sounds around them.

"I'm surprised you aren't asking questions about what I'm doing," Isaac said. "Aren't you curious?"

"I like surprises. My dad's horrible at them, so I like to savor them when I get a chance."

"You're one of those people who carefully unwraps presents, aren't you? Rather than shred the paper like a Tasmanian devil."

"There's nothing wrong with restraint and patience. Anticipation is half the fun. It's one reason I like making cider—the delayed gratification of months of growing, harvesting, and fermenting."

Isaac looked at her in a way she couldn't interpret in the dim light. She fiddled with her necklace.

"It can be. But it can also be torture." Isaac pointed to her necklace. "You play with your necklace a lot. What's the significance of it?"

"It's a cross section of a branch from one of the trees that was girdled. I made it before I went to college so I always had a bit of the orchard with me. It reminds me of what's important."

They were entering the Looms now and the branches were wilder, taking over all the open spaces.

"We're almost there."

Sanna nodded, but she wasn't sure he noticed in the dark. He took her hand and led her under the branches of one of the trees she'd spent hours repairing, one of the oldest in the orchard. The one, actually, that her necklace came from. The arching branches created a room. Just in case it didn't survive, she savored stepping under its leaves.

"Close your eyes."

"If I close my eyes, I might fall asleep."

He squeezed her hand and pulled his phone out of his pocket. "Trust me. I just need a few moments."

And she did. Full dark took over her senses. She heard Isaac tapping on his phone, then orange light seeped through her closed lids.

"Open."

Isaac had moved behind her so all she saw was her beloved tree lit up like a party. At least twenty mason jars hung from the branches filled with delicate strands of lights that blinked like fireflies, and Isaac controlled from his phone. He'd even tied a pretty blue ribbon around the tape holding the tree bark together. While she basked in the beautiful view, he fumbled more with his phone until a soft song crooned over the crickets.

"It's stunning, Isaac. Perfect."

He propped the phone in the crook of a branch and held out his hand to her.

"What?" Sanna looked at him blankly, unable to fathom what he wanted her to do.

"May I have this dance?"

Sanna covered her mouth with her hand. He had remembered her silly confession. "You don't have to do this." Protesting felt natural, even as she felt overwhelmed by how thoughtful he was.

Isaac still held out his hand patiently.

"I'm not going to dignify that nonsense with a response. Dance with me."

She licked her lips and set her right hand in his. He pulled her gently in, so barely an inch remained between them. He set her hand on the back of his neck and moved his now free hand to her waist. With his other hand he clasped hers tightly, but without force. His hand trembled at the small of her back, revealing the nerves he'd almost kept hidden. As they swayed to the gentle singing, Sanna resisted the urge to melt into him. She never melted.

"You didn't have to go to all this trouble for a pity dance," she said softly in his ear.

Isaac moved his head back so he could look in her eyes. "What?"

"I'm a thirty-two-year-old woman who's never slow-danced—"

"Before now," Isaac interrupted.

"Before now. This was too much work just because I mentioned that all the boys were too embarrassed to dance with me."

"You are striking and tall, yes, and all those boys were fools because you are gorgeous. I can't take my eyes off you. While I may not have thought of this without you mentioning it, that's only because I'm not that clever. If anything, it gave me the excuse I wanted, but didn't know I needed." He took a deep breath, deep enough that his chest pressed into hers for a brief, wonderful moment. "I came here to get away from complications, but I found so much more than an escape. I care about you, Sanna. I don't know what that means when Bass and I go back to California, but I know it means I want to spend more time like this with you. As much as I can." He brushed his thumb on the inside of her wrist, weakening her knees.

Before she could respond, he went on. "You're honest to the point of blunt, but I never question where I stand with you. Your love for this land is so deep, I want to be included in it, even if it's just for a moment. I've never met a woman so certain of herself and of what mattered most to her. When I'm with you, I want to make you smile, ease your worries, and solve your problems, but I know you'd hate most of that. Watching you suffer the last day has been torture, but I gave you space because I knew you wanted it." Isaac pressed his cheek to hers and softened his voice to a whisper in her ear. "Holding you in my arms right now is like holding a wish. You are magic to me."

The words filled her heart. It was too much. She'd accepted a life alone, even embraced its simplicity, but now this thoughtful and gentle man scrambled her all up inside.

"I don't know what to say to that."

Isaac pulled back and smiled, crinkling his eyes.

"Say what you feel, that's what I want to hear." His fingers circled the center of her palm. Sanna's mouth dried and she cleared her throat, but the words still came out gravelly.

"Part of me says I should go back to the house. I'm too tired, this is too complicated, and I'll only be sad when you leave. No good can come of knowing you better."

A worry line formed on his forehead, and it cracked her heart open enough for the rest of her words to tumble out.

"But the other part—the part that's winning—wants to stop time so this moment never ends. For so long, I've been just a cider maker, a daughter, a hermit. I've never really been a woman. I never really knew I wanted that. But I do. You make my heart reckless."

She took her arm from the back of his neck and touched his lips, soft and dry. He tensed his arm behind her back, but didn't move it. Sanna smiled and knew he was waiting to see what she'd do. She didn't know yet. She'd only been with one other man, and it was unimpressive at best, awkward and uncomfortable at worst. It had been bad enough that she had never felt the urge to seek another romance. But here was someone whose barest of caresses made her knees wobble, he delighted in making her day better, and he came right out and said he liked her for exactly who she was.

234 • AMY E. REICHERT

Her chest tightened and breathing became more difficult. She tried to take a deeper breath, but that didn't provide relief. The firefly lights still danced, their feet still moved, but all her focus was on her fingers pressed to his lips, as if the answer were there. She let her hand trail into his beard, grazing the black and silver scruff, so much softer than she expected it to be. Then she brought her lips to his, the faintest of kisses, and all the air rushed into her lungs and straight to her head. Isaac finally closed the distance between them and released her hand so he could thread his fingers through her hair. She set the freed hand on his chest, covered in a soft blue T-shirt, his heart racing with hers.

She wanted more. She pressed her lips against his, marveling at how they moved with hers, how sharing the same air with him made her more alive. She pulled him to her as he held her tighter, their lips opening to deepen the kiss—he tasted of cinnamon and apples from their dessert. The longer they kissed, the more certain she was that she could never stop, that she wanted all of him. She slid her hand from his chest to his back, right where his T-shirt met his jeans, slipping her hand under the cotton to his bare skin. His reaction was clear—walking her backward until the tree offered its support. She moved her other hand to explore his broad back, soft cotton on one side, strong muscle on the other.

She gasped when he moved his kisses down her jaw to her neck, his strong hands following her curves, tracing her lines. His kisses slowed as he found his way back to her mouth, then pulled away to look at her. Her lips beat with the wild pace of her heart, and her skin burned from his beard. Every part of her he had touched felt different, brand-new, and they still wore all their clothes.

He kissed her once more, more softly, then pulled back again.

"I want—" He breathed the words as his chest heaved.

"We are adults," she interrupted, leaving a trail of kisses from his ear to his lips.

He groaned against her lips and pulled back.

"I didn't intend for anything but dancing and I'm woefully unprepared." He grazed his thumb over her lips, then kissed her once more, at last stepping away. "And I'll regret it for the rest of my days."

The way Isaac looked at her in this moment made her feel more wanted, more beautiful than she ever had. She wanted him to always look at her like that.

"You aren't the only one. Maybe we leave these lights up and bring a blanket next time."

"Sanna Lund, are you flirting with me?"

She winked at him, and at last her exhaustion caught up with her as she grabbed the tree for balance.

"Thirty-six hours of no sleep just hit me. Time to get me to bed." Isaac raised an eyebrow. "You know what I mean."

He wrapped her arm over his and led her out, using his phone to turn off the lights behind them.

"Thank you for an unexpectedly enchanting evening."

"It was truly my pleasure."

Behind them, the firefly lights flicked back to life for a few seconds, both Sanna and Isaac turning in surprise.

"Did you do that?"

Isaac pulled his phone from his back pocket and showed it to her. The app said the lights were off.

Sanna shrugged.

"I never thought it'd say something so illogical, but it seems like a sign, doesn't it? I guess we need to come back soon."

"I didn't think we'd be back at our tree so soon," Isaac said, and enjoyed the pink spreading from Sanna's cheeks to her ears.

They were dressed to work in jeans, light long-sleeved shirts, and hats slung over their necks to use when the sun got high. The dew still clung to the grass and soaked the bottoms of their pants. He was close enough to grab her hand, but didn't. Sunlight made him bashful, and the memory of last night seemed like a dream filled with fairy lights.

"Gary wins the race." Bass dashed past them, sliding on the wet grass, grabbing at trees to keep his balance.

"Careful of the trees, they're healing," Sanna said.

"I like how you're more worried about the trees than him breaking something," Isaac said, and then he did reach out to squeeze her hand to let her know he was teasing. A rush of memories from last night sent his blood flowing. Last night he had lain in bed wishing he'd either been responsible enough to be prepared or irresponsible enough to not care.

"You and I both know he'll be just fine. That boy is made of rubber."

Sanna stopped to look at some apples, turning them in the sunlight without pulling hard enough to detach them.

"Everything okay?" Isaac asked.

"The green is almost gone. These will be ready in a week or so. We need to get the stand ready, and probably update the website." She scrunched up her nose.

"Not a fan of the website?"

"You made it really pretty, but no, not at all."

"Good thing I'm here, then. I'll get it all set up—but you'll need to learn how to work it eventually."

"I'll be in your debt forever, or at least until you head back to California."

She turned her head, but Isaac saw the frown.

"When are we going back, Dad?" Bass said. "Will we be back in time for Fall Ball?"

"Probably not. We'll leave when the Lunds don't need us anymore."

"But what about school?"

"I contacted your school, and they gave me the information I needed to do some homeschooling to keep you up-to-date before we go back."

Bass looked down at the ground.

"You okay with that, Barracuda?"

"It's just been a while since I've hung out with any of my friends or played baseball. I kind of miss them."

Isaac stopped in his tracks. Now that he and Sanna were finally connecting, he really didn't want to leave, but the whole point of coming here had been to do what he thought was right for Bass. Keeping him away from California was feeling like a decision he was less and less certain of.

Bass raced ahead again to slide, but he hit a spot where the dew had dried and flopped onto his face. Isaac started to jog to him when Bass rolled over, clutching his stomach with laughter.

"See, rubber," Sanna said. She glanced at him, then put her hat on her head, hiding her eyes in the shadows.

They'd arrived at the tree, where the mason jars still hung from the branches and the grass was still bunched down from where they danced. Sanna carefully unwrapped the tape to see how the tree was doing, then kept unraveling until it hung like noodles from her fingers. She ran her hand over the smooth bark.

"It's completely better." She said the words slowly. "But that doesn't make any sense . . ."

"Are you sure that's one of the trees that was girdled?"

Sanna turned to him, with a look he could easily interpret. She knew every tree in this orchard like her own face.

"How is that possible? I assumed it would take weeks to heal," he said.

Sanna's face scrunched in thought. "It should, but under just the right circumstances . . . maybe we got lucky. I need to check the others."

Isaac followed her, uselessly, as she inspected all the damaged trees. Those closest to the dancing tree were partially healed, those farthest looked the same as yesterday. Sanna didn't speak, but with each tree she pursed her lips tighter.

"Maybe we should kiss under all of them?" Isaac said, making sure Bass was out of earshot before he said it.

Sanna snapped her head to look at him.

"Don't say anything to my dad."

"You want me to lie about kissing you or the trees?"

"Yes. Both. Point blank. He has funny ideas about things— sometimes he thinks the trees respond to the people around them, this will only encourage him."

"I'm sure there's a valid explanation."

"If he thinks you being here helped heal the trees, he'll do everything he can to convince you to stay. And you don't want to be here in winter. Door County is bustling this time of year, but six months from now it's snow and wind and quiet. Sometimes it snows so badly, we can't leave our house for a few days. Sometimes the power goes out. Sometimes it's days before we see other people. It's lonely and isolating and not everyone likes it."

"Are you trying to get rid of me?"

"No. But I've seen what this place can do to those who aren't suited for it. It's devastating. My mom . . ." Sanna took a deep breath, and Isaac knew her next words would be ones she didn't share often. "My mom left my dad when I was six. She hated it here so much, she left us and never came back, never even called or wrote." She looked in his eyes with her pained blue ones. "If even a tiny part of you is thinking about staying—and I'm not saying you are—you need to know the facts."

He hadn't been thinking of staying—nor could he, because of Bass. But now he wished he could. Isaac didn't think the idea of being trapped in a house with Sanna sounded bad at all.

CHAPTER THIRTY

It had been two weeks since their dance under the tree and Sanna hadn't found a chance to sneak more time with Isaac. She didn't know where things stood between them. It was clear they were attracted to each other, but he was going to leave sooner rather than later. Everything she'd done since college was to protect her heart from this exact circumstance—but her heart happily ignored all the sensible advice her head shouted. Would a few weeks of bliss be worth the future heartache?

With her dad's physical therapy still going strong, too many thoughts about Isaac cracking her focus, and harvest starting, Sanna was up until two in the morning and awake again by six every day. She paid bills, prepped their meals, made calls to the bank, labeled the cider, and tried not to strangle her dad when he groused about doing his exercises. Today was the first day of harvest, and tomorrow they opened the farm stand, which would hopefully be the first day of cider sales to make a dent in the loan payments—but she tried not to think about it to avoid feeling nauseous.

"Bass, you almost full?"

Sanna looked down the ladder to see Bass, the harvest-picking bag strapped around his shoulders like a reverse backpack. The bags were actually long canvas tubes with the end folded up and secured to keep the apples from falling out the bottom. Once the bag was full, they unhooked the bottom end and the apples would roll out into a bin on the back of Elliot. Bass was in charge of the lower branches, while Sanna took the rest of the tree. When he walked, he waddled, not being big enough to move the bag to the side when walking.

"Yep."

"It looks like we've got most of the Galas. Let's finish up this section, then have our lunch."

They finished picking the ripe red apples off the arching branches, then gently released their cargo from the bottoms of the bags, careful not to bruise the fruit. Sanna pulled out the cooler where they kept their lunches. Isaac would be joining them shortly. He was helping set up the stand with Einars, then he'd spend the afternoon picking with them. Tonight, they'd sort and bag apples into pecks and bushels for customers.

As Sanna and Bass munched their peanut butter and strawberry jam sandwiches, the sun warmed the top of her head and the lack of breeze added to the warmth. She watched the little boy chew his sandwich, curious what he was thinking about in this rare, still moment.

"Did you and your dad start school yet?" Sanna asked.

"Yeah. I'm working on multiplying fractions. I can never remember which is the denominator and which is the numerator."

"I have the same problem. The good news is you don't need to remember the names when you grow up. You just need to do it."

"But why not just use calculators?"

"Sometimes you don't have them, and it's faster in your head. Like what's one-half times two?"

Bass rolled his eyes at her. "That's easy, that's one," he said.

Sanna handed him one of the apples. "Don't we need to wash these?"

"It rained last week." Sanna shrugged and bit into her apple. "I've been eating apples straight off the tree all my life, and look how tall I am. You'll be fine."

Bass took a huge bite, juice spraying to his cheeks.

"So who's your favorite superhero?" Bass asked.

"On to the important stuff, I see." Sanna gave the question some serious thought. A favorite superhero said a lot about a person.

"Mine is Iron Man. He's rich, smart, and gets the ladies," he volunteered. Obviously it had been on his mind for a while.

Sanna snorted.

"What do you know about getting the ladies? You're ten."

"I know things. And you didn't answer the question."

"I've always liked Wonder Woman. There's something awesome about Amazonian women. And an invisible jet would be baller, as you like to say."

"I can respect that."

Sanna finished her apple, flung the core under the trees, and tilted her head back to enjoy the sun. It was that kind of perfect late August day when the sun warmed your skin, but the air had a hint of the coming fall. Grasshoppers hopped in the long, dry grass, and the air smelled of sweet apples, dry earth, and smoke.

Smoke.

Smoke?

She looked around. They weren't far from the back of the property, by the guest trailer, and an oily black plume wound its way into the sky. What was happening? They were close enough that she could see some of the trailer's siding between the trees. She jumped up and sprinted with Bass close on her heels, but not for long. Her long legs covered the ground in gazelle-like strides, tree branches smacking her arms as she cut across the rows, then stopped dead in her tracks. Smoke billowed from the trailer's right side where the living room was. As Bass arrived, he kept running toward the front door, but Sanna grabbed him by the scruff of the shirt.

"You can't go in there."

His wide eyes flicked between her and the trailer.

"I have to get Snarf."

"You are not going in there." She kept a firm grip on his shirt. "What's a snarf?"

"It's my stuffed animal. A green dragon."

Flames flicked above the roofline. Everything rational in her brain said going into a burning building for a stuffed animal would result in certain doom. She looked down at Bass, tears brimming in his eyes, and he whimpered before making another move to the door.

Sanna pulled him back again. She needed to move fast.

"Where is it?"

"On the bed."

"Anything else important?"

He shook his head.

"Stay put, do you hear me? I can't do this if I have to worry you followed me in."

He nodded solemnly, tears streaming down his face.

Sanna took a deep breath and ran into the trailer. Smoke slapped at her face and she dropped to crawl on her hands and knees. Flames engulfed the couch and licked at the walls, moving in angry red tails toward the kitchen. Tears formed to wash the stinging smoke out of her eyes, but they dried almost as quickly with the heat intensifying in the small building. She saw Bass's iPad on the table and a small stack of chargers and books. Leaving them for lost, she turned to the left.

She didn't have much time before she'd be trapped—smoke burned her nose as she tried to breathe. She skittered into the bedroom and shut the door to minimize the smoke, grabbing the duffel bag strap from where it poked out under the bed. Luckily, the green stuffed dragon sat in the middle of the perfectly made comforter. She stuffed it in the bag. Books, toys, and other assorted items took over the surface of the dresser, she scooped them in, too, then opened the top drawer and crammed in as much as she could. Everything else would have to burn.

She grabbed the doorknob, then flinched back from the scald as if she'd clutched the handle of a cast-iron skillet on high heat. A blister formed where her skin touched the knob. Black, acrid smoke seeped under the door. She couldn't go out the way she came. For a moment, panic blanked out her mind. She was going to die. Shaking off the thought, she turned and looked at the window over the bed. She looked for something to break the window, then realized only a screen stood between her and safety—smoke already twisted its way to freedom, choking her along the way. Using the now-heavy duffel bag as a battering ram, she knocked out the screen, then clambered out behind it. She turned to see flames lick under the bottom of the door, up the doorframe, and across the ceiling. Soon the entire trailer would be lost. She grabbed the duffel and headed for the trees and safety.

"Did you get him?" Bass said, his face coated in soot like her own.

Sanna could only nod. Her heart raced and her throat burned from the smoke. She couldn't believe she'd done something so stupid—especially for a stuffed animal. Bass dumped out the bag, baseball cards, deodorant, and underwear forming a mountain. At the top sat the dragon, like Smaug on his treasure trove, along with some papers that must have been crushed at the bottom. He grabbed Snarf and hugged him tight.

She pulled her bandana from her back pocket and wiped the tears now streaming from her eyes—without the heat to dry them, they flowed unabated and she couldn't stop coughing. The sun still shone, the grasshoppers still hopped, and a gentle breeze began to pull the papers, so Sanna caught them before they blew away. Her mind struggled to reconcile the black smoke and blistering heat with the beautiful day around her.

She looked at the papers in her hands. One was a letter from Bass to his mother that hadn't made the journey home yet. The last, though, made her stomach drop. She covered her mouth with her sooty hand, adding this information to every conversation she'd had with Isaac over the past couple of months. Her heart broke for Bass.

"What is it?" he asked.

Her sadness was quickly replaced by anger at the man who could lie to this sweet little boy, clutching his stuffed dragon.

"I . . . You'll have to ask your dad."

Isaac and her dad arrived on the ATV. Isaac barely let the vehicle stop before running to Bass and pulling him into his arms. His normally heartwarming worry for Bass was tainted with the truth she now knew.

"Are you okay? Are you hurt?" he asked when he finally let go, searching him for any signs of injury.

"I'm fine. But Sanna said I'm supposed to ask you about something in the duffel bag?"

Isaac looked up at Sanna, and she stiffly handed him the paper and saw his eyes light in recognition, then the light disappear as his lie died. He held the paper to his chest and closed his eyes. Would he try to get out of telling Bass the truth? But when he opened his eyes, Sanna saw his resolve. At least he was making the right choice now.

Isaac knelt in front of Bass, holding both of his shoulders.

"I haven't told you everything that's been going on with your mom, Bass. She . . . she . . ."

He looked up at her for support, but Sanna had none to give him. He'd created this mess, he could get himself out of it. Her only concern was for Bass. He continued.

"She died. Right before we left for our trip. That's why we went on our trip, I—I didn't know how to tell you. I wanted you to have one last summer being little. I didn't want you to have to grow up so soon."

He handed the paper—Paige's death certificate—to Bass, who stood still, absorbing the words, clutching the paper. Sanna could see his world crumbling and readied herself to do whatever he needed, all concerns about her orchard or the fire didn't matter—only this little boy did.

"Is Mom really dead?"

Isaac nodded. He sat back on his heels, and ash from the nearby flames lined the creases on his forehead, making him look older.

"But you said she was sick and trying to get better. You lied!" Tears trickled down Bass's face, leaving trails through the ash. Isaac moved to pull him into a hug, and Bass stepped back.

"Don't." His voice cracked.

Einars limped next to Sanna and put his arm around her shoulder. "You okay?" She nodded. "I called the fire department, but I think it's a lost cause. They'll need to stay with us." He pointed at Bass and Isaac.

She turned into her dad's arms. "I can't even look at him right now. Poor Bass."

Einars watched her. She could feel him judging her—maybe

amused that the self-proclaimed kid hater had developed a soft
spot for Bass—and she didn't care. She couldn't stop thinking
Bass never had a chance to say good-bye, never had a funeral
for his mother. It had been months, and that little boy thought
his mom was waiting for him to return. He had written her
letters that would never be delivered. Sanna knew the pain of
having a mom excised from your life without a chance to say
good-bye. She knew it never went away.

"Parents sometimes make stupid choices. They make sense
at the time, but in retrospect, they're a bad idea. We can't know
why he made the decision," Einars said.

"He lied to Bass." And he had lied to her—or at least he'd
implied his ex was still alive. If she looked back on what he
said, his words were always so careful—he had said she was
sick a lot, or had avoided commenting at all.

Bass still clutched Snarf to him and his voice raised over the
sounds of the incoming sirens.

"You never think I'm old enough. But I am."

Isaac reached for him, but Bass stepped farther back. He
walked to Sanna, who put an arm around his shoulder. While
furious at Isaac and heartbroken for Bass, she was still relieved
she could be there for him. She wanted to keep him close. Isaac
moved to stand in front of him. His shoulders slumped and his
lips frowned.

"Minnow, I know you're angry at me and sad about your
mom, but I . . ."

Sanna didn't want to hear his excuse, because there wasn't
one good enough to justify his actions.

"His mom died and you didn't give him a chance to say
good-bye. You had no right to do that to him." She handed
him the letter he never sent because there was no one to
send it to, then looked down at Bass. "Want to head back to
the house?"

Bass nodded, she took his free hand, and they walked back toward the farmhouse.

Isaac gathered their belongings from the ground and slowly packed them into the duffel, careful not to bend the baseball cards or lose a single toy. What had happened that his life now fit into one duffel bag, and even that seemed like too much? He'd pushed away the truth for so long, he'd even let a part of himself believe that Paige was still struggling to recover, not that it was over. Bass had already had one parent fail him—now he had two. He couldn't even be mad that Sanna had taken his son back to the house without him. He deserved it.

The firefighters did their best to stop the blaze from spreading into the orchard. Two men pointed the hose, blasting water at the ravaging red flames, which hissed as it hit the heat. Siding melted off exposing blackened wood beams. As the firefighters moved around the building, the hose knocked one of the geranium pots into the muddy puddles forming from all the water.

Einars stood next to Isaac.

"The firefighters said there's no reason to watch them play with their hoses," he said. "Let's head back."

Isaac struggled to his feet, then rubbed his hands on his face, trying to erase the events of the past few minutes.

"They'll forgive you."

"They shouldn't."

"They don't understand. Sanna's sensitive to absent moms."

Isaac zipped the duffel and put it in the back of the ATV, making sure Einars safely eased into the vehicle.

"Yeah, she mentioned that."

"Sanna's mom left when she was young, without any explanation—though I had my highly educated guesses, she hadn't exactly been subtle about her unhappiness. Sanna was stuck with me and Anders." He rubbed his jaw and looked at the dark smoke still twirling in the blue sky as they turned the ATV toward the house. "Her teenage years were not fun."

He knew Einars was trying to make him feel better, but he didn't want to feel better. Bass had never rejected him before. They'd always gotten along, always been buddies. But then again, he'd always told him the truth before. He'd planned for months to throw the death certificate away—he could always get another one—but a part of him was glad the truth was out. Now he had nothing to hide. If Sanna didn't want him anymore, at least it was over. One less complication. His chest twisted at the thought.

"Maybe Bass and I should head home. We've taken up enough of your time, and it appears we've managed to burn down part of your property."

Einars waved his hand.

"Don't be absurd. Bass needs time before being trapped in a cross-country road trip with you." He looked over his shoulder at the smoldering trailer. "And something tells me you had nothing to do with that fire. Between the picked green apples, the girdling, and this—there have been too many weird things happening around here for it to be a coincidence."

They rode in silence, Isaac dreading yet eager to see the two people he cared most about. Idun's Orchard had been his escape from his poor decisions, and now he didn't want to leave. More than California, where he'd spent so many years, this place felt like home. Sanna felt like home.

Maybe Einars was right and they needed some space. He'd made a mistake—he wasn't arguing that. By the time they arrived at the farmhouse, Isaac had convinced himself he'd be forgiven and all could return to normal.

When he entered the kitchen, Bass and Sanna sat at the counter, drinking grape soda out of glass bottles, their hair wet and in fresh clothes. Bass wore an oversize white T-shirt, which must have been Sanna's as it almost reached his calves. Neither looked up at him.

"Bass, we should get set up in one of the spare rooms." Bass didn't move. "Bass."

Instead of his child hopping off the stool and running to his side, he remained seated, slurping his drink.

"Pa, can you please tell Mr. Banks that Bass will be sleeping on the floor in my room? And that he can get his own room ready."

Einars paused, looking back at Isaac to see if he really needed to convey the message.

"Bass, this isn't a joke. I'm still your father, and you still need to listen to me."

Sanna whispered in Bass's ear, and he hopped off the stool.

"Pa, let him know that Bass isn't joking. He needs some space."

Sanna went to a closet and pulled out a pile of blankets and pillows, then disappeared into her room, presumably to make up Bass's bed. Isaac dumped the duffel on the table and sat with his head in his hands. Einars sat in the chair next to him.

"He's never going to forgive me. He's been through so much with his mom. Seeing her sick, seeing her high—though he didn't understand what was happening. She'd been an addict for years—fentanyl." Einars made an O with his mouth, now understanding Isaac's concern about leaving his pill bottles lying around. "She was in her fourth rehab facility and had paid an orderly to sneak her some drugs. She finally ODed. When I got the call, I finished up my current job, packed the car, and we left. I couldn't tell him. I just couldn't tell him that his mom chose drugs over him. How can you tell a child that?"

He looked up to see Sanna standing in her doorway. Without a word, she closed the door.

Einars got up, pulled a bottle from the back of a cabinet, grabbed two glasses, and returned to Isaac. He poured a finger of the amber liquid into each glass and held his up to clink glasses.

"To doing your best," Einars said.

Isaac copied his movements and drank the liquor in one quick gulp. It burned going down, nearly singeing his nose hairs, but with a hint of apple at the finish.

"Apple brandy. I made it years ago. A very small batch—I don't have Sanna's gift. I pull it out when something stronger than cider is needed."

"Now is definitely one of those times." Isaac had taken another measure, wanting to feel the pain every second it went down his throat, and settled into the chair when there was a knock on the door.

"Come in," Einars shouted.

Two firefighters walked into the great room. They had taken off their heavy coats and hats, but still wore the pants with suspenders over T-shirts soaked with sweat from working in the heat under so much equipment.

"Hey, Einars," the older of the two said. "We've got some news."

"Doug." Einars nodded in greeting. "Should we go look at it?"

"Nah. I knew you weren't moving around too good, so I have pictures. Everything is already packed up as evidence." He pulled a digital camera to show the pictures. "Who'd you piss off? This is pretty clearly arson, unless your guests have a habit of lighting gasoline-filled bottles under the trailer."

"Not recently," Isaac said.

Einars and Isaac looked at the broken-glass pictures, squinting to make out the label, and Isaac's stomach dropped even more. It looked like one of his labels he'd made for Sanna. Another smack in the face.

"That looks like one of mine." Sanna's voice came from over their shoulders, then she walked out of the house, leaving her rosy scent behind. She returned in a few minutes, carrying an unburnt version of the bottle in the photo. "Someone took some bottles out of one of the crates in the barn. I wouldn't have noticed except I recently had to count to make sure I had enough."

Her voice rasped from the smoke.

"Why did you go into the trailer?" Isaac asked before remembering she wasn't speaking to him. He braced for her silence, but instead she looked at him with her cornflower-blue eyes and answered.

"Bass kept trying to run in for Snarf. I couldn't let him do that. I saw the duffel under the bed when I crawled into the bedroom, then filled it with whatever I could grab."

"Thank you. Losing Snarf would have devastated him."

"I think he's devastated anyway."

Bass emerged from Sanna's room. She grabbed a pack of Oreos and the milk from the fridge and spoke as the two of them went down the stairs and out the door.

"We're going back to harvesting. No need to join us."

CHAPTER THIRTY-ONE

Eva walked into one of the many small restaurants lining the main street of Fish Creek. She'd been to this one enough times that the waitstaff knew her order as soon as she walked in. Outside the window, the sidewalks teemed with strollers and older couples walking hand in hand. When she first arrived in Door County, the leisurely pace and pastoral scenes had made her antsy, but now she found it hopeful and reassuring—that there might be a different way to live.

By now Patrick had probably spilled the beans about her new plans, but she was hoping to beat him to it—too bad she was on hold with her own damn company. She hated the instrumental versions of eighties pop songs. She had heard them too many times while waiting for her father to answer his phone.

She slid into a booth with a smile and a wave from the hostess. Before she finished settling the tube containing the new drawings on the bench next to her, the waitress, Ann, set her black coffee down in front of her.

"Your egg whites will be out in a minute, Eva."

"Thanks, Ann."

254 • AMY E. REICHERT

During her last visit, she'd found out Ann had lived here her entire life. She went to college but found it didn't suit her. She came back and married her high school sweetheart, who was taking over the family's company, which rented watercraft to tourists. She and her husband had two kids under five and the grandparents helped watch them while Ann and her husband worked. They weren't rich, but they didn't need to be. Eva had always been rich—she worked to please her father, not for the money.

Eva envied Ann.

"This is Mr. Drake." Her father had finally picked up.

"It's Eva."

"Wonderful, the papers are signed then." There was an edge to his voice. Patrick had already told him, and he was baiting a trap.

"I've revised the original plan to make it more amenable to the sellers, but I expect they'll agree soon."

"I heard." The words contained even less warmth than usual. "So the papers aren't signed yet. I told you not to call until it was done."

"Dad . . ." She hated the begging tone in her voice.

"You know not to call me that at work."

"Sorry, sir. Money alone won't convince them. I've adjusted accordingly."

Her eggs arrived, and she gave Ann a thumbs-up.

"The clock is ticking. Do what needs to be done. Prove you can make the tough decisions. You're the one who wanted this deal. It has already taken much too long. Don't call again until it's done."

The phone went quiet. She set it next to her coffee cup. She'd get this damn deal done. She'd show them she was better than all of them combined and earn her spot at WWW. She sipped her coffee, letting the bitter liquid singe her throat as she swallowed—savoring the burn.

The door opened and in walked Anders, tall and handsome in the morning sun. She waved for him to join her. She started speaking before he even got settled, eager to show him the revisions.

"Thank you for meeting me. I wanted to show you the new plans I had drawn up. I'm hoping the designs are more amenable to you and your sister." She pushed aside her eggs and pulled the plans out of the canister, unrolling them over the table so Anders could see them. She ignored the uninterested expression on his face. "As you can see, I've kept a portion of the Looms and designed around them. I'm envisioning all sorts of ways we can incorporate them into our property—harvest fests, apple blossom balls, even stringing lights on them for the holidays."

She especially liked the idea of creating events around them—it was something that would be unique to the property. Anders held up his hand and looked over the drawings.

"These are impressive, but I'm not sure you understand my sister. I don't think I did until recently, either. It isn't just dirt and trees. She just spent thirty-six hours trying to save trees from something that is nearly always terminal. She'd have an easier time living without air than she would Idun's."

The unmistakable chill of failure spread from Eva's core. This couldn't be the end—not after everything she'd risked. Her father would send her to the mail room once he found out. Patrick would gloat for a year. Desperation sent tremors to her hands.

"Can you at least share the plans with her? Let her see them and then decide?"

Her voice cracked and Anders noticed—his eyes turned from

apathetic to sympathetic. Anything he said now would be only to delay his rejection. She'd given that look enough times herself.

"I'll think about it."

He left. Eva put the plans away, curling them tighter than necessary to fit back in the tube, to match the tightness constricting her chest. This had been it. The last stand. The final shot. And she had failed. Reflexively, she started to make a mental list of what needed to be resolved before she could go home, but found herself staring at the bakery case near the door. All summer she'd ignored its contents, telling herself she didn't enjoy sweets at breakfast time. But she did. She always had. She flagged Ann to take away her cold, dull egg whites and ordered a cinnamon roll the size of her head. If her whole life was going to change, might as well start now.

CHAPTER THIRTY-TWO

"If you're here to tell us to sell the orchard again, you can turn back around," Sanna said as Anders emerged from his black Lexus and entered the lower barn, where Einars, Bass, Isaac, and she were setting up. His normal suit was replaced with jeans and a button-down plaid shirt. He looked ready for a day working in the trees . . . or at least he would have if it weren't for his tasseled loafers.

Tomorrow was September first—their traditional first day of public sales. She had made it. They had made it. There was still a lot of work to do, but they'd harvested the first round of apples and tomorrow money would start trickling back into their coffers.

The barn doors to the farm stand were open to the warm day. It was about the size of a three-car garage, and that's what they used it as during the winter when the snow could bury their vehicles. But during the fall, it was open to the public to sell apples and Sanna's cider, hopefully more of both now that the website was up and running. Coolers lined the cinder-block walls, stocked with a paint store's worth of colors. White painted wood tables stood in three neat rows. Only one of the tables had apples ready for sale in bags. Right now, only the Gala and Viking apples were ripe. In a few weeks, the tables would be full with even more varieties. Neatly painted wooden apples identified the type, as did the white-handled paper bag that fit a half peck of apples. A few larger plastic bags contained an entire peck—a little over ten pounds of fruit.

Near the open entry, an ancient cash register sat on another white table. The manual keys still worked for their simple sales. This was the first year Pa had agreed—at Isaac's urging—to get a credit card device they could use with Sanna's phone. He sat near the register and filled bags from the large wood crate. Each apple sold was a success for her and Idun's. They were never overwhelmed like some of the other apple stands, but they always managed to have a steady clientele. The rest of their harvest was sold to the bigger stands who wanted a bit of apple variety. Because they were off the beaten path, most people stumbled across them while crisscrossing the peninsula between the bay side, which overlooked Green Bay, and the quiet side, which overlooked the expanse of Lake Michigan.

Once the season got under way, one of them would work the stand, while the rest would pick in the orchards, then they'd spend the nights getting the stand ready for the next day. This time of year was intense. Long days, late nights, and lots of people. For the first time, Sanna wasn't dreading the customers like she had in years past.

"Keep working. You're doing a great job," Sanna said to Bass. It had been two days since the fire, and she only spoke to Isaac when necessary, while Bass maintained his icy silence. This morning Bass had made eggs and toast for her and Einars, leaving Isaac to prepare his own. With each failed attempt to reconnect with Bass, Isaac's shoulders drooped more, his eyes following Bass's movements, longing to be a part of his world again. She'd need to help mend those fences. Bass and Isaac needed to be a family, no matter what happened. She, however, never needed to forgive him for being a shameful liar. She had shared more of herself with him than she had with anyone else. She'd told him about her cider-making gift and about the Donor—and he hadn't shown her the same level of trust. She'd simply resolved to consider him a bullet dodged—though that didn't take the sting away from knowing she'd never experience another kiss like she had under the dancing tree. Her lips tingled at the memory.

She looked up, waiting for Anders's response to her statement.

"I'm done with that idea," he said. "You're right that Idun's needs to stay in the family. But you, me, and Pa need to discuss how we're going to get through this mess and make money off your cider." Sanna resisted her urge to feign light-headedness at his admission—it wasn't her style—but it was still tempting.

"Go on."

Anders looked pleased that he was getting off that easy. At least she was making someone's day a little better.

"I got to thinking, if we don't sell, we still have the debt problem to solve. Your cider is good. You just need time to spread the word. Money will buy us time. What if we got some investors?"

"Doesn't that mean they would own a share of Idun's?"

"Yes, but the alternative is you lose the orchard completely."

Sanna thought about it. She didn't want anyone telling her how to run Idun's. She and her dad had lived here their whole lives, they knew best. She didn't want any non–family member owning any piece of it. But despite all her pleading and hard work, if they didn't get some cash, and they needed more than they could make off the farm stand in the first few weeks, they would default on their loans—and that would mean zero Lunds running the orchard. Sharing ownership was definitely the lesser of two evils.

"Okay, why weren't we thinking of this before? And where do we get these investors?"

"We'd need to raise over two hundred thousand, at least. More if we can get it. We could get a lot of small local investors, or a few larger investors. And I didn't think of it before because I was blinded by the huge offer from WWW." He looked down at his feet. "Taking the money was an easy out, this will require a lot more work. Pa told me about the girdling and how you worked to save the Looms. Idun's is where I grew up—past tense—but it's your home, your livelihood. I get that now."

"I'm in," Isaac said from behind her.

Sanna turned, torn between wanting to glare at him and wanting to hug him for his enthusiastic offer. Though he might be offering to get back in her good graces, which she was willing to sell to him if it helped the orchard. Against her better judgment, she softened toward him.

"I'll consider your offer." She turned back to Anders. "Who else?"

"Julie and I have a bit saved, too. We talked about it and thought this would be a good investment. With luck, it might pay a sizable portion of the girls' tuition in ten years."

"How did you convince her?" Sanna asked.

"The reason we don't spend more time here isn't just because of Julie, it was because of me, too. I needed to separate myself—prove I was more than this place. She actually saw way before I did how much Idun's means to you, and what I would be forfeiting to give up on this place."

Sanna covered her mouth with a hand and closed her eyes

to keep tears of gratitude from falling. They'd had so many dif-
ferences over the years, and he and Julie still wanted to help.
Too often, she and her father seemed to be two against the
world keeping the orchard running, but knowing Anders and
Isaac had her back felt like the reinforcements had arrived.
Maybe there was hope for them yet. She stepped toward Anders to give him a hug.

"Don't hug me yet. You haven't heard who the final investor
I have in mind is."

Sanna shook her head.

"I don't care who it is if it means Idun's is still ours. Done."
Sanna looked at her dad, but he was watching Anders warily.

"Who's the last person?" he asked.

Anders took a step back and swallowed slowly before he said
the last possible person Sanna ever would have guessed.

"Mom."

"No. Absolutely not. We'll find someone else."

Isaac stood behind Einars and Bass in the shaded stand
while Anders and Sanna glowed like angry Norse gods in the
sunlight. "Sanna, she wants to help. I've told her all about the
cider business—she thinks it's a great idea."

"Since when are you and the Donor chummy?" She poked
him in the chest, her face reddening with each emphatic jab.
"Is this why you wanted to separate yourself from us? You're too
busy living the high life with her? Traitor."

Anders caught her hand, his mouth a grim line, then gently
moved it to her side, where she let it stay.

"First, stop referring to her as the Donor—you're more
mature than that. If you don't want to call her Mom, call her
Susanna. Second, I started seeing Mom in college. She reached

out to me, just like she reached out to you." Sanna gave her father a quick glance, and Isaac could tell from Einars's pressed lips that he understood everything. "I chose to listen to her, to try to eventually understand why she left us."

"I know why. She was too busy with her new husband and new life."

Isaac didn't like watching Sanna have to relive these painful emotions from so many years ago. He wanted to help, but knew there was nothing he could say to shield her from the truth any longer. She and Anders needed to have this fight to get all the ugly truths out on the table.

"Wrong. She tried over and over again to see us. Dad wouldn't let her. Ask him."

He pointed to their father, whose face had drained of color, reminding Isaac of the day he had fallen from the ladder. Perhaps he and Bass should head back to the house and give the family privacy, but he didn't want to draw attention to themselves by leaving.

"Pa? Is this true?"

Einars's shoulders melted even lower and he rubbed his hands over his eyes.

"She left us," he said. "She didn't deserve to see you two if she wasn't willing to come here."

"The D—Susanna wanted to see me and you didn't let her." Sanna fought to keep tears from falling.

"Sanna-who, she could have seen you if she would've come to Idun's. She refused. We were happier without her."

Sanna stepped away from Anders and away from her dad until she bumped into the garage door's frame. She clenched the wood for support until her knuckles whitened.

"Don't call me that. Not now. You were happier without her. Not us. We weren't happier. I wasn't happier. A part of me has been missing my entire life, and now you tell me it didn't have to be that way?" Sanna used the heel of her hand to wipe the tears on her face. "How could you?" She turned back to face her brother. "And why didn't you tell me any of this earlier?"

"You seemed happy," Anders said.

"Sometimes what looks like happiness is just people making do." She started toward the house. "Does everyone have deep, dark secrets they are keeping except me and Bass? No investors. You don't deserve to be a part of Idun's Cider."

Five months ago Sanna had stepped into their clean, remodeled barn, ready to start planning the new season, sketching out ideas for new ciders to create with all the shiny equipment. She could make huge batches of her most popular versions, while still making smaller specialty batches. She could make bottles of any size, or a quarter barrel for a bar to serve her cider on tap. A cold room and a walk-in freezer could store pallets of cider and juice—enough for her to keep cider production going year-round. It was way more than she needed, but if her dad believed she could do it, then she believed, too.

Back then, she wouldn't have said she was happy, but she was content. She had a routine of breakfast, chores, lunch, cider, dinner, reading, and planning—or more chores, depending on the time of year. Baking apple treats with Pa, and a movie sometimes with Thad. It was predictable and simple, and now she knew that none of it was happiness.

As she walked back to the house, she replayed every major life event in her mind and wondered how it would have been different with her mom there. Or how many times her father and Anders had lied to her? Why couldn't they rewind the clock before they remodeled the barn and purchased all the cider-making equipment? If she had been content to continue with what she had had, they wouldn't have the debt looming over the orchard, they wouldn't have needed Isaac to help them, and Anders would be staying out of their business. Everything would be simple.

In the house, she went into her father's bedroom and found the box he kept full of pictures of Susanna and took it to the loft. It looked worn at the corners, as though weary from too many years of holding in sadness. Sanna curled her feet under her on the couch, set the box on her lap, and lifted the lid to her greatest pain.

On top sat the picture of the four of them, smiling faces frozen in time. She sorted the contents into piles—photos and letters. At the bottom was a box containing their wedding bands, still shiny like new, since they had only been used less than a decade. A wedding band should have nicks and scratches, like the great dining room table downstairs, but these were polished and bright. As she removed each photo, she studied her mom's face for signs of Susanna's unhappiness—a downturned mouth, a creased forehead, a brittle smile. It was so obvious now.

She returned the pictures to the box and picked up a letter. It was dated around her thirteenth birthday.

Dear Einars,

I know you will never share this with Sanna, but I'll regret not trying even more. She is nearly a teenager and I'm sure she has questions best answered by a mother. I would love a chance to see her. I can come to Green Bay. Just name the date and time.

I know you want me to return to the orchard. I tried. I made it as far as Algoma and had to pull over from the panic. I know

you can never forgive me and I'm truly sorry for how I hurt you,
but please don't let our children grow up without me.
Please.

Susanna

She looked through the letters and they were all similar. Excuses for why she couldn't make it to the orchard and pleas to see her children. Sanna couldn't make sense of either of her parents' actions. How could her dad keep these from her all these years? And why couldn't Susa—her mother drive those last few miles? It seemed the height of selfishness. What made seemingly rational adults make such stupid choices? Anger made it impossible to cry for all the years she lost. Her head hurt without the emotional release of tears.

Now that Sanna had briefly glimpsed a little happiness with Isaac and Bass—seeing the joy the right family created—she didn't want to settle with getting along anymore. And now her mother wanted to invest in the very place she hated so much. When did everything get so complicated?

CHAPTER THIRTY-THREE

Sanna heard someone come up the steps and braced herself for another confrontation. At least she knew it wouldn't be her dad—he still couldn't make it up the spiral stairs with his crutches. She had intentionally come up here because she knew it was difficult for him to walk up the stairs.

"Sanna?"

It was Bass.

"What's up, bud?"

"You okay?"

She gave a little chuckle that he was checking on her. Shouldn't it be the other way around?

"I'll be fine." She wrapped her arm around him and gave him a little hug. "Thanks for checking on me."

"Dad always says that when a lady says she is fine, she's really just angry at you that you don't know the real reason she's angry."

Sanna snorted at that. It was always interesting to hear what Bass gleaned from listening to the adults.

"Your dad said that? He's not too wrong. But in this case, I didn't say I was fine. I said I'll be fine. There's a difference—do you see it?"

Bass nodded and looked up at Sanna.

"Is the orchard really in trouble?"

Sanna shifted so she could look at his face while they spoke.

"It is. My dad borrowed a lot of money from the bank, and we don't have enough cash to make the monthly payments. Haven't had enough for a few months now. To get the money, we promised we would make the payments on time and if we don't, then they could take the orchard. We don't have enough money to make those payments right now, so unless we get some fast, the bank will take it."

"That sucks big hairy balls."

Sanna gave him a look. He was too young to be talking like that—at least around adults.

"Okay, it just sucks."

She nodded at the improved language. "It really does."

"Our dads really screwed up, didn't they?"

"They didn't think we were tough enough, I guess."

Bass put his finger to his lips like he was holding his words in until they were ready to come out.

"Maybe you should let your mom help."

"I'm not sure I can do that."

"But she's still there and wants to help. Even though my mom chose drugs over getting better, I still wish I could see her again—and I don't ever get to do that again. Maybe it's different when you're old, but that's how I feel."

Sanna brushed a curl off his face, astounded at how right he was. He wasn't complicated by years of hurt feelings and a scarred heart.

"First, your mom was sick. She didn't choose drugs over getting better. She was sick and she couldn't fight it any lon-

ger. Second, it's not any different when you're grown up."
She propped her feet on the coffee table and leaned into the
squashy cushions. "Do you think we need to go back down?"

"Nah—let them finish the work."

"Good idea."

They looked out the window at the orchard. On the far right
an unusual movement caught her eye. She scanned to find it
in the Looms, not spotting it right away. Something was wonky
with the Dancing Tree—as she'd come to think of her favorite.
Branches pointed up and wobbled, and they knocked into the
branches on the tree next to it. She saw a figure in tan walking
toward the back property line.

Without realizing it, she squeezed Bass's hand as her heart
stopped. What had happened?

"Ow."

She let it go. She needed to get out there immediately.

"Sorry."

She ran down the stairs, slipping on some clogs to race
across the lot, and climbed into the ATV, praying the keys
were in it. In the farm stand, the three men watched her
as she revved the engine and tore through the orchard. She
prayed she was wrong, prayed the stress and exhaustion of
harvest season were messing with her vision. But as she pulled
into the row, she knew. What should be a clear view to the
property line was instead full of green, leafy branches crisscrossing at odd angles. The hollow feeling in her chest grew
and grew as she approached her beloved tree. She stopped the
ATV and walked slowly around the vertical branches that still
wobbled in the breeze, unaware they would soon be dry and
brittle.

She knelt on the ground next to the naked stump and ran
her hands over the fresh cut revealing well over one hundred

rings. Even with such a long life, it was too soon. Tears slid down her cheeks as the fresh, damp sawdust clung to her jeans. Who would do this to her beautiful tree? Could it have been Thad?

Sanna wasn't sure how long she rubbed her hand over the newly sawn wood like a mother rubbing a sick child's back, but the sun dipped to the horizon and the air chilled her bare arms. She'd rushed out of the house without a jacket. While she still didn't understand how her mom could abandon her and Anders, losing this tree made it clear to Sanna that she would do anything to make sure she didn't lose Idun's. Happiness without her orchard would be impossible. With that knowledge, no compromise or sacrifice was too much to ask.

She gave the stump one last pat and stood, confident in what she needed to do next. Using the tree clippers in the vehicle, she collected a small mound of new-growth clippings, each about a foot long, adding more to a bucket until she couldn't fit another stick. As she emerged from the wreckage, her foot clanked against something hard. She picked up the item and held it in her hand—it was one of the mason jars with fairy lights. Isaac must have missed it when he collected the others. Another reminder of what she couldn't stand to lose.

When she returned to the house, she carried her bucket of sticks into the kitchen, where everyone, including Anders, had gathered around the TV to watch a baseball game. With a clatter, she dumped the sticks onto the table, then went into the kitchen for a box of gallon baggies.

"Sanna, what did you do?"

When she spoke, her voice scratched from all the spent tears.

"Someone chopped down the Dancing Tree." Isaac met her eyes, and he looked as heartbroken as she felt.

"What's the Dancing Tree?" Anders asked.

"It's Sanna's favorite tree," Bass had answered for her. She gave him a wink as Isaac moved to pat his shoulder, but Bass stepped away. He still hadn't completely forgiven his dad—that would take some time.

"The one you made your necklace from?" Einars asked. She nodded. "These are for grafting?" he said, referring to the sticks. "It hasn't worked any other time we've tried."

"It has to work this time. I'm going to start some as soon as I have new rootstock, I'll save some in the barn, in the house. It has to work." She stuffed handfuls into a baggie until it was full, then began another. Without a word, Isaac, then Bass, then Anders and Einars joined her.

As they filled the bags, Anders asked the question Sanna had been turning over in her mind. "Who would chop down one of the Looms?"

"I'm pretty sure it's Thad. Ever since I turned down his proposal, he's changed. I think I saw him walking toward the border right after the tree came down. I don't have real proof, but I definitely saw a figure in tan walking off the back of our property and onto the Rundstroms'."

"I'll talk to Sheriff Dibble," Einars said.

Sanna nodded, her mind on her work.

"I spoke to Eva Drake aga—" Anders started.

"Really, Anders?" Sanna said.

"Let me finish. I promised I'd tell you even after I gave her a very firm no. She seemed a bit desperate, and I felt bad. But she did something that was interesting—she listened to what I said during the first meeting and reconfigured the plans to save most of the Looms. It was a clever idea. Anyway, I fulfilled my vow to pass that information on to you both."

Sanna hadn't expected that piece of information, but it gave her an idea, well, really a twinkle of an idea that she hadn't caught, but might once it formed.

When they were done, they had fifteen full bags of potential scions. Fifteen bags of fresh starts, if only she could save Idun's.

The next day started chaotic and fuzzy. Sanna had dreamed of waking to find all her trees broken on the ground. Even with the relief that it was just a nightmare washing over her, she couldn't shake the off-kilter feeling as she walked to the barn for the start of the day, catching sight of something she never thought she'd see: when they opened the farm stand for the first day of business, customers were already waiting in the lot.

"Where did all these people come from?" she heard her dad ask Isaac.

"I checked the website last night. Your visitor count is up, and your site shows up in the first page of Google results when someone searches for Door County orchards."

"All that fiddling you did, you did that?"

"It's what I do."

Sanna didn't know how to feel. Grateful for the customers, irritated because she wasn't ready to completely forgive her dad or Isaac, wanting to celebrate this tiny success with them. Sometimes it was difficult to let go.

"Can I help with the cash register?" Bass asked Einars.

"Sorry, Wahoo. You're too little for that. They need a grown-up to handle the money," Isaac answered before Einars could. "Can you go run and get Anders from the house? I think we'll need all hands on deck from the looks of this crowd." Bass scowled at his dad and stomped to the house.

As they opened the door to the waiting patrons, a brisk wind whipped Sanna's hair. She checked the weather on her phone.

"Pa, let's move the register back a little from the entry. It's sunny now, but they're saying we might have some bad storms late—we don't want the register to get wet." Isaac hurried forward to help her lift it, catching her eye and bringing a reluctant smile to her face.

The morning flew by in a blur, helping customers, selling over half of the apples they'd set out and even several six-packs of cider. Sanna had even forgotten about her felled tree until she wiped sweat off her face with the neck of her T-shirt and her hand brushed her necklace. The loss hit her again, reminding her she still needed to grab that twinkling idea from last night and see where it led her.

They needed to do some restocking, and she needed Bass's help. She looked for his mop of curls in the stand but didn't see them. Stepping into the sun of the parking lot and raising a hand to her forehead, she saw that he wasn't there either. Einars and Isaac huddled around the laptop, talking website and social media. Now that Einars had seen how effective it was, he wanted to know more.

"Have either of you seen Bass?"

Einars shrugged and returned to studying the page, while Isaac stood up with his head on a swivel.

"He should be here, but it's been a while since I heard him. Actually, I asked him to get Anders but neither of them ever came out and that was hours ago." Isaac ran both hands through his loose waves and checked around the barn's corner. "I'm going to look in the house."

He'd probably gotten distracted in the house, or Anders had let him play on his iPad.

Sanna ran upstairs to the storage for more bags to fill with apples. When she came back down, Isaac's face was pale.

"I can't find him. He's not in the house or out here. And I found this."

He handed her the notebook she had given to Bass when they'd first arrived—opened.

Miss Lund told me about this awesome place where she and her brother used to jump into the bay. There was a huge cliff of rocks and you could jump right into the water, like flying. She said she'd take me sometime because you needed to be big enough to do it and she wanted to make sure I was a strong swimmer. I am.

"I told him just this morning he was too little to help with the cash register, remember? I have a feeling he's gone there to prove he's big enough."

"But this was from weeks ago," Sanna said.

"And he's trying to prove something. How many times have I told him he's too young? And he's still mad at me."

He paced outside the barn. If he went to the swim spot, he could be in real danger.

"Let's get in the truck," Sanna said. "This spot isn't far, but we'll get there faster by driving." She paced to where Elliot was parked under the large oak tree near the house.

"I can go," Isaac said. "You need to watch the stand."

Sanna glared at him and continued to walk.

"Don't be absurd. I love that boy, too, and I know exactly where we need to go. You'll get there faster with me. Now, get in the truck."

As he climbed in, she snatched the dragon keychain from the open ashtray, inserted the key, then gave Elliot a little rub—praying he would start. He leaped to life and they bumped out of the gravel parking lot onto the road in front of the orchard.

Isaac held on to the door handle to keep from shaking like a bobblehead doll in an earthquake, as the truck hit every pothole and crack on the road.

"Tell me more about this place."

"My brother and I used to go there when we were teens. It's a cliff about ten feet high and you can jump into the bay. You have to know where the rocks are under the surface, but once you do, it's pretty safe."

"You told Bass you'd take him there?"

"Supervised. I wasn't going to do it without your permission. I made it very clear you needed to be old enough."

"Which is why he went there. Oh God, he's going to hit a rock, and he's only used to swimming in pools, not open water."

"We'll get there in time. He'll be fine." She hoped she sounded more confident than she felt. Seeing Isaac shaken when he'd always been strong and calm disconcerted her. Maybe he wouldn't notice the sky, where a line of dark clouds pushed toward them like an alien invasion in a science fiction movie.

"How did he even know how to find it?"

"There's a trail from the corner of the property that leads there. You just need to follow it." Sanna thought back to the day they ate Oreos and caught fireflies. "I was remembering what it was like with my brother, how we'd run through the orchard after we'd finished our work."

"How could you be so shortsighted? You can't tell a ten-year-old boy about something cool and dangerous and expect him not to do it."

"Don't yell at me. I'm not the one who lied to my child and still hasn't apologized properly to him. You need to make that right sooner rather than later." She squeezed his hand, pouring as much comfort into it as she could, and being calmed in return by the contact. If something happened to Bass, she'd never forgive herself. "And I'm sorry for telling him about the swim spot."

They stopped the truck at the end of the road. They'd have to go the rest of the way on foot. They both set off at a run, Sanna leading the way, letting stray branches whip their faces before they burst into the small clearing at the end of the trail. Above them, gulls rode the wind like a carnival ride, swooping and dipping on the invisible roller coaster from the approaching storm. Foamy whitecaps tipped the waves like strips of lace, playing a game of hide-and-seek as they came and went with the choppy surf. Sanna couldn't tell the difference between the roar of the waves on the rocks below and the wind in the nearby trees. Lightning tore across the sky like a strobe light. Scanning the water, she spotted Bass's head bobbing, then dipping below the waves. She knew from experience how brutal those waves could be on a calm day. It wouldn't take long before he smashed into the bottom of the cliff.

"Where is he?" Isaac said.

Sanna had already kicked off her shoes and pulled down her jeans, tearing off her flannel shirt as she walked to the edge, leaving her in just her white T-shirt and underwear. Memory served her well as she jumped off the edge, knowing where the gap between the large underwater boulders made diving in safe. The water was deep enough that even she didn't touch bottom when plunging down, so she used her long legs to slow her descent into the water and break the surface in a few quick upward strokes. Though it was still summer, the water had a bracing chill, especially with the vicious storm churning up the water from colder parts of the bay toward the cliffs. She spotted Bass's head dip beneath the waves and swam to the spot, looping a long arm under his armpits and pulling his body to her. Large drops started to pock the surface of the already rough water as a larger wave went over both their heads. Sanna gulped for air and checked to make sure he was still conscious. His brown eyes were wide, then slammed shut as he coughed up water.

She turned her body so the waves would break over the back of her head.

"I've got you. You're safe. If you can wrap your arms around my neck, that'll make it easier for me to get us to shore. Can you do that?"

Bass nodded his head and used his arms to pull himself tight. He winced when his legs bumped against her.

Isaac stood at the brink of the cliff. He spotted her and started to kick off his shoes. Treading water with one arm, she pointed to her right. She needed him to find the path down—she couldn't get Bass up the face of the rocks without his help from land, but her strength was fading fast in the rough waters. She aimed for the spot where she had pointed, where the limestone had created a natural slope they could use to get out of the water. As she moved closer to the rocky shore, the riptides started to pull at her. She focused on keeping both their heads above water. Thank goodness, Isaac had found the path to the stairs and scrambled toward them. Just a few more feet and they'd be there, but the waves kept pushing her toward the wall. She turned her body so it was between the rock and Bass. The largest wave yet crashed into them, smashing her into the wall, and whooshing the breath out of her—she barely had enough time to tense her body for the impact. In the break between waves, she used the slimy wall to push her and Bass toward his waiting dad.

In an instant, Isaac pulled Bass from the water and he was safe in his father's arms. Isaac looked at Sanna, and she waved him on to the safety of the cliff top, grateful to be rid of Bass's weight. Another wave battered her as she clung to the ragged steps. In the next lull, she pulled herself out of the water into the cool air. Her legs and arms quivered with the effort to crawl up one more step to get away from the next crashing wave. The rain poured and thunder cracked, as lightning wrote letters across the sky. She longed to rest, as shivers trembled from her core. She needed dry clothes and hot tea.

Using the natural handholds on the jagged and cracked limestone, she hauled herself to standing and staggered to the top. As she pulled on her soaking shirt, Isaac emerged from the trees.

"I'm sorry, I had to get Bass in the truck. His leg . . ."

Sanna waved him off, but he picked up her jeans and shoes despite her wordless protests. She was grateful for that. As they walked to the truck, Sanna, barefoot, stumbled on a tree root and Isaac caught her, scooping her up in his arms, his hand grasping her bare, wet thigh.

Her body still trembled from the chill and exhaustion, and Isaac pulled her closer to him. Sanna had never been carried by a man—she had never needed or wanted to be—but she'd be lying if she said she didn't savor the sensation. She didn't feel unwieldy in his arms. She fit.

At last they were at the truck and Sanna was tucked into the warm interior next to Bass, who shivered on the seat next to her. She looked down at him. Scrapes and bruises covered his legs, his wet curls pressed flat to his head, and big, wet tears welled in his eyes. Carefully, she eased the blanket covering the vinyl seat from under him and curled herself next to him.

"You okay?"

He nodded.

"Nothing broken?"

"I don't think so," he said with chattering teeth.

Isaac opened the door and slid behind the steering wheel. She pulled Bass close and covered them both so their body heat could work together against the chill and residual fear their bodies needed to work out.

As Isaac drove back to the farm, Sanna looked down at Bass.

"For a fish, you're an awful swimmer."

Bass looked at her, then they both burst into laughter.

Isaac looked at them both like they had gone insane, and maybe they had.

CHAPTER THIRTY-FOUR

Isaac couldn't stop the hammering in his chest. Within minutes he thought he'd lost the two people he cared about most and now those same people were safe and laughing. Could a person have whiplash of the heart? He couldn't even speak until they pulled into Idun's parking lot and were greeted by rows of cars.

"What did you say on our website?" asked Sanna.

"The truth—that Idun's has been family owned for generations and you make unique craft ciders. Clearly, there's a market."

"Pa. He must be overwhelmed." Sanna reached to get out of the car to go help. Isaac grabbed her arm.

"You can't go out like that."

Sanna looked down at her all-but-see-through T-shirt and underwear, then blushed. "Shit." She took the blanket and wrapped it around herself. "Tell him I'll be right out to help."

He didn't avert his eyes as she covered up. Under different circumstances . . . Isaac let the thought go. He had something more important to address.

Bass slid to follow Sanna out of the truck, but Isaac held

him back. Sanna was right about him, he hadn't given Bass a real apology and that would change now.

"Bass, I'm sorry." Bass faced him and those brown eyes tore at him. Could he make things right? "I was wrong and I never really explained to you all that happened. I thought I was protecting you, but that wasn't fair. You had a right to say good-bye to your mom in your own way. I took that away from you. I hope you can forgive me. When you're ready."

Outside the approaching storm finally crashed over the orchard, turning the air into water, which thundered on the truck's roof. Bass blinked down at his lap, his face screwed up to fight the tears. Isaac needed to remember he hadn't had three months to mourn. To him, it was like his mom had just died.

"Did you know she was going to die?"

"I didn't. I really thought she was getting the help she needed. But when people are addicted to drugs, sometimes that's all they can think about. If I'd known she wasn't going to come home, you would have seen her. I promise."

Bass's eyes sparkled with tears ready to fall, and he tucked his face into Isaac's side.

"I'm mad because I didn't know I should be sad. Before we left, I was happy I wasn't going to see her for a while. The last time I saw her she yelled at me and threw my Legos away after she stepped on one. I should've told her I loved her. Maybe that would have helped her."

Isaac wrapped his arms around Bass.

"You didn't do anything wrong at all, but you deserved better from me." Isaac pulled him tight, and they sat in silence as Bass's body shook.

"We should have a funeral for her. We should say good-bye the right way."

When did his son get so much smarter than him? He'd been

so busy telling him to be young that he hadn't seen the thoughtful young man he was becoming. Isaac couldn't have been prouder.

"Of course. Why don't you get into some dry clothes and come back out? It looks like Mr. Lund could use some help."

Bass rubbed his eyes and nodded.

"I love you with all my heart, Bass. I'll do whatever I can to be both your mom and dad from now on." He kissed his forehead.

"Love you, too, Dad."

They'd be okay.

Bass ran to the house, and Isaac took a deep breath before dashing through the rain to help Einars. But when he entered the farm stand, he discovered Einars had plenty of help already. Anders was there with Mrs. Dibble, Sheriff Dibble, and her grandsons. Anders worked the cash register, while Mrs. Dibble and the boys refilled bags of apples. Einars stood at a table in the back, offering cider samples to those who wanted it. A short, dark-haired couple—though everyone he saw these days seemed short compared to the Lunds—helped him with the tasting. They smiled and laughed with the customers as they filled small glasses. Einars saw him and waved him over.

"Isaac, meet Lou and Al. They're up from Milwaukee for the weekend and found your brilliant website about Idun's."

They all shook hands.

"Where's Sanna? They want to meet her."

"I'm right here."

Her hair was still wet, and she wore a lightweight gray sweater that went halfway to her knees over a pair of jeans. Her cheeks flushed pink when she looked at Isaac. Einars made the introductions.

"I'm in love with this cider. Actually all the ciders," Lou said. She had wavy, dark brown hair, and the way Al watched her—it was as if the world would end if he stopped. "You have so many different types. I would love to build a menu around it."

Sanna looked confused.

"A menu?"

"I have a restaurant in Milwaukee, and these ciders would make a fantastic pairing for a special tasting menu. For example, Toasty Dark Brown would go beautifully with roasted chicken and root vegetables—I'm thinking beets, parsnips, and fingerling potatoes—with a sauce made from the cider." She took another sip of the cider and smacked her lips—her eyes drifted off to another place, the same way Sanna's did when she envisioned new ciders. "And thyme, maybe rosemary, I'll need to play with it. Anyway, you get the idea."

"So, you want to buy my cider?"

Lou smiled and touched Sanna's arm.

"I want to buy a lot of your cider. Should we set up an appointment for tomorrow to talk pricing?"

Sanna used her phone to schedule it as the two women continued chatting about flavors and possible pairings.

"We'll be taking a bit to go today, too," Al said, grabbing four six-packs from the cooler, carrying them to where Isaac had taken over the register from Anders. "How long have you two been together?" Al tilted his head toward Sanna.

"Just friends," Isaac said. "Why do you ask?"

"She's looked at you no less than five times since she walked in—quick little checks to make sure you were still there. You're doing the same thing to her." Al paused. "Whatever you're not saying—don't wait. It's absolutely worth the risk." Al's eyes moved to Lou, and he glowed.

"It's complicated."

"It always is, mate."

Lou and Al paid for the cider with promises of returning tomorrow. Sanna's eyes sparkled with excitement as she watched them go, then turned back to the tables, her eyes flicking to Isaac. He considered Al's advice. Did it even make sense to confess how he felt for Sanna? They needed to head back to California for a funeral as Bass had said and to pick up their lives.

"Boys, why don't you go see what's taking Bass so long?" Sheriff Dibble said.

Einars began closing down the stand as the last few customers walked out. They'd sold a lot of stock.

"This is a start if we're going to make our payments," Anders said. Isaac knew he was trying to keep the peace with Sanna, but one good day wouldn't solve their debt.

Sanna tucked her hands into her sweater sleeves.

"I've been thinking on that and I have an idea. Anders, you're right about investors, but we also need someone who knows how to make money and sell an idea."

As she shared her plan with them, the screen door on the house slammed as Bass finally emerged with the Dibble boys, singing a rude song at the top of their lungs. Perhaps Bass wasn't one hundred percent grown-up yet.

As they approached, Thad drove in with his giant truck, forcing the boys to run toward the patio.

Seeing the silver monstrosity on her property, Sanna remembered him walking away from her fallen tree—or at least seeing a figure wearing his signature beige. Up until now, she hadn't had the emotional space to process what she had seen, but now that she had a viable path to saving the orchard, and all the secrets had been laid bare and dealt with, Sanna could give the matter her full attention.

And she was pissed.

Anger burned her from the bottom of her feet to the top of her head. In her heart of hearts, she knew he was responsible for the fallen apples, the fire, the girdling, and the demise of the Dancing Tree. This ended now.

As he got out of the car, she swooped at him, the rain having slowed to a drizzle.

"You. I know what you did. How dare you set foot on Idun's? How dare you?"

Thad stopped in front of her, his red face equally angry, finally adding color to his taupe visage.

"You've ruined everything," he said.

Sanna hadn't expected an accusation back. What could he possibly be complaining about?

"What are you talking about? You aren't still upset I won't marry you?"

"You've ruined the deal. WWW planned to buy my property, too, but only if you would sell. We could have each had millions, and you've wrecked it."

Pieces clicked into Sanna's head. As someone who saw money as a means to keeping her home, she didn't need more beyond that. Thad had only been after her property for money. When marriage wasn't a viable option, he wanted the cash. Any sympathy she had for him or guilt over how their friendship ended dissipated with the rain clouds clearing above them.

"You son of a bitch," Sanna said.

"Literally," Einars said under his breath.

"You really did do it all, didn't you? The apples, the girdling, the fire. You cut down my tree. You knew how much that would hurt me. I loved that tree."

She stood inches from his face, forcing him to look up at her, yet he still had the balls to deny it.

"I have no idea what you're talking about." He said the words evenly, like he'd practiced saying them in the mirror to make them convincing.

"You. Lie."

While they argued, Sanna noticed the boys climb onto the back of his truck, using the tires to drag themselves up, then jump off into a large puddle, splashing the side of his previously immaculate exterior.

"Hey, Sanna," Bass called after his second or third jump. "Are these the missing cider bottles?" He held one up so everyone could see the custom Idun's label.

"Get out of my truck." Thad started toward the rear, but Sanna followed, recognizing her bottle.

"That is one of mine. Why do you have that?"

Thad turned to explain to her as if she were a child.

"Because I always drink your cider. You gave it to me."

"I've never given you bottles that have labels on them. I just got those labels last month. You took those from my barn—they were missing. What else do you have back there?"

"He's got a chain saw," Bass said.

Thad moved his glance from face to face.

"This is ridiculous. I'm leaving." He pointed at Bass in the truck bed. "Get out."

He moved toward the driver's-side door, but Sheriff Dibble converged.

"I don't think so. You and I are going to have a bit of a chat."

As Sanna watched Thad get shoved, none too gently, into the back of Sheriff Dibble's squad car, her anger and hurt and stress melted into the puddles covering the parking lot. Everything was finally falling into place, but she had one more leap to make.

CHAPTER THIRTY-FIVE

Eva pushed her sunglasses off her face as Sanna approached the table, her head almost bumping the red and white awning above them. She carried two sundaes in her hands and a tote bag over her plaid-covered arm. Sanna had asked her to meet here, alone. Given how their last meeting had gone and then the one with Anders, Eva had been intrigued to say the least. Perhaps she'd get a chance to show her the new plans and prove to her father she was good enough after all.

"Mint and fudge or butterscotch and fudge?" Sanna nodded to the glass dishes of ice cream in her hands. Eva pointed to the smaller butterscotch sundae—relatively smaller at least. "Good, mint is my favorite," Sanna said, setting the butterscotch sundae in front of Eva.

Sanna settled into her own chair, taking a big bite, then an even bigger breath. Eva recognized the signs of someone pretending to not be nervous. What could unsettle this woman?

"Thank you for meeting me. I had a few things I wanted to discuss with you."

"Is it about the plans I shared with Anders? Because we can be flexible to get this deal done."

"Sadly, no. But if it helps, that is partly why I'm here." Sanna's eyes closed as she savored another bite. She pointed at Eva's sundae. "At least try it. Wilson's has the best. You can't say you've been to Door County unless you've had their ice cream."

Eva scraped off a bite of whipped cream and ate it. She paused to enjoy the sweetened topping. It had been a long time since she'd had ice cream. She took a bigger spoonful, one that had butterscotch and marshmallow on it. Bliss.

"So, if you aren't going to take the deal, why are we here?"

"You made new plans that kept the trees. Why?"

"You seemed attached to them, and I thought keeping some of the Looms would make the sale more palatable for you."

"You listened and compromised," Sanna said.

"Back to my question—why are we here?"

Eva took another bite of the sundae. Now that she'd started, she couldn't understand why she'd ever stopped eating ice cream. Everything seemed a little better—even hearing there was no way Sanna would sell the orchard didn't seem as tragic with ice cream.

"I have a different business proposition, which could use a smart businesswoman like yourself." Sanna paused. She was finally getting to the point. "As you know, Idun's is very important to me. One of the many reasons is because I make cider from the heirloom apples, the Looms, we grow." She pulled a bottle and two plain glasses out of her bag. The label on the bottle was a black-brown. She opened it and poured an inch into both the glasses. "I don't mean this in a boastful way, but it's very special cider. This batch is called Fudge, and you'll find it goes surprisingly well with ice cream."

Sanna took a sip and ate another bite, so Eva did the same,

288 • AMY E. REICHERT

skeptical that a hard cider would go well with dessert. She sipped the dark amber liquid, which had a lazy effervescence. It was sweet, and the subtle fruit notes enhanced those in the hot fudge and vanilla. There wasn't any bitterness or dryness to confuse the taste buds. Closer to a port, really, but easier to drink.

"Why do you need me? I know nothing about cider." Sanna finished her cider and rolled the empty glass between her hands. Eva reached over and took the glass from her hands. "You're showing me you're nervous. Don't."

Sanna smiled.

"See, that's why I need you. I can make cider and grow apples forever. I could teach you all about making it and drinking it, but I don't know anything about selling it. And, as you know better than most, the orchard is in massive debt. For me to keep doing what I love, I need people to buy it. Lots of it. I know it's good. I know customers would love it. I just don't know how to connect the two. Already, I have interest from a restaurant to purchase a good amount, but I have no clue how to negotiate a deal like that. You know business. And I need an investor. Someone who can provide enough cash to get us over the growing we need to do and guide me on the business side of things."

Eva sat up. Now they were talking. Thoughts of water parks and architect drawings disappeared. Work had never been about the money. She had plenty sitting in her trust fund. With it, she could invest in ten different companies like this, without it affecting her life—but it could change the course of business for some small companies. Her mind already had seven, no, eight ideas for research she wanted to do about the industry and how they could market the cider. They'd need a business plan, of course, and she'd need to better understand Sanna's goals. Her mind whizzed with possibilities and the thrill of creating something from nothing.

At WWW, it was always someone else's plan, someone else's process. She was the go-between who had to ask permission to change drawings or suffer the consequences. Never good enough for Dad, never as ruthless as Patrick.

Sanna was offering something better than a deal: autonomy.

"I'm intrigued." She pulled a napkin from the nearby holder and started writing down percentages and dollar amounts. Sanna countered with her own. While Sanna had claimed ignorance in business, she knew her worth and Eva respected her more for it. They eventually agreed on a forty percent stake each in the company, and to sell the other twenty percent to community investors.

"Trust me, even if it's a thousand dollars, if a community member has a stake, they'll work just as hard as a majority holder," Eva said.

Sanna studied the paper.

"I'll share this with my dad and brother, but I think we're close to something." Sanna stood to leave. "I'll call you in a day or two to discuss what we need to do next."

As she walked away, Eva scooped another bite of ice cream and fudge. If this worked, she could stop working for her father. No more Patrick lording his position over her. No more being put on hold before being allowed to talk to her own father. She watched traffic scooching by on the nearby road and the boats bobbing in the marina. A new peace settled over her. Under the table, she kicked off her heels, propped her feet up on a chair, and savored every bite of her sundae.

CHAPTER THIRTY-SIX

Sanna's nerves skittered and bounced. It had been a week since she signed the deal with Eva that saved Idun's—but that wasn't why she tingled more and more as she cleared the dinner plates with Bass's help. Her dad had moved into his favorite chair and was using a bent coat hanger to scratch his leg under his cast. Isaac had gone to retrieve the lesson Bass needed to work on now that dinner was finished.

"How's the homeschooling going?" She scraped their dinner scraps into the trash then handed the dishes to Bass to put in the dishwasher.

"Pretty good. Dad says I should be way ahead of my friends when we get back."

There it was. She knew it was coming, but that didn't stop it sinking to the bottom of her stomach.

"Do you know when that is?"

"Soon, I think. He can tell you." Bass pointed his chin at his dad as he returned to the room.

"What can I tell you?" Isaac said.

Sanna tossed the empty cider bottles they had with dinner into the bin to wash and reuse.

"I'll ask you later."

As Sanna served up the apple cobbler, she watched the two get started on Bass's geography lesson. She brought her dad a plate and set one next to Bass. Once Isaac had Bass settled on what he needed to do, he joined Sanna in the kitchen.

"No dessert for me?"

Sanna ran through all the possible responses to that, all flirty and saucy and not her.

"Can I steal you for a while?"

Isaac took note of her fingers tapping the counter, then met her eyes with his warm brown ones, probably trying to discern why she was so nervous.

"Of course."

"Pa, Isaac and I are going out for a bit. You got things under control. I have my phone if you need us."

Einars raised the hand holding his fork to acknowledge he had heard them, then continued to enjoy his cobbler.

She grabbed Isaac's hand and led him outside to Elliot. As she drove through the orchard, he watched her silently, his gaze like little caresses. The sky had no clouds, only a billion stars being chased by the rising moon. When they arrived deep in the Looms, Sanna parked the truck where the Dancing Tree once stood.

She got out and opened the tailgate to reveal a thick cushion of blankets and pillows. With a shaky hand, she flicked the switch to turn on the Christmas lights strung along the sides and started the romantic playlist she'd stayed up late last night to create.

"What is this?" Isaac said from behind her.

Sanna turned to face him, thrilled to see him already only inches away. Her hands cupped his face.

"I have wasted too much time this summer. We have wasted too much time." She kissed him, his lips instantly joining hers, his arms wrapping around her back. With the fingers of one hand she dug deep into his soft curls, while her other hand traced the muscles on his back as they flexed with each movement. His breath still tasted of her cider, leaving her breathless and seeing fireworks. He trailed kisses from her lips to her ear, giving her time to inhale—but barely.

"Sanna." It was hardly a whisper, more like a silent prayer. He put his hands on her hips and lifted her so she was sitting on the tailgate. She rejoiced that he was the exact height so when she pulled him in tight with her legs, their bodies aligned just right. They both moaned as their lips found each other, more frenzied than before.

Isaac pulled back, her lips pulsing in his absence. His chest rose and fell to the same tempo as her own.

"I find myself woefully unprepared again," he said.

With her fingers, Sanna traced his jaw, over his lips, then to the back of his head. She could lose herself in his fiery gaze.

"Good thing I'm not. I made a trip to Sturgeon Bay so my purchases wouldn't be fodder for the gossip monsters."

Her lips followed her fingers' trail over his jaw and lips to his ear, giving him time to adjust to what she proposed. She nibbled his ear, enjoying his quick breath. Her hands slid under his sweatshirt so she could feel the heat coming off his back.

"Sanna." He kissed her forehead and took her face in his hands. "I want this. I want you so very much. I have since almost the first day I saw you, but you need to know that Bass and I are going back to California soon. That's why I've been so hesitant. I didn't want to be another person who leaves you here—and I will be."

She smiled—he was trying to protect her.

"I know. And I love you for it. I'm not making this choice blindly." Her hands traced circles on his back. "I realized that never making love with you would be infinitely worse than knowing our love is short-lived. I'd rather have the memories of these magical moments than regret my lack of courage."

She kissed his lips again, just once. She wasn't done explaining.

"Before you came here, I was content, but I didn't know the joy of being part of something bigger and more special. You've shown me I want more than contentment. I want happiness. I may never find it outside of these moments, but at least I'll always have them in my heart.

"I'm not going to ask you to stay. I know you have to get back home. I only ask you to not tell me until the day before. That way I'll be forced to savor each day as if it were the day before the last. Can you do that?"

"You love me?" Isaac's grin spread wide.

"Of everything I said, that's what you remember?"

He touched his forehead to hers, tracing his hands along the skin at the top of her jeans.

"I remember every word, and I'll never forget any of it. I love you, too."

Sanna knew he had more to say, but she'd had enough of words. She grabbed the bottom of his sweatshirt to pull it over his head. He watched her face as she memorized the lines under her touch, his heart thundering under her fingertips. She tugged at his waistband and when she slid back onto the soft bed she'd made, he followed. As the moon rose higher and the temperature dropped, neither of them noticed.

The back of the barn was wide open to Sanna's work area as the noon sun warmed the top of Isaac's dark curls on the cool early October day. He wore a thick, cream cable-knit sweater

294 • AMY E. REICHERT

over his jeans, the kind perfect for a fall day spent in an orchard. Inside, huge crates of apples were resting, or sweating, as Sanna had referred to it. Only a few varieties of apples were ready to be pressed, but Sanna would be working for the next few months to get all the different juices she wanted using her new apple mill and press, then she'd spend the winter creating new blends. Her workspace had been organized for photos he had posted on Instagram. They'd also discovered its height was similar to that of the pickup's tailgate. Isaac's skin heated at the memory.

Outside, tables were covered in food, from smoked whitefish to Mrs. Dibble's homemade chili. All the Lunds and Dibbles, as well as people from the community who had invested in Sanna's cider, were there—even Eva Drake. They were here to celebrate the official launch of Idun's Cider and to help Sanna with her first press of the season. Isaac was proud to be a part of it and stood next to Sanna surveying the process, wanting to spend as much time with her as possible while he could.

Einars and Mrs. Dibble joined them.

"Sanna, can you tell Eileen about the process?" Einars said to Sanna.

"Who's Eileen?" Sanna asked, looking around for another person.

Einars blushed.

"I'm Mrs. Dibble to you," she said.

"Pa, when did you learn her first name?" Sanna said.

"When she sat with me at the hospital and spent fifteen minutes scolding me for climbing a ladder at my age. If she was going to yell at me like a wife, I thought I should know her first name."

Pieces clicked into place in Sanna's head.

"Are you two dating?"

"We've been stepping out together for a few years. Not my fault you never noticed or asked." Her dad avoided eye contact, but Mrs. Dibble winked at her and patted her dad's arm.

How had Sanna missed that? She thought Mrs. Dibble might have had a crush, but it hadn't occurred to her that feelings went both ways. She smiled at her dad—good for him. He deserved someone as kind and loving as Mrs. Dibble . . . as Eileen.

"So, are you going to explain what we're doing today or what?" her father said.

The three of them followed Sanna to the beginning of the process.

"We have three stations set up. The first is for washing. The apples go into this large trough, where they get washed. Any rotten ones will sink, so the clean, good apples can move to the second station." They walked to a conveyor belt moving apples toward a huge funnel six feet above the ground. "The apples go into the apple mill, where they are crushed into tiny pieces, called the pomace, or *pa-moose*, as Bass likes to say." Sanna smiled when she said his name. She pointed to the bottom of the funnel where a black hose stretched toward the third station. "When we're ready to press, we use this hose to fill the press with pomace. I have a hydraulic press I'll use inside the shop, but for the party we're using this one. It's the bucket press the L1s used. The pomace goes into a bucket, then a flat plate presses down to squeeze out the juice when the large screw is turned. When the juice slows, we dump out the used pomace and start with the next batch. The collected juice is dumped into storage containers and put in my cooler."

The boys took turns twisting the screw, showing off their strength and making muscle poses.

"I'm very impressed, dear," Mrs. Dibble said, patting her arm. "Make sure to get some chili before it's gone." She walked off with Einars to where Sanna's nieces scooped apples out of the water to send up the conveyor to the mill. Even they looked like they were having fun.

"It really is amazing," Isaac said.

Sanna turned to face him, her glowing smile warming him in the chilly fall air better than the sunlight. Over the last couple of weeks, they'd spent every spare moment they could in each other's company—occasionally sneaking around like teenagers through the orchard. He'd told her all about his marriage to Paige and her tragic addiction. Sanna had shared her painful history with her mom. Every moment was a stolen drop of bliss. He needed to talk to her privately, and soon.

As he reached for her hand, a woman he'd never seen before appeared by their side. She was petite and casually dressed in jeans, a green sweater, and a quilted black vest. Her light brown hair was pulled into a ponytail. Isaac noticed Anders walking toward them at a slow pace, but ready to spring in case he needed to get there quicker.

"Sanna." Her voice was soft.

Sanna stiffened when she noticed the small woman. Anders sped up to stand by Sanna's side, Einars hobbling behind with a cane.

"Mom? What are you doing here?"

"I like to see what I'm investing in before I put money down." Her eyes looked at all the people helping out her daughter. "This is impressive."

Her mom waited for Sanna to say something. Even though she was easily a foot shorter than Sanna, she held her gaze steadily.

"Susanna, maybe we . . ." Einars started to say, but didn't finish.

"This is just for the party. Let me show you the real operation," Sanna said, waving over Eva to join them and leading the two other women into the barn.

Anders hovered near the barn entrance in case he needed to intervene, and Einars tottered back to Mrs. Dibble—content that he'd done his part to maintain the peace.

Isaac motioned for Bass to join him by the mill, and he raced over, his shirt covered in apple chunks and wet from spilled juice. Some things never changed.

"I spoke to Einars earlier. We're going to head home tomorrow. It's time. You ready?"

Bass looked over his shoulder at the Dibble boys.

"I'm going to miss them, but I miss home more. It'll be good to see my friends. And to see Grandma again."

"You can chat with them whenever you want, I promise. And Grandma can't wait to have you back." Bass's face brightened. "Now get back to work, and try to keep some of the apples in the bucket."

Speaking of his mom, Isaac should probably let her know they would be home soon.

We're heading back tomorrow. We should be home on Tuesday or Wednesday.

Her reply was instant.

IT'S ABOUT TIME!!!!!! TELL BASS I'LL MAKE HIS FAVORITE CUPCAKES. I'LL PUT SOME GROCERIES IN YOUR FRIDGE, TOO.

Thanks, Mom. See you soon.

LET ME KNOW WHERE YOU'RE STAYING EACH NIGHT. LOVE.

Leaving felt more real now that it was in writing. He just had to tell Sanna. It was her one request.

Sanna emerged from the barn with her mom and Eva, who both joined Anders at the food table.

"You okay?" Isaac asked.

Sanna looked at him and her blue eyes shone.

"I am. I don't know if we'll ever be close, but I understand her a bit better. It means a lot that she came here. Her setting foot on the orchard is the redwood of olive branches. I'm not going to take her money, though. It doesn't feel right for her to be tied down in any way to a place she hated—at least not yet."

Isaac hugged her. "It sounds like you've found some common ground. I'm happy for you."

Isaac took a deep breath. It was time to tell her. He took her hand, still chilly from the barn, and led her back into its shadows, so they could be away from the crowds and nosy neighbors. He stopped in front of her workbench, where this had all begun, the window finally repaired with his and Anders's help.

"I need to say something to you. Something I've been dreading." Sanna crossed her arms. He loved how she could say so much without words. "Bass and I are going to be leaving early tomorrow. You said you wanted to know just the day before. It's time."

She dropped her hands and pressed her lips tightly together. After a moment she spoke and took his hand.

"I assumed it would be soon." She smiled. "Come to my room tonight?" Sanna's voice cracked.

"Yes." He didn't trust himself to say more.

She squeezed his hand and walked back into the party.

He took a few moments before following her out, joining Einars at one of the tables.

"You tell her?" Einars asked.

"Yes," Isaac said.

"You know you can come back anytime, son."

Isaac smiled.

"It would be fun to come back for a visit. Bass would love that."

"I'm not talking about a visit. California might not be what it once was for you." Isaac opened his mouth to respond, but Einars silenced him with a hand and continued. "I know you have a lot of things to settle. I just wanted to let you know you have a job and a home here if you want one. Whenever you want one."

It was after midnight when Isaac finally knocked on Sanna's door. Bass had been so excited that he'd had difficulty falling asleep—so Isaac had lain next to him until he dozed off. By that time, the rest of the house had gone to sleep, and he prayed that Sanna hadn't drifted off without him. But his fears were unfounded. She opened her door wearing a silky blue nightgown that made her blue eyes electric. On a woman of average height, the gown would have hit midthigh—on Sanna it was scandalous and delicious. A single candle flickered behind her. Without a word, she grabbed him by his collar, shutting the door behind him and crushing his lips to hers. He gave into the whirlwind of kisses and caresses, knowing this would be their final night. He pulled her tight against him, walking her back to the bed, running his hands down the short length of her gown before slowly pulling it over her, like he was unwrapping the one present under the Christmas tree he'd put on his list. Right now, no words were adequate. He'd have to show her how he felt.

• • • • •

Sanna lazily traced a path with her fingers from his throat to where the sheet lay across his stomach, her naked body stretched out next to his. Isaac lifted her chin so he could look squarely into her eyes. Time was running out.

"I love you, Sanna Lund. When I came here, I didn't recognize myself anymore. Everything in my life had been put on pause for so many years. I came here to hide, but I was found. You found me. Thank you for sharing this place—for sharing yourself—with me."

His heart thudded. There was so much he wanted to say, but he struggled to find the words. She waited, seeming to know he had more to say.

"I need you to promise me something, will you? You were so guarded when we first met. Don't go back to that. You have so much to offer someone. Promise me you'll keep your heart open. I need to know that I didn't make your life worse, because you have made mine immeasurably better."

While it crushed him to think of his darling Sanna in someone else's arms, he needed to know she would move on— knowing she could find the happiness she deserved meant he could move on, too.

She looked into his eyes, then responded, her lips wavering as she spoke.

"I promise. Someone very wise once told me that happiness is always worth remembering, even when it was temporary." She took a deep breath, her chest pressing into his. "At dawn, please just kiss me one last time and go."

He made the promise. But when the first hint of light seeped through the window, his heart cracked in half. Leaving her behind would leave his heart broken forever—he would never find love like this again. But he wasn't free to follow his heart. Bass always came first, so he kept his promise and ignored the tears glinting in Sanna's eyes. He kissed her one last time, both of them savoring this last moment, and walked out her bedroom door.

CHAPTER THIRTY-SEVEN

Sanna searched the refrigerator for the extra butter she knew her dad had bought and opened the crisper drawer to a surprise—a bag full of twigs from the Dancing Tree. She'd stashed one in the house, hoping one of her storage options would make a difference in the success of the grafts. She pulled a stick out of the bag and smiled when she realized it was still viable. It hadn't dried and shriveled like all her previous attempts had—in fact, each baggie that she and Isaac and Bass and Einars and Anders had packed that horrible night had been viable. Somehow, grafting the Looms had become possible. Was she crazy to think it was the kiss that did it?

She set aside the bag with the stick on top of the counter. She'd deal with it after she found the butter.

"Pa, where'd you put the butter?"

Einars sat in front of the fireplace with Anders. Gabby and Sarah played hide-and-seek in the bedrooms with the Dibble boys, their occasional giggles and racing footsteps eliciting laughter and reprimands from the adults. Mrs. Dibble had promptly taken over the kitchen and bossed Sanna and Julie around like the miniature general she was. She'd even put Eva to work creating a centerpiece for the table from a box of table decorations. Mrs. Dibble had been horrified that Sanna had been letting Einars cook, what with his injuries and all. Sanna tried to point out that the injury was almost five months ago, and he cooked every night, but Mrs. Dibble put a peeler in her hand and pointed to the potatoes. She'd been assigned to the safe mashed-potato duty while Julie got the much more complicated gravy assignment.

It had been over a month and a half since Bass and Isaac had left, and Sanna still felt the hole in her chest where they belonged. She missed Bass's unending questions and silly fart jokes. She missed Isaac's brightness—especially now that the days were getting shorter and she'd be spending so much more time indoors. They'd connected online now that she had to take charge of the orchard's site—so she saw the occasional picture of them, but it wasn't the same. She couldn't smell him through a picture or run her fingers through his hair.

She thought back to their last night. She didn't regret one second of their time together—the memories had held her together when their absence almost pulled her apart. She'd tried to keep her heart open, like she'd promised. She even went on a horrible date. She'd spent the entire evening comparing the poor guy to Isaac, and the unsuspecting fellow came up short in every category. He wasn't tall, he wasn't funny, he wasn't dark-haired. He wasn't Isaac.

"Pa, where is the butter? How many times do I have to ask?"

As she spoke, Mrs. Dibble ducked under Sanna's arm that held the door wide open and grabbed it off the top shelf.

"Here, honey." She handed the blue box of butter to Sanna. "Sometimes it's hard to see things in front of you when what you want to see is so far away."

Then she returned to buzzing around the kitchen.

Mrs. Dibble was right. Sanna wasn't heartbroken, but she wasn't whole either. She peeled the butter out of its wrapper and slowly chopped it into sad, misshapen slices.

"Can't you ever cut things even?"

Sanna set down the knife and turned, a part of her worried her fantasies had now progressed to hearing his voice aloud, because she wanted to so badly.

But Isaac and Bass really were standing at the end of the counter. Snowflakes dotted their dark curls and his beard, which was neatly trimmed. His warm eyes soaked her in as she stood and stared. All the other adults gathered around to greet the returned pair, and the kids whisked Bass off to play. Sanna still just stood there, happily drowning in the sight of him as he smiled and laughed, bending down to let Mrs. Dibble bestow a kiss on his whiskered cheek. Einars took his coat, and Anders poured him a glass of mulled cider. As the crowd dispersed, Isaac stepped closer, his eyebrows raised in question because Sanna still hadn't said a word.

Finally she spoke. "Can you stay for Thanksgiving dinner?" But that wasn't what she meant. She took a deep breath and tried again. "How long will you be visiting?"

Isaac took another step toward her until he was only a foot away.

"Yes, and I'm not just visiting." Another few inches closer. "Einars offered me a job. I accepted." Another few inches.

"You're here to stay?"

"I'm here to stay."

The hole in Sanna's chest didn't fill up, it healed as if it had never been there to begin with. She closed the last few inches between them and wrapped her arms around his neck, drawing his face to hers. She heard her family snicker, but she didn't care. Isaac's arms found her back, his broad hands pulling her closer to him, and then she didn't hear anything. She only felt his warmth and love, and his beard tickling her cheeks between kisses. He pulled away.

"We had to go all the way home to realize we had just left it. That's not home anymore, this is. You are. I love you. We love you. Are we too late?"

She touched the curls on his head, his scruffy beard, his broad shoulders. She could barely believe he was real, that he was really here to stay.

"No. No, you're not too late. I love you, too. You bring everything around you to life. You brought me to life."

She kissed him one more time as he nodded, recklessly, knowing this time, it didn't need to last her a lifetime. She now had an endless supply of kisses and plenty of time to give them.

Eventually, Sanna and Isaac joined everyone at the table, not even noticing that the stick she'd laid on the counter, still poking out of its plastic bag, had burst into full bloom sometime in the last ten minutes.

Only Einars noticed the white petals with the soft pink blush and delicate yellow center that popped open when it had no right to. He turned to look at the large, happy family circling the turkey, laughing and smiling, bigger than they'd been in twenty years.

Happiness had returned to Idun's.

CARAMEL APPLE BREAD PUDDING

I've made almost every kind of apple dessert, and this one is among my favorites—made even better with cinnamony apples and a homemade caramel sauce. Homemade caramel sauce isn't difficult, but there is a technique to avoid a grainy texture. Feel free to use a high-quality store-bought caramel instead.

Sautéed Cinnamon Apples

You can make these up to a day ahead.

   1 tbsp unsalted butter
   1 large Granny Smith (or tart baking apple), peeled,
      cored, and chopped into 1-inch pieces
   2 tbsp white granulated sugar
   ¼ tsp cinnamon
   ¼ cup cider, preferably dry or semi-dry (good apple juice
      can be used instead for a non-alcoholic version)

1. Melt the butter in a small skillet or saucepan over medium heat.
2. Add the apple and sugar, stirring to coat. Cook until the apple softens and caramelizes, stirring occasionally, about 15 minutes.
3. Add the cinnamon and cider, cooking until the sauce is syrupy, about 2 minutes. Remove from the heat and set aside.

Bread Pudding

  1 tbsp brown sugar
  ¼ tsp cinnamon
  6 tbsp plus 1 tsp white granulated sugar
  8–10 ounces challah, or similar egg bread or firm,
    high-quality sandwich bread, cut into 1-inch cubes
    (about 5 cups)
  5 egg yolks
  3 tsp vanilla
  ½ tsp table salt
  1 ¼ cup heavy whipping cream
  1 ¼ cup 2% or whole milk
  Caramel sauce (recipe following, or use high-quality
    store-bought)

1. Combine the brown sugar, 1 tsp white sugar, and
   cinnamon in a small bowl and set aside.
2. Preheat oven to 325 degrees. Arrange bread cubes on
   a baking sheet in a single layer. Bake for 15 minutes,
   gently tossing once halfway through until the cubes are
   toasted and dry. Let cool.
3. Whisk yolks, 6 tbsp sugar, vanilla, salt, cream, and milk
   together in a bowl. Put the dried bread cubes in a 2-quart
   baking dish and pour custard mixture over the bread. Press
   bread cubes into the custard and set aside for 30 minutes.
4. Sprinkle the top with the sautéed apple and cinnamon
   sugar mix. Bake in 325-degree oven for 45–50 minutes,
   until the custard has set (no liquid should be visible
   when you press in the center of the pudding). Cool for
   45 minutes. Serve warm with warmed caramel sauce
   drizzled on top.

Caramel Sauce

1 ½ cups white granulated sugar
¼ cup water
1 stick unsalted butter, cut into eight pieces at room
    temperature
¾ cups heavy whipping cream, room temperature
½ tsp vanilla

1. Combine sugar and water in a stainless steel saucepan.
   Turn heat to medium. Do not stir anymore to avoid
   crystalizing the sugar, which will cause a grainy caramel
   sauce.
2. If sugar crystals start to form while the mixture boils,
   dip a brush into water and brush the sides of the pot
   so the forming crystals dissolve into the boiling sugar.
   The brush should not touch the boiling mixture. Boil for
   13–15 minutes, or until the sugar turns a caramel color.
   Be careful not to let it get too dark.
3. Turn the heat to low and whisk in the butter, careful not
   to splash as the sugar mixture is very hot. Add the cream
   and continue to whisk until combined. Remove from
   the heat.
4. Whisk in the vanilla. Cool the caramel before storing in
   a sealed container. Leftovers are great on ice cream, in
   frosting, and on desserts.

ACKNOWLEDGMENTS

While much of my time is spent alone in my room, these books would never make it beyond the figment stage if it weren't for the following essential people in my life.

Rachel Ekstrom, my truly magnificent agent, you are always a voice of reason and my staunchest advocate. I know that no matter what happens, you'll always have my back.

Kate Dresser, *Cider* never would have happened if it weren't for your gentle encouragement and (almost) always accurate comments. You've found the magical balance between criticism and cheerleading, and somehow always know when I'm just about to lose it. I'd be lost without you!

Kristin Dwyer and Theresa Dooley, I just love you. It's a bonus that you help spread the word about my books.

A huge thank-you to all the glorious folks at Gallery: Louise Burke, Jennifer Bergstrom, Molly Gregory, Gina Borgia, Chelsea Cohen, Liz Psaltis, Melanie Mitzman, Diana Velasquez, Mackenzie Hickey, and Akasha Archer. I'm so proud to be a part of this amazing team.

Gracias to Baror International for their excellent foreign rights work.

This book required a bit of research, so thank you to Jay Williams for teaching me about orchards, Rick Stenson for talking me through an ambulance visit, and Paul Asper of Restoration Cider for sharing the craft of cider making with me, with bonus expertise on emergency medicine. Any mistakes I made in the book are my own.

Kelly Harms and Nina Bocci, you've been so generous with your wisdom—thank you!

My favorite part of being a writer is getting to know other writers. We talk ideas, share early drafts and writerly wisdom, cheerlead the good news, and provide shoulders for the bad news. I hope I never learn what it's like to write without these women in my life. I love you: all the Tall Poppy Writers—there are too many to list (though I will mention the founder, Ann Garvin, because everyone needs to know her), Sarah Cannon, Gail Werner, and Carla Cullen. A special thank-you to Karma Brown, who helped me nail down an amazing synopsis for *Cider* and is all around magnificent. And Melissa Marino, my Mel—soul sister, partner in crime, and future Hallmark Christmas movie script-writing partner—thank you for being my friend.

To all my family, especially Mom, Pam, and Sandy—you are all so supportive, if it's cheerleading from afar or helping at the house during my busy times—I love you all!

My beautiful children: Ainsley and Sam for understanding that what I do is a real job, but also reminding me that I need to take a break and do something fun, too. Sam—I had to capture your special age in a book before you got taller than me. Ainsley—don't worry, your book is coming.

To my husband, John—you are my first reader, ultimate supporter, and partner in all things. I wouldn't have the freedom to do what I love if you didn't work so hard. I hope to give you the same opportunity. And thank you for helping me determine lip placement during a rather important hug.

Lastly, to all the craft cider makers who made my research so delicious and inspired me to write this book.

the
Simplicity of
Cider

AMY E. REICHERT

This readers group guide for *The Simplicity of Cider* includes an introduction, discussion questions, and ideas for enhancing your book club. The suggested questions are intended to help your readers group find new and interesting angles and topics for your discussion. We hope that these ideas will enrich your conversation and increase your enjoyment of the book.

INTRODUCTION

For Sanna Lund, change doesn't come easy.

Sanna is perfectly content with her quiet life, living and working alongside her father, Einars, as a fifth-generation orchardist on her family's apple orchard in Door County, Wisconsin. Although the business is struggling, she cannot be persuaded to sell the land and start anew somewhere else. Idun's Orchard is her home and the only life she's ever known.

For Isaac Banks, change is what he needs.

Isaac is a single dad who has spent years trying to protect his son, Sebastian—or Bass—from his troubled mother. Then when tragedy strikes at home, Isaac and Bass flee, heading off on a road trip with no destination in mind. As luck—or fate— would have it, they end up at Idun's Orchard.

There, Isaac secures a job, proving himself to be a blessing to the Lunds, and even more so when Einars is injured in an accident. But when an outside threat suddenly infiltrates the farm, surprising revelations are exposed. Just as Sanna and Isaac begin to find solace in each other, their lives become increasingly complicated—and anything but simple.

TOPICS AND QUESTIONS
FOR DISCUSSION

1. How does the alternating narrative between Sanna and Isaac influence your understanding of the events and characters in the novel? How did you feel about the few chapters from Eva's perspective? How would the story have been different if it was just from Sanna's point of view? Isaac's? Eva's?

2. What kind of a father is Isaac? What is his motivation by withholding the truth from Bass regarding his mother's death? Is Isaac trying to protect his son, or himself, from the difficult reality? Can you understand his choice?

3. The author represents Sanna's connection to her ancestors through magical realism. In what ways does Sanna feel a strengthened bond to the orchard "like another root digging into the soil, finding nourishment" (p. 17)? Did you find this literary element to be authentically woven into the story? How did it change your understanding of Sanna's devotion to the orchard?

4. Is there a proper way to grieve after tragedy? Like Isaac, have you ever taken a trip to escape from your troubles? Was it cathartic? Do you think going on an adventure to somewhere new helps the healing process?

5. Why is Bass the only person who's able to soften Sanna? How does Bass change her impression of children?

6. Examine Sanna's relationship with her mother. Why does Sanna refer to her as "the Egg Donor"? Despite her mother's past attempts at reconciliation, Sanna refuses to allow her back into her life. Is Sanna being unreasonable? How would you react if you were in her position?

7. Sanna is very resistant to change, telling Anders, "The changes I don't plan for are the ones that I hate" (p. 119). How do you react to changes that occur in your own life? Do you understand Sanna's struggle to sell the land? What would you do?

8. *The Simplicity of Cider* offers plenty of insight into life on an apple orchard. Have you ever been to an orchard or tried cider? What have you learned about the cider-making process?

9. Why does Isaac describe finding Einars's fentanyl bottle as "seeing a cobra in a baby's crib—unpredictable and deadly" (p. 160)? Why is the sight of the bottle so painful for him? Do you think the anguish he feels is something he can overcome?

10. Describe Sanna and Thad's friendship. Why does Sanna keep him around? Are you surprised by Thad's disloyalty to the Lunds?

11. Betrayal manifests itself in a few strong ways in the novel: Isaac not telling Bass of his mother's death; Thad sabotaging Idun's Orchard; Anders not telling Sanna of his rekindled relationship with their mother; and Einars preventing Sanna's mother from communicating with her throughout her life. Who has been most affected by betrayal? Can some of these instances also be interpreted as acts of love? Can love and betrayal intersect?

12. Discuss the role Eva plays in the novel. How are she and Sanna similar? Were you surprised by their ability to come to an understanding? How does their new business deal benefit both of them?

13. How do Sanna and Isaac evolve individually, and as a couple, over the course of the novel? How do they each deal with their own fears of vulnerability and disappointment? What have you learned from their experiences?

ENHANCE YOUR BOOK CLUB

1. Plan an outing to a local cidery or apple farm. Have fun apple-picking and taste-testing all the different varieties!

2. Share with your book club: Do you cherish memories in specific ways, just as Einars does with his shoebox of family photos? Einars says, "Happiness is always worth remembering, even when it was temporary" (p. 3). Do you agree? What can you do to always remember the happy times of your life?

3. Bring your favorite apple dessert to your next book club meeting. Then, choose one of Amy E. Reichert's other books for your next pick: *The Coincidence of Coconut Cake* or *Luck, Love & Lemon Pie*.

4. Bass's green dragon stuffed animal, Snarf, holds particular significance to him because it was a gift from his mom. Have each member of the group discuss a special gift or keepsake that they treasure. What do these objects represent for them? What memories do they hold?

5. Learn more about the author, Amy E. Reichert, at http:// amyereichert.com. Follow her on Facebook (https://www .facebook.com/amyereichert) and Twitter (@aereichert) for more updates about her books.